Arielle Immortal Struggle

The Immortal Rapture Series
Volume 7

Lilian Roberts

Cover Design by Shari Ryan
Edited by Jacy Mackin

This is a work of fiction. Names, characters, places, brands, media, and incidents are either the product of the author's imagination or are used fictitiously. Any resemblance to similarly named places or to persons living or deceased is unintentional.

ISBN 978-1945415142

Library of Congress Control Number: 2015901859

 *Chapter 1*

THE LAST COUPLE of days had crawled by, lasting forever. Worse, Sebastian knew that this fight was not nearly over. Jorrit was getting ready to unleash a horde of goons with the sole desire to hurt Sebastian, his business, and those he loved. And then there was Annabel, Sebastian's ghastly immortal ex who had vowed to make him miserable by destroying anything that made him happy. Arielle made him happy so she was going to die, a promise Annabel planned to keep. He felt like he was being dragged under, deep into a helpless place and desperate for resolution.

He leaned his forehead against the steering wheel and closed his eyes. There was absolutely nothing that Sebastian had ever loved or wanted in his five hundred-plus years on this planet more than he desired Arielle. Memories flickered, pounding against his brain, like watching a horror film being played in slow motion right before his eyes. He was facing two evils, and Arielle was right in the middle of both. His mind was muddled, unable to believe what was happening. The thought of her being captured by the Russian Mafia and tortured until Sebastian released the information they wanted drove fury straight into his bones. And Annabel succeeding in her promise to kill Arielle drew the breath out of his lungs. Anger took over, and he increased the pressure of his grip on the steering wheel. Troy's eyes narrowed worriedly.

Sebastian felt something nudging his senses and snapped out of his horrid thoughts. He realized that he was sitting in the car at the airport parking lot, lost in thought while Troy and Nathan watched him carefully. Silence wrapped all three in a thick blanket for a long moment.

Sebastian sighed vastly and shook his head in frustration. He swept a quick glance over his friends and muttered under his breath, "Sorry." He didn't clarify any further. Nathan opened his mouth to ask a question, but noticing the expression on Sebastian's face, he let his mouth snap shut. Troy gave him a quick stare and Nathan shrugged his shoulders; he had no idea how to make Sebastian break out of his quiet mood.

"Anything wrong?" asked Troy.

Sebastian scoffed. "I wouldn't know where to begin," he replied, and his mouth fell into a fierce scowl.

"We just had a successful outcome against some of Jorrit's goons," Nathan said, trying to improve Sebastian's mood.

After a few moments of staring into the distance, he nodded in agreement. "Yes, we did, but they will come back for more."

Sebastian pushed on the gas and the car roared to life. He pulled away, a fretful expression on his beautiful face, as though his thoughts weighed him down. The silence stretched again inside the small space and Troy's mouth settled into a hard line. He knew that Sebastian was worried about Arielle and her safety. He didn't need to read his mind to understand his concerns.

By the time, they pulled into Nathan's driveway, all Sebastian wanted was to get home to Arielle as soon as possible.

"Sebastian, I understand the issue here," Nathan said, "but you must have some positive reaction to the events that took place in the last two days. We did deliver a hard hit to Jorrit and Rainer."

This time Sebastian nodded in agreement and a satisfied glare danced in his eyes. Troy laughed out loud, happy to see Sebastian snapped out of his dark mood.

"Thanks, Nathan, I appreciate your help," Sebastian said sincerely. "Please tell Jasmine hello and I hope she feels better soon."

Nathan nodded and looked immensely relieved at being home. "I'll make sure to tell her. I'll see you both tomorrow." Shutting the door, he tapped the roof of the car with his hand and, turning away; he strode toward the front door.

When they reached Troy's house, Sebastian turned and gave him a grateful look. He cleared his throat and managed a smile. "Be sure and say hello to Gabrielle for me," he muttered. Troy stepped out of the car and shut the passenger door. He hesitated long enough to take a deep breath and, bending down; he motioned for Sebastian to lower the window. Sebastian tilted his head to the side to glance at his friend's face as he was given a meaningful stare. Sebastian raised an eyebrow quizzically and, quickly, he glanced at the rearview mirror, muscles clenched.

"What's bothering you, man?" Troy asked with clear concern.

Sebastian dropped his eyes to his lap and sat as motionless as a stone wall.

"Sebastian!" Troy persisted. "I can see something is wrong, so come out with it. It'll make you feel a lot better, man."

He finally turned, gave Troy a restless stare, and grimaced. "Ugh… Troy, I've made a mess of Arielle's life," he said brusquely. "I feel guilty for being so selfish. I'm a selfish man. I should've never come to Brighton. I would have just been a guy she met on her holiday and nothing more. She would have forgotten about me. And she would now have a carefree life with no anxieties, without crazy people trying to kill her because of me."

Troy saw a shadow of discomfort on Sebastian's face. "Sebastian, Arielle loves you," he muttered quietly.

Sebastian groaned. "This has turned out to be a horrible nightmare. Some nights, I stay awake suffocating in my own thoughts." He winced once again at the elusive gist of his words. Troy was motionless with incredulity while leaning into the car, resting his elbows on the windowsill.

"Well," he said calmly with a shake of his head. "I think you've got this whole thing terribly wrong."

Sebastian raised his gaze to Troy. "How so?"

Troy snorted. "I don't think that Arielle could or would have gotten over you that easy. Gabrielle told me that when she came back from St. Jean last year, she was a mess. She thought that you just didn't care. You had smashed her heart into a million shards and had spread them all over St. Jean. That's not a girl that would just forget about you. You are more than a guy she met on the beach, Sebastian. She's in love with you, man."

"I hope you're right, because right now, I have a hard time forgiving myself."

Troy scoffed. "Arielle told me a while ago that she was ready to take on any crazy immortal who tried to get between you and her."

Sebastian couldn't help grin at Troy's words. "She's feisty, isn't she?" he asked, joy in his voice.

"Yes, she is." Troy laughed, delighted. "Go home, man. Take her in your arms, and be thankful for having her in your life. I know I'm thrilled to have Gabrielle in mine. I had been sure that I would never find true love. Don't you hate the thought of moving through eternity searching for, but never finding, what we now have with Arielle and Gabrielle?"

Sebastian made a face. "You're right, you're right. I guess I just feel sorry for myself," he said stiffly.

Sebastian shifted uncomfortably, still smoldering, in deep thought. Minutes passed and Troy wished that his friend would get his head straight before he drove home. He pulled away from the window and, straightening up; he tapped lightly on the roof of the car. "Go home," he called out.

Sebastian snapped out of his murkiness. He looked up and nodded in response. "Thank you. I'll see you tomorrow," he said quietly.

Troy stepped away from the car and stood in the driveway, staring blindly as Sebastian pulled away. The worry on his best friend's face, the urgency in his eyes, sent unease flooding through him. For a long moment, he remained quiet and unmoved. A magnificent mixture of colors burnished the clear sky to orange as the sun chased the horizon. Suddenly, Troy's head ached, and he gazed into the distance, blinking away the sun's glare. He was concerned about Sebastian. He was more like a brother to him than a friend. He knew the battle Sebastian was waging against the Mafia and Annabel while trying to protect his company from ruin and keep Arielle safe. With a minor shake of his head, the immortal decided to go inside. Turning around, his eyes fell on Gabrielle. She stood at the door watching him, dressed in a pair of shorts and a sexy tank top. She was a vision of beauty, lovelier than anything he could remember. He smiled appreciatively, his lungs were locked, and his eyes burned with hunger. She hesitated for a moment before she ran, fell into his arms and buried her face against his muscled chest.

"I miss..." she started to say, but Troy interrupted her. His arms came about her, and pulling her hard against his body, he bent down and crashed her lips beneath his, leaving her breathless.

"God! I missed you," he murmured against her mouth. Something inside of him tugged at his senses, and he held her tighter. The warmth of her body and the sweetness of her lips sent a scorching sensation over him and left him breathless.

Gabrielle gazed into his eyes and saw beyond the passion to the deep concern etched inside. "What's wrong, baby? Did something happen in Brussels?"

Troy nuzzled her hair, and clasping her hand; he pulled her toward the house. "Nothing for you to worry about, love. Let's go in. We need to make up for lost time." He saw the satisfied grin on her face and her blissful giggle washed over him like a summer breeze. He pushed the door shut, and his hands skimmed her thighs as he leaned forward and pressed a gentle kiss on her lips. She scrabbled for an intelligible thought, but all she could do was moan with need. Troy draped his arms around her thighs and threw her over his shoulder, making her squeak with delight.

"What are you doing?" she asked, giggling.

Troy groaned softly. He wanted her like he had never wanted another woman before. "It's time for bed," he answered, his voice filled with need.

Sebastian drove away; his head completely engulfed with heart-wrenching thoughts. Arielle was exposed to danger, and his selfishness put her in that situation. He felt a lump of nausea climbing up his throat, and a surge of anxiety coursed through his veins and spread like wild fire. He let the rage slither far into the deepest corner of his mind

All he craved was to spend every single moment of his life loving Arielle. He never knew ecstasy until he bathed in the blue waters of her sapphire eyes, submerged himself into the wonder of her vigorous existence, and experienced the feeling of her sensual body. He was sure the sun rose in the marvel of the endless sky only for her and that she was the one and only bright star in the center of his universe. The car hit a bump, shaking him brusquely and bringing his mind back to the present. His arms ached for her, and the thought of her body was so intoxicating his mouth lifted at the corners and his foot pressed the gas pedal harder. His single and most steadfast need right now was to get home.

They had spoken on the phone as soon as the plane landed and he knew that she was waiting for him at the beach. His mind unwittingly went to their last encounter on that beach and his lips curled up into a mischievous smile.

He pulled into the garage and jumped out of the car anxiously. He went through the house with his immortal speed and now he stood at the edge of the garden gazing down at the shore. He scanned the area and his eyes found her lying on a beach towel, soaking in the sun's warmth. He descended the wooden steps to the ocean and, taking his shoes off, he smiled wide as soon as he felt the cool sand between his toes.

Several people walked along picking up shells and others were just sitting or sunbathing enjoying the day. He strolled slowly toward her and, reaching her side; he looked down at her. The sun reflected off her beautiful alabaster face, leaving him breathless.

Her eyes were closed, a small iPod on the beach towel, earbuds plugged into her ears. She was listening to a beautiful slow song and she looked peaceful. His gaze roamed her face carefully and moved down to the white column of her long neck, over the mounds of her breasts, her tiny waist, down across her flat stomach, her curvy hips, and finally over her beautiful long legs. His mouth went dry at the sight of her beautiful body, barely covered by a tiny, white bikini.

He dropped to his knees and, placing his hands on either side of her body, he bent down and pressed his lips against her sensuous mouth. She tensed for a short second, but the familiarity of the kiss made her heart pick up speed, and she lost herself in a great passion that took her breath away. He traced her bottom lip with the tip of his tongue and she parted her lips, giving him access to the sweetness of her mouth. He deepened the kiss, filled with eagerness and desire. Sebastian moaned blissfully, finally pulling back to glance down into a bluer than blue scorching gaze, a face that reflected clear hunger, and lips burning with a lure. A smile tagged his lips and he dove right back into that kiss with vaster need. He decided to take her home. He pulled back reluctantly and, sitting back on his heels; he watched her carefully. Her eyes were closed again and a smile of contentment painted her face. Silence spread around him like the stormy rain on a dry field, He waited for a short moment and felt giddy at the sight of her. Arielle blinked and, opening her eyes slowly, she gazed into his flawless face and bit down onto her lip.

"Hey," her voice coded with want. He reached out and pulled the earbuds out of her ears.

"Hey, baby," he replied, running his finger across her lip line. "What were you listening to?" His immortal hearing had already picked up what she was listening to, but he wanted to hear it from her lips.

"Oh," she giggled, "it's just an audio book I bought yesterday."

"Love story?" He was grinning, fully aware of her reply.

"Of course, what else?"

He arched an eyebrow amusingly, and his eyes flashed. "And the book is?"

"*East of the Sun*," she replied evenly.

Pleasure washed over him. He gazed out toward the ocean in thought. His mind flipped through copious information and, finally turning back, he gave her a thoughtful look. "I don't think I'm familiar with the book."

"It's not new, but it's really good. A great love story," she said passionately.

"Indeed!" he replied gently and, leaning back down, he pressed a kiss to her forehead. "I love you, baby."

Arielle smiled wide, "I love you, too."

"Did you miss me?" He angled into the question with extreme eagerness. He was surprised at the want in the tone of his voice. *Why am I so insecure? That's not an immortal emotion. I shouldn't feel that way.*

"Yes," she replied genuinely, but a bit startled with his question. It wasn't so much the question, but the way he asked it. "Do you doubt that I missed you?" she asked, trying to suppress laughter.

"No," he replied quickly through narrowed eyes, knowing that he got caught. She understood his insecurities, and she watched him closely. "I'm sorry, baby," he muttered. "I just wanted to come home and be with you."

She raised an eyebrow inquisitively and, taking a deep breath; she gave a tender smile. She sensed his uneasiness, but curiosity made her ask the next question. "Did something happen while you were away?"

"Why?"

"You sound different," she said firmly.

He looked completely unnerved. "We don't need to talk about this anymore, Arielle, do we?"

She remained silent, gazing into his eyes in surprise. "No, we don't," she muttered nonchalantly. She curled her fingers around the music player and rose to her feet slowly. Sebastian moved quickly and, taking the beach towel; he gave it a hard shake. He threw the towel over his left hand, and turning around, he faced her, giving her a stern gaze. He moved closer. Cupping her chin with his right hand, he tipped her head back, and his mouth came down on hers with unbelievable vigor.

"God!" Every time he took possession of her mouth she lost control of her senses. She melted against his hard body and surrendered to an in-depth and fierce kiss. The pleasure was shattering, the spark grew into an inferno in a matter of seconds, and her knees buckled. Sebastian felt her wobbling; he let go of her chin and wrapped his arm quickly around her waist, holding her steady against him. She sighed contently and he groaned, feeling every muscle in his body contract.

Even though he wanted to prolong the pleasure of the kiss, he stopped and pulled his lips a hairpin away. "Let's go home," he breathed against her lips. "I want you, but I don't want to put us on display." He gathered her into his arms and held her tightly, feeling the warmth of her body that made his blood rush wildly through his veins.

"I can't sleep without you," she murmured, resting her head on his shoulder. "I fell asleep at six o'clock this morning and I'm dead tired."

"I'm sorry, love. It wasn't easy for me, either." He licked his lips, trying to preserve the sweetness of her mouth on his just a little longer, or at least until they got home. He smiled to himself.

"Did you finish your business in Brussels?" she asked quietly.

"Yes." He was still smiling.

"Are you going away again?"

"No, not if I can help it," he replied and gave her a soft squeeze. "I don't want you to worry about that."

"But I do." Her voice was a soft whisper.

"I'm here right now."

Arielle looked up and fixed her eyes on his beautiful face. The corners of his mouth lifted into that amazing smile that made her heart skip a beat.

"You don't know how happy I am to be home," he muttered.

She snuggled even closer. "Why don't you tell me?"

Sebastian grinned like a small child, his voice tantalizing. "I would rather show you."

"I think I would rather hear it right now," she teased.

Sebastian couldn't hold back laughter. "You'll soon find out," he breathed against her ear, his voice a husky whisper. Their gaze was locked and Arielle's breath held at her throat. The wolfish grin on Sebastian's face made her stomach quiver as if an army of butterflies surged through her body, and she felt suspended in time. She was lost in the passion that simmered out of his emerald eyes. She was delighted! And he was home!

He clasped her hand and thrilled shot up his arm and slipped into his bones, leaving him breathless. He looked into those blue pools in her eyes and got lost. He shook his head and managed to say. "What are you doing to me?"

She looked up, a mirthful glint coating her eyes. "I have no idea what you mean?" Suddenly, she giggled outright, and jerking her hand away from his; she didn't hesitate before running toward the house without as much as a glance back.

A shocked moment passed. Sebastian eyes opened wide and his brows arched as he watched for a short moment, and then he smiled lustfully. *So she wants to play. Game on, Arielle…*

Chapter 2

ARIELLE DIDN'T HEAR Sebastian's footsteps, so she risked a glance over her shoulder and saw him still standing in the same spot she left him, utterly unmoved. He was watching her run with a shocked look on his face. She felt giddy, overcome with excitement, and nearly out of breath. Two more running strides and she would reach the wooden steps leading up to the house. She closed her eyes and laughed out loud, dazed by exuberant pleasure. One...two...and she collided with a hard, muscled, solid body. "Aaaaa..." she yelped, and her eyes flew open.

Sebastian towered over her with a lustful expression on his face. "So you want to play!" His voice drove an eager flutter down her spine.

It took a few moments to gather her scattered thoughts. "You cheated!" she squealed and broke out into a hearty laugh. "You have to stop doing that."

"Doing what, baby?" he murmured, his voice husky filled with amusement.

"Using your immortal speed," she stuttered. "One of these days, you are going to give me a heart attack."

He chuckled blissfully. "Well, you raised the excitement bar when you ran. I wanted to make sure you didn't run away from me."

Arielle sighed but grimaced at him playfully. Lust sank in the pit of her stomach as he pulled her into his arms, bending her to his body.

Sebastian felt his need throbbing beyond any reason. This sexual game was unfolding between them, and he wanted to play. Arielle focused on his lips and felt a scorching heat surge through every muscle in her body. His mouth came down on hers, and passion exploded. The kiss deepened and he drank her sweetness, delving and searching with his tongue even deeper. She moaned, and he groaned blissfully as their breaths mingled in a sensual dance.

Suddenly, sanity dropped into his brain, and he pulled back. Despite being in a public place, he was ready to take this further. He stared at the glow lingering on her face and smiled. Arielle's eyes were closed, but her lips remained parted, tempting, inviting. Reluctantly, he released her and straightened to his full height; his hands still on her hips held her wobbly body steady. Her eyes flew open, and her gaze met his wolfish smile.

"Ooooo...Don't stop," she protested.

Sebastian drew a deep breath. "You're becoming insatiable," he mocks admonished.

Her eyebrows rose in disbelief. "You think?" She snorted.

"I'm taking you to bed, now..." he advised inflexibly, unable to hide the seductive purr that coated his voice. She yelped as he scooped her into his arms, overwhelmed by the thrill that coursed through his body. The warmth of her body against him felt good, and he moaned blissfully, knowing that she belonged there. She belonged to him and him only. Using his immortal speed, he entered the house, through the hallway, into the bedroom and, setting her on her feet; he began removing her bathing suit while his mouth came down on hers with brazen fervor. His eyes shimmered with sexual intent, and she drank him in. Frantic hands removed his clothes, and he groaned into her mouth. It had been two very long days without her. He was not going to wait any longer.

Arielle cupped his face and pulled him down to her with a low sigh. Sebastian took her mouth in a voracious kiss and groaned with anticipation.

He wrapped his steely arms about her and pulled her firm against him. Her lips relaxed beneath his, and he took complete control, deepening the kiss until a tender shudder surged right through him. The tip of his tongue pressed softly, coaxing her lips apart, then delved deep into the softness of her mouth. He explored and tasted the sweetness like a starving man until heat seeped deep into his bones. Arielle's hand left his face and trailed down his muscled chest and over his flat abdomen, stroking, squeezing, and heading south in a slow, enticing motion. Sebastian sucked in an audible breath, and his jaw tensed. He felt himself harden and, shifting, he set his hands on her naked bottom and pulled her against him, moving suggestively. A loud moan escaped her lips and washed over Sebastian, heating and burning every nerve in his body.

"What are you doing to me?" he stammered and set his mouth to her throat, trailing open-mouthed kisses down the column of her neck, across her shoulder, and down to her breast. Arielle's shiver was palpable, making Sebastian groan with desperation. She wanted him, and he was ready to accommodate her. They were both lost in the haze of the passion while struggling to reach the bed. Her legs hit the edge of the bed, and she fell flat on her back, giggling. Sebastian followed her down and draped the full length of his body over hers, pressing her into the mattress. He dropped his head and set his mouth on hers with uncontrolled hunger. She parted her lips and their tongues met and dueled, stroking and sucking with savage craving. The kiss deepened as she gave him complete access to the softness of her mouth. She tasted like floral wine and honey, emanating from desire, and he thought he would go mad.

Sebastian braced his weight on his elbows and stared at her bluer than blue eyes, now swimming in a sea of desire and lust. She gazed back at him, and a slow sexy smile lifted the corners of her lips.

"I love you," he breathed.

"Then love me," she replied and rocked her hips suggestively against him. His muscles tensed, and his teeth clenched trying to suppress release.

He bent down. With his tongue, he trailed wet kisses down to her breast and lingered over them for a short moment. He then drew one of the hard buds into his mouth, and sucked firmly. A guttural sound rumbled from his throat. Arielle wriggled beneath the heat of his mouth and she dragged her fingernails down his back. His mouth moved to the other breast, and she let out an incoherent sound.

His hands skated over her soft skin, and she gasped with pleasure, letting the rest of the world fade away as scorching fire spread and burned every part of her body. Her hands left his back and traveled south, exploring and touching along the way. His lungs were locked, and he stopped breathing when her hands rested on his lower abdomen for a short second and then began to explore his erection eagerly. He felt himself grow harder and pressed his eyes shut, trying desperately to prevent an early climax. He brought his hand between them and tagged on her wrist.

"Arielle, for the love of God, stop!" he gasped.

"Why?"

"The way I feel right now I'm not going to last very long, baby." He pulled back from the kiss and gazed down at her. Her silky hair was splayed across the pillow, and her eyes were murky with arousal. "God! You are beautiful!" he breathed and dove right back into the kiss, devouring her mouth. Her taste was maddening. Settling between her thighs, he thrust in, and time stopped for both of them. He trapped her gaze in his, and they surged together. Passion swelled like a tidal wave, and they matched each other stroke for stroke. Startling desire rippled through their muscles, and they soared until they grasped the crest of the wave and rode it to a magnificent, breathtaking, sensuous peak.

The shattering of their exultant release whooshed the air from their lungs in harsh quick gusts, and the return to reality was slow. Sebastian rolled over on his back and pulled her into his arms, folding himself around her. She rested her face against his shoulder, and he pressed a soft kiss on her forehead.

"I love you," he murmured. Her reply was a muffled word, and he gave a short laugh of pleasure. Passion rumbled through him; it was a spectacular encounter. He glanced down, and his gaze roved her face, as a possessive emotion gripped him, stole his breath, and left him bewildered. He squeezed his eyes closed, enjoying the enveloping warmth of her. He was a strong immortal. Bewilderment was a human emotion. What was happening to him? His eyes snapped open again and settled back on her face. Her eyes were closed, her lips luscious and swollen from his kisses lightly parted. Her chest rose and fell. She was in deep sleep. He laid back and smiled wide. She was his, and he was going to keep her safe if that was the last thing he ever did. Turning his head one more time, he pressed a kiss on her temple and, lifting his hand; he pushed a stray lock of hair behind her ear with his finger. She shifted, moaned softly, and moved even closer to his body. Oh! The feel of her silky soft skin made him shiver. His lips curved, and exhaustion seeped into his bones. He pulled her gently against him and closed his eyes.

The next few days went by without incident. Sebastian and Troy had rejoined their friends in attending classes. Both now had irrefutable proof that Jorrit's thugs were observing Arielle and her friends, pausing for the right moment to strike.

"I haven't detected anything unusual," Sebastian said to Troy when they met in the parking lot the first morning after returning from Brussels. He scanned the surroundings vigilantly to make sure it was all clear; however, he couldn't shake the feeling that something was slightly off around campus.

"Neither have I," Troy replied skeptically. "That's exactly what I don't like. Something is not right," he furthered. He spoke in that inaudible immortal manner, so Arielle and Gabrielle couldn't catch a single word.

"I'm not surprised. Keep in mind that they move deviously. They are watching all of us, waiting for the moment one of us is alone," Sebastian hissed.

Troy nodded his head in agreement. Something about this whole situation didn't seem quite right to either of them, but they had to keep an eye on them and wait. Every one of their immortal friends had been given the details about the threats from the goons. The only people utterly unaware of the danger were Arielle, Gabrielle, and Paul.

On Friday morning, Sebastian held to the same routine. He steered the car to the parking lot at the east side of the enormous campus. This was also the place where they had all agreed to meet each and every morning before classes commenced. He noticed Troy's car already parked and pulled into a spot a few cars away. Before he opened Arielle's door, he scanned the area carefully. He then clasped her hand, and they made their way to where Troy and Gabrielle were standing.

They had just reached their friends when a quick movement of a black car approaching caught Sebastian's eye. The car slowed for a short instant and then it sped passed them. The windows were tinted, but his immortal eyes could clearly see the interior. He didn't recognize the two men, but he was sure that they were not students on their way to class. Sebastian eyes narrowed and his jaw muscles clenched. He could barely restrain his anger. The car was a black Mercedes and left his view when it quickly took a sharp turn at the far corner of the lot, disappearing behind the engineering building. He instinctively tightened his hold on Arielle's hand, keeping an attentive eye over his shoulder in the direction where the car disappeared. It was by the grace of God that he didn't take off after it.

Arielle's tense voice snapped him from his reverie. "Sebastian!" she cried out quietly, pointing to their intertwined hands. "You're crushing my hand!"

His head snapped around at the tone of her voice, and he instinctively loosened his hold but didn't release her. He stared down at the pained expression on her face. The realization that he could have crushed her bones with his immortal strength drove the air out his lungs. "God! I'm so sorry, love."

Shock and pain still lingered in the depth of her eyes. "What in bloody hell is wrong with you?" she asked again and winced. She had stopped walking, looking up into his baffled and somewhat cautious eyes as she listened for his answer. She slipped her hand from his, and using her other hand; she tried to bring some life to her numb muscles. "I think you shattered a few bones," she whimpered.

"I'm sorry. I didn't mean to hurt you." His arms came about her, and giving a gentle tug, he pulled her forward and into his warm embrace. She felt his breath against her skin. "I'm sorry, love." He nuzzled her hair, feeling extremely guilty for losing his perspective for a short moment. He could have hurt her, and the thought made him shudder. "Are you all right?"

"I'll be fine, but you need to tell me what is going on."

Forcing his worrisome thoughts away, he feigned ignorance and quickly replied. "Nothing, baby, nothing at all. Let's go and meet Troy and Gabrielle. They have been waiting for us."

"I'm still in pain."

Sebastian blew out a long breath. He was angry with himself. "I know, and I'm truly sorry about that. I wasn't thinking. Can you forgive me? Will you ever forgive me?" He held her gaze steadfastly, a worried expression on his face.

What is he up to? What's on his mind? This was one of the times Arielle wished that she could read Sebastian's thoughts.

"You haven't answered my question," he insisted.

His tone brought her sapphire gaze to his eyes. "What question?"

"Will you forgive me?"

She made a dismissive movement with her uninjured hand. "Oh, of course, I'll forgive you." She was sure that something was amiss. The frown in his eyes said a lot more than his voice. She shut her eyes tightly. For a moment, Annabel's image flashed before her eyes, and she shivered. *Could this all be about Annabel? What happened in Brussels?* She felt that she was standing in the middle of a deep canyon screaming out her fears. The thoughts were bouncing against the walls of her skull and echoing back into the far corners of her mind. Snapping her eyes open, she shook her head, and Annabel's image vanished. Arielle decided that she was going to let it go for now, but she would resolve this later. Much later. She rubbed her throbbing hand once again and focused on his beautiful face.

"I'm sorry. I don't know what came over me," he murmured, brushing his lips against her ear once again. Clasping her hand gently in his, he placed a kiss on her nose and pulled her softly to him. "Are you ready to go?" She nodded, and they made their way toward their friends.

"What's wrong?" Gabrielle asked as they approached. "You look awful!"

Arielle smiled and hugged her friends. "Nothing is wrong," she lied. "By the way, thanks for the compliment." She feigned displeasure at Gabrielle.

A small smile quirked Troy's lips, and Gabrielle snorted. "I was just kidding."

Sebastian and Troy exchanged meaningful glances as they made their way to their first class. Sebastian remained absorbed in his thoughts through the duration of the lecture. The black car had darkened his mood. He was sure that Jorrit's men were close. His hands tightened into fists, and he felt anger rippling through his body.

Arielle slightly turned and checked out his profile, instinctively knowing that something tormented him. She leaned closer and tugged on his sleeve, but he was lost in thought, his expression mysterious, deadpan, and unreadable. A wave of unease coursed through her body and her throat went suddenly dry. This was worse than she thought. *What in bloody hell is going on?* She reached over and grasped his hand in hers, pressing her right leg tightly against his left. He then turned and, raising an eyebrow, he let his emerald eyes burn into hers, causing Arielle's lips to purse, wondering what his expression meant. She suppressed her wild thoughts and gave him a soft smile. His lips curved with longing and her body sank as a sigh of relief escaped her lips. "Are you all right?" she whispered.

He nodded and stared into her eyes, his expression draped in apology. His hand curled around hers, and his warmth enveloped her. He realized that all the negative thoughts about Jorrit's goons weighed him down, overwhelming his mind with an uncomfortable sensation. He needed to snap out of it. He took a deep breath, gave her a soft smile, and pressed her hand affectionately before turning and fixing his gaze on the professor standing at the podium.

Arielle had missed the last part of the chemistry lecture, but she was sure that Sebastian hadn't heard a single word of it. Not that he needed to hear it. He knew the subject better than the professor. He had attended this type of class many times in his five hundred plus years on this planet. But she needed him to snap out of his sullen mood.

At the end of the lecture, they stayed back, waiting for the others to walk out. His intense gaze roamed over her, and his lips lifted. Her eyes narrowed. "Don't you even think for a moment that I'm happy with your rubbish explanation that there is nothing going on in there," she said and pointed to his head.

Sebastian's eyes widened, mirth emanating in his gaze, and his face lit up like the summer sky. "Rubbish? Did you say rubbish?"

"Yes, that's exactly what I said, and don't make me laugh." She wrapped her arms around herself and tried hard to suppress a giggle.

"I thought we moved passed this, love."

"You may have moved past it; I'm still waiting for an explanation."

Sebastian chuckled softly. She was not going to give up. He adored her relentlessness. She was going to hound him until she was satisfied with his answer.

"Let's go. We are the last people left in here," he mentioned quietly. Professor Colt Allworth was watching them indiscreetly. As an immortal, he was able to hear every word spoken.

She continued chatting, utterly amusing him. "I'm truly sorry that I can't read your thoughts."

He smiled at her. "Why is that so important?"

Arielle sighed. "Because you are notorious for keeping secrets."

Sebastian stood up and reached for her hand. "Let's go. Professor Allworth is watching us."

She tilted her head back and peered up at him. "And what if he is?"

"Arielle, he's immortal; he can hear a pin drop from miles away. Do you want to discuss your issues right here?"

Her eyes widened, and her gaze immediately moved down to Professor Allworth's desk. He was gazing up, his expression that of amusement. Arielle flushed, and taking Sebastian's hand; she rose to her feet, and they hurried out of the auditorium.

When outside, he draped his arm around Arielle's shoulder and pulled her toward the Pavilion, where they met Eva, Ian, Lauren, and Paul. They fell into feverish chatting, trying to make plans for the weekend while waiting for Gabrielle and Troy to finish their class.

Students clustered the grounds of the university each day and today was not any different. They gathered at the auditoriums, the library, the hallways, and the Pavilion. People were busy talking, laughing, and rushing across campus to their next destination. Others were just relaxing while waiting for their next class. It would be easy to hide among all of those bodies and faces, to disappear in the throng. Sebastian used his immortal abilities to scan the large groups and spent a short second on each face, scrutinizing their next move or thought. He couldn't find anything that spoke of danger, and he smiled, obviously relieved.

Chapter 3

AFTER ANOTHER WEEK of their usual routine, Arielle was quite fed up with Sebastian's secrets. She was going to resolve her unanswered questions. While driving toward campus, Arielle noticed the strange flash in Sebastian's eyes and the tightness on his face. She stared at him for a long moment with pure curiosity. This was going to be the right moment to find out what has been eating him up for the past two weeks. "What's wrong?" she asked, nudging him softly.

It had taken a few minutes before her question sank into his mind. He immediately forced a smile and, taking her hand, he brought it up to his lips and kissed each fingertip tenderly. His jaw muscle twitched, and his voice came out a bit edgy. "Nothing, baby, just work."

She raised an eyebrow in disbelief. "You know, Sebastian, I'm getting pretty sick of the same bloody stupid answer."

Sebastian tried hard to suppress his disconcerting emotions. He knew that this duel of conversation with Arielle could go on for a very long time, or at least until she was satisfied with the answers. He successfully forced a serene expression on his face. Glancing over at Arielle, he let the corners of his lips elevate into a warm smile. "Don't you trust me?"

"It's not a matter of trusting you, Sebastian. It's your expression that worries me. You had the same expression on your face last week, and when I asked you, I receive the same answer. I'm not an idiot, and you are quite obtuse. I know you better than you think I do, so come out with it!"

The tone of her voice made him chuckle. She was human, but she was a force to reckon with. She took his breath away, and she was right. She knew him better than anyone else. But he couldn't let her know of the danger that was lurking around them.

He wasn't worried about himself or the other immortals. However, he was very worried about her, Gabrielle, Paul, and their families. He would have to resolve this situation and soon. For now, he had to make up a story, and it had to be a good one. "I'm worried about our company's future."

"Why? Did something happen in Brussels?"

"Dylan rang while I was in Brussels and he said that the Russian goons have come up with a new device to infiltrate our company's secret documents."

"What are you going to do? You're an immortal, for Lord's sake."

"Arielle, I know how eager you have been to find out what's going on, and all I'm trying to do is to protect you. Troy, Nathan, and I are working hard to find out where they plan to strike first and discover the details of their plan. The company buildings and laboratories are global, therefore vulnerable. We have to stop them before they strike, and we have to be smart about it. The outcome could be disastrous if those documents fall into the hands of dangerous people like this group."

"Is there anything I can do?"

"Absolutely not." Sebastian noticed that Arielle had accepted his explanation. She fell quiet, having nothing more to say. He checked out her profile and couldn't help feeling quite uncomfortable for not telling her the whole truth. She was sitting motionless, focused somewhere out in the distance. He reached over, took her hand in his, and pressed it softly.

"Are you all right?"

"Yes, I'm fine, I just wish I could help." She was keeping her voice light, despite the fact that she was a bit anxious.

In class, Arielle was busy taking notes and following the lecture.

Sebastian gave in to the overwhelming rage. Jorrit's guys were taking their time. This long, torturous wait was not something he was familiar with. Anger had settled deep into his bones, and he wanted to have this over with.

On Friday morning while in the shower, Sebastian thought for a moment that it might have been a good idea to go into the office for a little while. His eyes fell on Arielle, still standing very close to him, letting the warm water engulf her body. Her eyes were closed, and a beautiful smile spread across her face. His eyes followed the rapid movement of the water in clear wonder. It touched her long, silky hair and glided over her curves like a secret trespasser caressing her thighs. After finally touching her pink painted toenails, it disappeared into the drain.

He watched her for a while, and it looked like a ritual of some sort. His mouth went dry, and his arms ached for her. Mesmerized, he reached over and pulled her into his embrace. His mouth came down on hers in clear longing. Her eyes snapped open, but shortly, she gave into the heat of the kiss and melted against the wonderful wall of muscles that enveloped her. Standing too close to her burning desire, he immediately knew that he wasn't going to go anywhere; he'd stay with her until everything had been resolved and she was safe.

He licked the droplets from her lips and held her tight. "How you can drive me crazy by just standing there I will never understand." He gave his head a soft shake and chuckled inexplicably. They were lost in each other, enveloped by deep desire and sizzling passion.

"We have to get ready for class," he murmured.

She giggled with pleasure. "I don't think I want to go to class today."

"Arielle, it is rather late to be making such a momentous decision. You can't miss the test. It will count for a large portion of your grade."

She wrinkled her nose and pressed her lips together glumly. "Oh, very well. You know how to spoil a great time."

Sebastian chuckled blissfully, cupped her face, and settled his lips to explore. Warm, tender, sweet, extraordinary. *Oh! Lord, I'd rather take her to bed than to class.* Reluctantly, he drew back and heard her sudden intake of breath. He pulled her tenderly out of the shower and wrapped her in a huge bath towel. He loved her powerfully, unconditionally. She stirred emotions in him that he never knew he possessed. She had to be the most passionately alive human being he ever encountered. He adored her, and she was in danger. Too many people wanted to destroy him, and she had become the target to their endeavors.

While getting ready for class, they fell into a pleasant conversation. She was leaning over, adjusting her Nike laces, when his next question hit her like a ton of bricks.

"Have you seen that black Mercedes lately?"

She jerked her gaze from her shoe to Sebastian, and her smile slipped. For a short moment, she couldn't move. *Where did that come from? Why would he even ask a question like that?* "What?" she squeaked. Silence fell over the room while she stood there stunned and studied his face. She noticed the same tension that she had seen plaguing him for the past two weeks.

She had pushed the fact that something was terribly wrong into a far corner of her mind, and now was the perfect time to bring all the questions back and make him fess up to the truth. Her eyes were closed, and she took a deep breath. Anger flared and stripped her self-control. "So you lied...you lied...you lied!" she shouted, the blood draining from her face. "You made up rubbish about Dylan and the Mafia and the company. You're hiding something from me, Sebastian."

His eyes widened in unmitigated surprise. He opened his mouth and closed it again.

"What in bloody hell is going on?" she continued, clenching her fist to her side.

Sebastian stared at her, utterly astonished at her outburst. Of course, nobody had ever accused him of being a liar. As an immortal, he couldn't lie. He could only give a different explanation of the issue in hand. The fact that Dylan had cautioned him about the Mafia goons, that they were after his company, and that they were going to do everything in their power to achieve their goal, all that was true. He merely left out a small detail, because he didn't want to frighten her. Jorrit's goons were going to try to use her as a bargaining chip to accomplish what they needed from him. So she was in grave danger.

Another long moment of silence passed before he finally spoke. "I have no idea what you are talking about?"

Arielle stood up, and their gaze locked. She saw a bewildered shadow flash across his eyes, and she felt a piercing twinge of remorse coursing through her. She didn't have to yell at him in such a harsh manner. Her words came out with more anger than she had intended. She sighed, exhausted from trying to learn the facts. This had been going on for two bloody weeks.

"Arielle, you know that I can't lie, so please have faith in me. I have my reasons for not giving you all the facts, and if you love me, you'll have to trust me. Can you do that?"

She rose from the bed and gazed at him across the room. "I'm sorry, Sebastian. I'm just worried that something is going on, and as usual, you keep me in the dark. I'm a strong person, in case you haven't noticed. *You* just have to trust *me* and give me a chance." *And if this doesn't have something to do with me, I'll be a monkey's uncle.*

Sebastian raised his brows; all pretend innocence and shock. "Why, Arielle, I do trust you. This has to do with both of us. It is our company in danger and, therefore, we are in danger." He didn't like arguing with her. He pushed away from the dresser--his eyes warm, loving--and slowly closed the distance between them. His shirt was still unbuttoned, exposing his beautiful muscled chest. He was stunningly handsome, and she swallowed past the lump that lodged in her throat. Her eyes roamed over him, desire settling, drinking him in. He was now towering over her, and her mouth went dry, utterly transfixed by his nearness. Placing a finger under her chin, he lifted her face up to his, his lids half-mast. Lowering his head, he brushed her lips with his gently. "I do trust you, my love. Please put your clothes on; we'll be late for class." He lifted his eyes from her lips and the corners of his mouth kicked up.

She fixed him with a firm expression on her face. "You are not going to tell me, are you?"

"No," he replied, a smile playing on his lips. "I have said all that

I am going to say. And you have to accept it."

She scoffed at his reply. She opened her mouth to argue, but he cut her off by lifting his index finger and pressing it against her lips. "Go—get—ready." His voice was gentle, not annoyed. The composed gaze in his emerald eyes resigned her to the fact that this conversation was over. After several seconds of silence, he released her reluctantly. She frowned and, shaking her head in exasperation, she turned and stormed into the bathroom.

"This conversation is far from over," she mumbled, shutting the door behind her. She heard his soft chuckle.

As they drove on, heading for the campus, the silence in the car fell thick and intense. Arielle was pouting. Reaching out, he clasped her hand and pressed it softly. "I wish that you'd stop being mad."

She sighed and kept her eyes on the road. "I'm not mad."

"Funny way to show it."

"Sebastian, stop."

"I will when you stop acting as you are right now."

"And I will stop when you start including me in your troubles, which apparently you're not doing right now," she snapped.

"Arielle, you shouldn't be so quick to judge me. I'm trying to keep you safe and happy. That's all I'm trying to do." He pulled her hand to his mouth and pressed feather kisses against her knuckles.

"Fine," she said petulantly, unable to prevent mockery from touching the tone of her voice.

Sebastian's jaw tensed. A sinking sensation gripped him. *What the devil is she thinking? I absolutely cannot, and will not, divulge all the grim details about the danger that is about to be thrust upon us.* He was sure that he would be able to take care of all the problems that came along and avoided putting additional anxiety and discomfort on Arielle. He was going to keep her safe, but in the meantime, he hated to see her troubled and worried. He shook his head and muttered his exasperation in that immortal way that she was never able to follow.

Silence stretched. She felt the weight of his gaze on her, but she turned away, resting her head against the headrest.

"Are you all right?" he asked.

"Yeah. I'm fine." She fell silent again, her thoughts churning wildly. *Oh, how I wish that I could read his thoughts.* She knew it was an outlandish thought that would go unsatisfied, but she could dream. She released a soft sigh and closed her eyes.

Sebastian's mobile ringing broke the silence. He let go of her hand and hit the accepted button on the screen.

"Hello," he answered blankly.

"Sebastian, it's Nathan. I have the report that you asked for."

"Hi, Nathan, I'm in the car with Arielle, going to class. I was planning on coming to the office later this afternoon. Is it urgent?"

"No, it'll keep."

"Fine. Thanks, Nathan."

He pressed the disconnect button, set the mobile back down on the hand rest, and clasped her hand gently once again. He didn't miss that the tightness in her lips was increased.

"What?"

She glanced at him; eyes narrowed to slits. "I'm bloody sick and tired of being kept in the dark." *There, I told him.*

His eyes widened. "What the devil are you talking about?" he asked. She could hear the surprise in his voice.

"Um," she started to say, but she stopped. She just stared at him.

"What?" he pressed on.

"What did Nathan want?"

He didn't answer right away. The question clearly surprised him. He shook his head in exasperation. "Is this really about Nathan's call or is there something else that's bothering you?"

"Um...well, it is that, and Dylan's calls, and all the other calls with Troy in that weird immortal language of yours. I want to know what's going on."

Keeping his eyes on the road, he started to laugh. "You think that I'm weird?"

His laughter was contagious, and she tried to suppress hers. It was impossible to remain angry with him. "You have to stop making me laugh. I'm mad at you."

"Are you now?"

"Yes." she said petulantly.

"So…you don't trust me."

"Don't you try and turn this on me. It has nothing to do with me trusting you. It has everything to do with you keeping secrets from me."

He kept quiet for a short moment and when he spoke, his voice was measured. "Arielle, I have no secrets from you. Nathan wanted to brief me on the report he obtained this morning about the security systems we purchased. The vendors are flying in, and I needed to know all the details before our tomorrow afternoon's meeting. Dylan's calls were about the people who are trying to destroy our company and my calls with Troy are mostly about the plans we are putting in place to handle the jerks who are planning to infiltrate our company. That is *our company*." He emphasized the last two words. He pulled her hand to lips and pressed a soft, warm kiss on her knuckles. "Why can't you just trust me?"

Arielle felt terrible. *Why do I keep doing this?* "I… I'm sorry about that." She ran her fingers over her amulet and tried desperately to understand why everything was so intricate when it came to Sebastian.

"Are you ready to go to class or do you want to go home?"

Arielle blinked in surprise. "What?"

"We are here. Do you still want to go to class?" he asked again.

She didn't even realize that they had arrived on campus, and he had already pulled into a parking space.

He flashed one of his amazing smiles and hopped out of the car. She watched him walk around with that mesmerizing, seamless walk and shook her head in wonder.

"Why are you smiling?" she asked when he held her door open.

"Because you're a funny girl," he said and reached in to help her out of the car. Arielle struggled to pull herself together, shoving her mobile, a book that was laying on the floor, and her jacket into her book bag. In the process, she spilled most of the contents out. She groaned in disgust, and she heard his faded chuckle. She ignored him and gave one of her pitiful efforts to play it cool, but she failed miserably.

"Why don't you put all that stuff back in your book bag?" he asked, a smile still playing on his lips.

Arielle snorted in frustration. "Um…what in the world do you think that I'm doing? It's not that easy." Frustration coated her voice.

Sebastian grinned. "Yeah, I can see that." He kept his amused eyes on her, and when she was finished, he reached for her book bag with one hand and held out the other for her to take. His fingers closed tightly around her wrist, and he pulled her right out of the car and into his arms. He bent his head and pressed a chaste kiss on her lips.

"Are you ready now, my love?"

She didn't answer; she just followed alongside him as he turned and headed toward the buildings. With every step, she felt her anxiety-- along with her anger--wash away.

"Do you still love me?" he asked, leaning closer and brushing his lips against her ear. She nodded, and he tightened his hold on her. "Can I have a kiss?"

She reached up and pressed a soft kiss on his lips.

"That was a peck, not a kiss," he murmured.

"Oh!" she slanted a glance over at him. "Do you want to make out right here in the parking lot?" she said mockingly.

"I don't mind if you don't."

The hint of a smile touched her lips, and she continued walking. "Come on. I see Troy and Gabrielle waiting," she said softly.

"Am I forgiven for whatever I did or didn't do wrong?"

"Yes…yes…yes, let's go."

They crossed the parking lot and walked across the grounds with Troy and Gabby where they met Eva, Ian, Loren, and Paul. They had a few minutes before classes began and it was a perfect time to make plans for the weekend. They decided to go out to dinner, see a film, and spend all day Sunday at the Polo Club, horseback riding.

In the calculus auditorium, they took a seat together with Eva, Paul, and Loren. Troy, Ian, and Gabrielle had general biology this morning. It was in the middle of the lecture that Sebastian's mobile vibrated. He reached into his jean pocket, fished it out, and pressed the unlock button. Glancing at the screen, his jaw tensed. It was a text from Madeline, his private secretary. "Dylan wants to see you. Very important." He bit back a curse and his fingers curled tightly around the mobile.

Arielle glanced over and noticed the intensity on his face. She raised an eyebrow, her expression momentarily unclear. He forced a smile, trying to appear unruffled. "Work," he murmured, leaning close to her. She seemed to accept his explanation as she turned and wrote down the last of the professor's instructions. When outside the auditorium, he called Madeline.

"Hi, Madeline, did Dylan say what he wanted?"

"No, sir, he didn't, but he did say that it was quite important. He would like to see you this morning if possible."

"Did he give you time?"

"He said eleven o'clock would be his preference. Can you make it?"

"Yes, I'll call him back. Make sure you tell Nathan to meet me at Dylan's office at eleven."

"Yes, sir, I will."

"Thank you," Sebastian said and ended the call.

Chapter 4

MADELINE PUT THE PHONE down and sighed deeply. She had fallen in love with Sebastian from the very first day she accepted the job as his private secretary. His voice had become the air that she needed to breathe each day. She knew it was hopeless. He was madly in love and engaged to be married to a beautiful girl. She placed her arms on her desk and intertwined her fingers restlessly. She bent her elbows and rested her chin on her hands, closing her eyes. Oh, how she wished that she could be Arielle. Jealousy struck like a scorching stream, right through every nerve in her body.

Every time she thought of him, she felt steel clamps squeezing her chest. Unfortunately, she thought of him every single moment of every day, and there was nothing she could do about it. She felt pressure behind her eyelids. Her breathing became difficult, and tears burned the back of her eyes. She stood up and walked to stand in front of the large window, afraid that someone would come through the door and catch her crying.

The image of his remarkable green eyes pushed to the forefront of her thoughts and her breath hitched. She wondered what it would be like to be loved by a man like him. He was perfect. She stood in front of that window utterly unmoved, transfixed by the vision of his flawless face. Maybe it would be better if she resigned and put a stop to this torture, but her heart was not going to allow that. She gave an involuntary shiver and returned to her desk. She wiped her cheeks with the back of her hand. She would never allow her feelings to be exposed. She would just have to endure the pain to be able to see him and be near him whenever possible. She would hang on to this job and enjoy the sight of him, for as long as was allowed.

Troy regarded Sebastian with curious eyes. "What's up?"

His green eyes had swept over Arielle's face before he replied. "Dylan wants us at his office at eleven o'clock this morning."

"Hold it," Arielle snapped.

His eyes narrowed at her outburst. They glared at each other for a short moment. He leaned closer and whispered, "Didn't I just explain about Dylan and his calls in the car?"

She gave a curt nod. "Yes, you did."

Sebastian averted his gaze to Troy. "He has received important information from his surveillance team in Brussels and he would like to chat in person."

"I'll drive," said Troy. "The girls can use your car to go home." Sebastian nodded in agreement.

He wrapped his arms around Arielle and, placing his fingers under her chin, he tipped her head back and pressed his lips to hers tenderly. "Please don't go anywhere alone and set your mobile on vibrate," he murmured against her lips. "I'll call you as soon as I'm finished with Dylan." Dropping his keys in her hand, he winked and strolled away, following Troy. Troy looked back and sent Gabrielle a sweltering glance full of promise. Gabrielle gasped at his silent message and, hugging herself tightly; she giggled gleefully.

Arielle rolled her eyes at their retreating backs. "Bloody duty calls," she groaned. She bit her lip and glanced at Gabrielle glumly, who grinned and shrugged her shoulders.

They stood there for a long moment in complete silence, lost in their own private thoughts. Gabrielle was the first to break the silence.

"I need to go to the library. Do you want to come?"

"Sure, what else is there to do until our next class?" she replied and sighed moodily. By the time they walked out of the library, it was time to head to their eleven o'clock classes.

Arielle was a bit bored with physics and not very happy being in class without Sebastian. This was not how she planned her day. She stared at the professor impassively, her mind a million miles away, wondering what Sebastian was doing. The memories of their morning's scorching encounter made her smile and sigh audibly. Several of the students turned and stared at her with amusement. A little embarrassed, she stared back and shrugged her shoulders, pretending boredom.

Time dragged excruciatingly and drearily slow. The clock was moving backward. *Good God*, she thought, *is this class going ever to end?* She intertwined her fingers and tried to think of anything else but physics. Finally, she heard Professor Mayfield voicing the most wonderful and the most anticipated words of the moment. "I'll see you all next time."

She leaped out of her seat and ran out of the auditorium. She took a few deep breaths and, straightening her shoulders; she walked unhurriedly toward the cafeteria. She was to meet Gabrielle outside for lunch.

"Arielle," she heard Gabrielle's voice calling and, turning to her right, she saw her leaving the medical building, walking toward her at a fast pace. She waved in acknowledgment and smiled wide. She loved Gabrielle like a sister and spending time with her was like balm to a restless soul. At least that is how she felt without Sebastian. Waiting for Gabrielle to catch up, she noticed Christian and Isabella crossing one of the quads, heading for the cafeteria. She chuckled quietly, knowing that they were doing this only for her benefit, for her protection. They never ate a single item they set on their food tray.

"Hey," Gabrielle said as she approached. "How was class?" Arielle made a face, and Gabrielle laughed. "I felt the same way," she admitted as they entered the cafeteria. They stood in line and, after getting a sandwich and drink, they walked over to the Pavilion. They both had their last class at one o'clock and quite a bit of time to kill. Following Gabby with their food trays in hand, they walked over to the table where Loren, Paul, and Ian were already sitting. A tray filled with food was in front of Paul, but nothing in front of Loren or Ian. Arielle chuckled again, shaking her head. How things had changed. They joined them, and immediately, the group engaged in a lengthy conversation about the weekend coming up. They were trying to pick out a good film and a club for dancing. Eva walked up in the middle of their very lively conversation and took a seat next to Arielle.

"Are we on for the secret society meeting next Tuesday?" Arielle asked in a low voice.

"I can hardly wait," Eva replied and chuckled blissfully. She glanced around the table and greeted her friends cheerfully. "Where is Sebastian? Where is Troy?" she asked, glancing between Gabby and Arielle.

"They had to meet an Interpol inspector or officer or something like that," Arielle said blankly.

"You mean you didn't bug him for details; that's not like you," Eva snorted.

"I did, but he didn't elaborate, so I had to let it go."

"Do you have an inkling of what is wrong? He wouldn't be meeting an Interpol officer for a simple issue."

"I think it has something to do with his company and the issues he had last year. You know Sebastian; he never talks about stuff. He wants to keep me from worrying. What he doesn't understand is that I'm worried more about him when I don't know what's going on." She pressed her lips together anxiously. "The last time he had problems, he had to go to New Zealand. I'm sure you remember that" Arielle furthered.

"Yes...yes, I do remember. You don't need to be anxious. You seem extremely worried, and I can feel it," Eva said softly. "Sebastian is a very smart guy. He hasn't become rich by not making sound decisions or knowing how to handle problems," Eva reminded, nudging her softly on her side with her elbow.

Arielle gazed at Eva and smiled. "I know. I just miss him so much when we are apart."

"How long ago did they leave?"

"About an hour ago."

Ian leaned over and pulled Eva closer, getting her attention. They fell into an immortal chitchat. Arielle blew out a breath and picked up her sandwich. She tried to focus on her friends and the conversations. Gabrielle was nibbling on a peach while into a deep discussion with Paul. Loren was listening to them, going back and forth about the new films that were showing, trying to come to an agreement.

Arielle let out a soft snicker; she loved her friends and their conversations. She sank her teeth into her ham and cheese sandwich and took a large bite. She remained quiet while chewing in clear delight. She partook a sip of her beverage and proceeded to finish up her food.

"Arielle!" Paul said, drawing her attention to him. "Will Sebastian be able to go to the cinema tonight?"

"I don't see why not. He said he was coming home right after the meeting."

"All right then. We have agreed on a film, and we should meet at seven-thirty at the Towne Square Cinemas," Loren said, glancing around the table. "It starts at eight, so we should go there just a bit earlier. It is, after all, the weekend, and it'll be busy."

They all rose to their feet, and taking back their food trays, they spread out, heading for their classes. Arielle noticed Christian and Isabella walking the opposite way and smiled. What Arielle didn't know was that Sebastian had asked everyone but Eva, who was already in class when he left, to make sure that Arielle arrived at her classes safely.

Arielle crossed the threshold of the auditorium calmly and smiled at Professor Allworth. He nodded politely and returned her smile. In route to her seat, she reached for her mobile. She stopped mid-step, anxiety spreading quickly across her body. She quickly patted her jean and jacket pockets, but no sign of it. She frantically searched her book bag and her purse with no results. Inside, alarmed, she scowled. She thought back, trying to remember where she left it. *What in bloody hell have I done with it? Sebastian will text, and I won't be able to see it.*

Her thoughts moved wildly. *Where is it?* She remembered that the last time she used it was in the car. She had texted Gabby and then she put it back into her book bag. But she just checked, and it wasn't there now. *It must be in the car.* She glanced up at the clock and noticed that she had another ten minutes before the lecture began. All the emotions she had held at bay rushed in, and she clenched her teeth. Without further thought, she decided to run to the car.

She lifted her head and glanced toward Allworth's direction, but he was busy thumbing through his papers. Exiting the auditorium, she picked up her pace. Reaching the parking lot, she pointed the fob and pressed down caused the car to blip as it unlocked. She pulled the passenger door open, and leaning halfway inside; she started to search feverishly for her mobile. She smiled when she finally located it wedged between the seat and the center console. She forced her fingers in the small space and pulled it free. She set it on vibrate and, pushing herself out of the car, she straightened up and shut the passenger door. Mobile in her left hand and books in the other, she turned around, ready to run back to class. That was the last thing she remembered.

A little after two o'clock, Gabrielle came out of her class and walked over to the chemistry building to meet Arielle. She leaned casually against the wall and waited patiently. The lecture finally ended and most of the students exited the auditorium in groups. She scanned the crowd as they hurried to their next destination, but Arielle was still a no show. She gazed down at her watch in disbelief and, pushing away from the wall, she moved toward the door. She entered the auditorium in a bit of a hurry and collided with Professor Allworth, who was exiting with his briefcase clenched in hand. She bit back an oath and blinked, a startled expression on her face.

"Excuse me, sir," she murmured. She sidestepped to move out of his way and looked around the room. She was startled to realize that the auditorium was empty.

"What the…" she started to say, but closed her mouth, realizing that Allworth had not moved an inch. Completely puzzled, she humphed.

"Good afternoon, Miss Taylor. Are you searching for someone in particular?" Professor Allworth asked calmly.

"Yes, sir, I was waiting for Arielle Lloyd."

"Miss Lloyd didn't come to class today," he said inflexibly.

"Oh!" she said, totally confused, eyes wide open.

"Is there a problem?" he asked interestingly.

"Well, yes, sir…I watched her enter the auditorium earlier, and we were to meet here at the end of the lecture." She was still probing around, outright baffled.

"She did come in for a short moment. She seemed to be searching for something, and then she turned around and ran out," he said gently. "She never came back to class. Is there a problem?"

"Oh! No!" she muttered worriedly and ran her fingers through her hair.

"What is it?" Allworth pressed on and eyed her quizzically.

"She's…she's…" Her mind was whirling wildly, unable to say much. She was standing unmoved, glancing around guardedly. She finally saw Eva and Ian crossing the walkway by the administrative building, and she called out frantically.

"Eva!" she practically screamed. Allworth watched her, outright stunned. Eva and Ian followed the sound and saw Gabrielle across the way. They immediately knew something was amiss. They walked at a fast pace toward her, and when they reached her, she fell in Eva's arms.

"Eva, something is terribly wrong. Arielle is nowhere to be found. I was to wait for her here," she made a hand gesture pointing where she stood a few seconds ago. Her fear was intensified, and her voice came out in a soft whimper. "She never went to the lecture."

"But…but I watched her go inside," Eva said astoundingly.

"She did, for a very short moment, and then she left. She seemed to have forgotten something." They all turned to follow the voice. Allworth was still standing there, watching them with an analyzing expression on his face.

"Oh, no!" Eva murmured, pressing her index fingers against her lips. She shot a glance at Ian, unable to hide her agitation.

"Is the car still in the parking lot?" Ian asked Gabrielle.

"I don't know. I didn't check," Gabrielle replied.

"Let me go and check. She may have had to…" He didn't finish his sentence; he just darted toward the parking lot. He found the car, but where the hell was Arielle? Ian frowned, trying to put his thoughts in order, and bit back an oath. He turned his head and took a quick glance around, scanning the surroundings cautiously. He then walked around the car slowly, and putting his face against the window, he peered inside, puzzled. Nothing seemed to be out of place. He pulled on the door handle and gaped in astonishment. The car was unlocked. *Well*, he thought to himself, *that is a bit strange*. He had had several conversations with Sebastian in the past about leaving expensive cars unlocked. Sebastian was adamant about locking his car and promoted his opinion to his friends. Ian winced at the thought and gave a last hopeful scan around the parking lot, wishing that he would catch sight of Arielle.

He dug into his jean pocket and, pulling out his mobile, he pressed Arielle's number. He listened very carefully, using his immortal ability, and caught an unusual faded sound coming from somewhere around him. Surprise shot right through him mixed with intensity. He opened the car door, but the noise was not coming from inside. He closed the door, and his body moved slightly toward the front of the car. By that time, the noise had stopped, and Arielle's voice mail picked up.

He ended the call and pressed her number again. This time, he followed the noise carefully, and his eyes focused on the ground right on the passenger side. He dropped down on one knee, placed one hand against the car with the other on the ground, and lowered the upper part of his body to peer underneath. His jaw dropped at the sight, and cold fingers crawled down his spine. Arielle's mobile was flashing with each vibration, and books were spread across the ground. He found himself in utter shock. It seemed like they had been pushed under the car purposely in an attempt to conceal them from clear view.

Ian pressed his eyes shut in pure frustration. A loud, explicit oath escaped his lips, and a sick feeling settled in the pit of his stomach. He raked his fingers through his thick hair, and for the first time, the realization that Arielle was in danger slipped through his skin, saturating every part of his body. He examined the area in a puzzled haze one more time, but everything seemed peaceful, not a hint of a fight outside the car. But what about her books and her mobile? Who shoved them under the car? And why? Where in the world was she? It had been over an hour since the last time he saw her walking into the auditorium. Rising to his feet, he took another careful look around the parking lot and, releasing his strong immortal ability; he tried to sense the presence of another immortal. He thought that Annabel may have something to do with this, but nothing there indicated that that was the case.

After a few more seconds had passed in absolute silence, he decided to head back. He reached underneath and scooped up her mobile. He then gathered her books one at a time. The blood froze in his veins when he lifted the last book. Arielle's gold amulet and the car keys were obscured beneath it. He picked them up and couldn't help shuddering at the thought that she was out there with no protection at all. Tons of questions clattered his brain. How did she lose it? Was she forced? But if she had it on and she was touched, she would have been protected. What happened to her? How did the amulet end up on the ground? Did the person that took her use a gun? *Oh, my God! Where is she?* He put her mobile and the keys in his pocket, clutching the amulet in one hand and her books in the other. With a few large strides, he crossed a couple of grassy quads and reached the front of the auditorium just as it started to drizzle. He saw that Paul and Loren had joined Eva and Gabrielle, and they were standing in a close huddle. Professor Allworth was still there, interested in Arielle and her whereabouts.

"You do know that she couldn't be harmed, right?" Allworth said emphatically. Every head snapped his way.

"What?" Gabrielle muttered.

Allworth raises an eyebrow. "The necklace…of course," he added in a hopeful declaration, giving them a meaningful glance and gesturing at his own pendant that was the same as Arielle's.

Gabrielle opened her mouth to say something, but she quickly changed her mind. She stared at him, letting his words resonate through her mind. He was right. Arielle was wearing her necklace. Hope sparked in her eyes and, silently, she nodded in a perceptive way until they heard Ian's shattered voice.

"Do you mean this necklace?" he asked as he reached the group, raising his hand and letting the chain dangle from his middle finger.

They all paled at the sight of the pendant. Shocked gasps escaped the group, and Allworth appeared mortified. Arielle was not just his student; she was a fellow member of his secret society. Protecting the safety of their fellow members was the number one law in the society book of governs.

"Do you think that they used a gun?" Eva said uneasily. "They don't have to touch her to hurt her."

"Let's hope that this is not the case," Allworth said calmly.

"We need to call Sebastian," Loren said. Shock spread across every face, as the thought of Sebastian, had escaped the equation for a short while.

A sick feeling settled in the bottom of Gabrielle's stomach. "Oh, God," she whimpered.

"Where in the devil could she be?" Ian muttered, eyes drifting over his friend's troubled faces. "It couldn't be Annabel because I didn't smell the scent of an immortal around the car," he furthered.

"Oh, God…Oh, God…" Gabrielle's voice trailed.

Eva pressed Sebastian's number on her mobile.

Chapter 5

SEBASTIAN AND TROY had left Arielle and Gabrielle right after Sebastian received Madeline's call. They moved in an intense stillness. The silence did very little to cloak the severe alarm in their expressions. Troublesome matters were burning through their brains.

"He must have something important in his hands," Troy finally broke the quiet.

Sebastian gave him a quizzical glance. "I can't envision anything better than the photos we already have," Sebastian said flatly.

"I guess you're right." Troy flicked his glance back on the road. "There must be something important, though. He wouldn't be asking you to meet him right away, otherwise," he muttered.

"You may have a point at that. I just don't hold my breath when it comes to Dylan. He had ample time to deal with the lowlifes after Nathan, and I handed them over," he said thoughtfully. "But we're not going to make the same mistake again. We'll have to handle this our way," he spurted.

"What made you bring in the Interpol to begin with?' Troy asked curiously.

"I never did. The security team contacted them when the goons broke into the vault at the headquarters building in London. They couldn't contact me because my phone was off. It was during the time Arielle was hospitalized after Savanna tried to kill her during her birthday party. You do remember that, don't you?" he asked Troy, sending him a quick glance.

"How can I ever forget something like that?" Troy snorted.

"Well, I turned my mobile off, because I spent a lot of time by Arielle's side in the hospital. When finally Nathan found me, it was too late. Interpol had already assigned two agents to the case. So we had to play along."

"Apparently," Troy snorted again.

Fifteen minutes later, they arrived at their destination. Pulled into a visitor's spot in front of the huge building. Walked through the glass front doors and crossed the lobby in large strides, taking the elevator to Dylan's office. Exited into the receptionist area and the elevator doors closed behind them with a weak click.

Immediately, they noticed Dylan standing in front of his secretary's desk reaching out for a large brown envelope. He turned at the sound of the elevator doors and smiled courteously, acknowledging them politely.

"Sebastian, Troy, thanks for coming." He strolled toward them, holding an extended hand out to both of them. He then turned, gave his secretary a nod and a reassuring smile, and directed them to his office.

"Please sit," he said, gesturing at two large leather chairs, while he took a seat behind his enormous desk.

"So what's up, Dylan?" Sebastian asked evenly. Dylan seemed to twirl a pen between his fingers tensely, as he glanced between Sebastian and Troy, and dragged in a long breath.

Sebastian raised an eyebrow while Troy appeared cloaked in quiet anticipation.

"Well?" Sebastian asked again, eyes narrowed.

"Sebastian, I have information right here." He lifted the brown envelope from his desk and shook it lightly. "The boys from Belarus are on the way to Brighton. They are what the Mafia calls the execution squad."

Sebastian read the significance in Dylan's voice. He cocked his head to one side, and his eyes focused on it. Dylan followed his gaze and, leaning over his desk, he handed it to Sebastian.

"Take a look at this," he said blankly, and resting his elbows on his desk, he watched Sebastian vigilantly.

Sebastian took it and stared at the name hand-printed in black ink. *Sebastian Gaulle*

"Where did you receive this?" he asked Dylan, still staring at down at the cover.

"I had set up surveillance on a group of young criminals known to deliver extortion letters for money. A couple of my agents followed one of them carrying this," he said, pointing to the envelope in Sebastian's hands. "My agents had no idea who the thugs had targeted this time around. But they had strict orders from me to confiscate each and every package and bring it to me. They noticed the young lad creeping up to the front door of your building, acting completely out of place, and they apprehended him." He took a deep breath and rose to his feet. He walked slowly around his desk, never taking his eyes off the envelope, and stood in front of Sebastian and Troy. He leaned against his desk, crossed his feet at the ankles, and pointed at the name on the top of it with his index finger.

"As you can tell, he was on his way to your office." Crossing his arms in front of his chest, he remained silent, waiting anxiously for Sebastian to lift the flap and inspect the contents.

Sebastian broke the shield and pulled out a handful of photographs, along with a piece of paper folded in two. He scanned through the photos carefully. Most of the photos were taken while Arielle was alone at various locations and going about her daily routine around Brighton. He stared at each one of them for a very long time and then passed them on to Troy, pressing his lips into a thin line. Anger grew and grew, spreading across every muscle in his body while anxiety gripped him by the throat, making it difficult for him to breath. Photo after photo displayed Arielle at the store, at the cleaners, at the beauty salon, or walking on campus with her friends. He was astounded to see one photo taken while she was with her father in her parents' garden. *What in the world?* He thought to himself.

One thing was very clear. They were watching Arielle twenty-four hours a day every day. He was not surprised about the photos. What he was surprised about was that these photos didn't include any of Arielle's male friends or Sebastian. Why was that? He shook his head in frustration. He then flipped open the single piece of paper and groaned through clenched teeth. The note was typed in caps.

"GAULLE, THIS IS OUR ONE AND FINAL DEMAND.

YOU MUST RELINQUISH ALL THE DOCUMENTS AND DESIGNS OF THE NEW IIRL PRODUCTS.

YOU HAVE FIVE HOURS TO ARRANGE AND COMPLY.

WE WILL CONTACT YOU AT THE END OF THE FIVE HOURS WITH THE PLACE AND TIME TO MEET.

YOU MUST COME ALONE AND UNARMED. DO NOT TRY TO BE A HERO IF YOU CARE ABOUT THIS GIRL.

OUR INSTRUCTIONS ARE TO BE FOLLOWED TO THE LETTER. ANY DEVIATION WILL COST YOU DEARLY.

THERE WILL BE NO EXTENSIONS TO THESE DEMANDS OR RENEGOTIATIONS."

"You have got to be kidding," Sebastian breathed, setting his mouth in a hard line.

"What is it?" Dylan and Troy ask simultaneously.

"It's an extortion note," he replied shocked. He passed the note to Troy, who read it carefully and handed it to Dylan, utterly mortified.

"Sebastian," Dylan said quietly after reading the note. "This clearly tells me that the goons that are here already have their orders to move on with the abduction. The five hours are up. Arielle's life is on the line!" he emphasized.

Fury coursed through Sebastian's body and settled deep into his bones. His eyes moved to Dylan, but his expression gave nothing away. He was determined to handle this problem the immortal way.

He wanted it over and done with. He didn't want to have to deal with this issue ever again. These people had absolutely no idea who they were messing with.

His mind was now far away from Dylan's office. He was already thinking about the immortal friends he needed to gather to end this mess. Troy's friends from Italy, his friends from France, Ian and Eva, Loren and Troy, Christian, Isabella, and himself made a total of thirteen fearless, unbreakable immortals who could take down a whole army with no problem at all. He was ready to attack the goons and their bosses, and at that thought, he realized that his anger was fueling the fire burning deep in his gut.

"I want to set up a security team around Arielle and your friends," Dylan furthered, interrupting Sebastian's runaway thoughts. Sebastian gazed up at him again and smiled politely.

"You don't need to do that, Dylan. I already have private security providing the required protection," he said stiffly.

Dylan frowned and, pushing away from his desk, he interlaced his fingers on his back and started to pace across the floor thoughtfully. The silence stretched for an uncomfortably long moment, and finally, Dylan stopped in front of Sebastian, watching him cautiously. "I still think you'll need police officers in case something happens," Dylan insisted. Sebastian's expression remained indecipherable.

"If something happens, my security officers will call the police for assistance. However, right now we are okay," Sebastian replied in a clipped tone.

Dylan shook his head in disapproval. He opened his mouth, determined to insist on protection, but taking in Sebastian's expression, he decided against it. "Okay, Sebastian, I don't seem to be able to convince you. However, if you change your mind, you know where to find me."

Sebastian glanced at Troy, giving him a meaningful look, and they both stood up at the same time. Sebastian put all the photos inside the envelope and handed it back to Dylan, forcing a smile. "Thank you, Dylan. I promise to let you know if I need help." Dylan smiled kindly and shook hands with both of them.

"I want you, Arielle, and your friends safe," he called out, as Sebastian and Troy walked out of his office, heading for the elevator.

Arielle's concerned face from this morning loomed over Sebastian's thoughts. "Son of a bitch," he muttered. The thought of Arielle abducted and imprisoned made his muscles tremble, and he suddenly struggled to breathe.

Troy turned to face him. "What is it?"

"I wonder where Jorrit's man are at this moment. Are they waiting for her to be alone? Will I be able to get to her before they do?"

"Sebastian, we are going back. I am sure Arielle is fine."

He let out a deep sigh and nodded. There were so many things he wanted to tell her. He had to let her know that the bad guys were in Brighton, and she was in danger.

For over a week now, Jorrit's shady goons had set up surveillance and monitored every move in Arielle's daily routine. They had spent hours upon hours doing a mind-numbingly dull job successfully. They had taken hundreds of photos and surreptitiously determined her every move without being seen.

They paid attention to each detail, such as which route she took to school, which places she frequented, who she talked with, and what she liked to do.

Each morning, they began by following her while she drove to campus, interacted with her friends, and ran her daily errands after class. They ended their surveillance after Arielle went home for the day. They knew every little thing about her routine. They never allowed themselves to be distracted and never took unwarranted chances. This was an assignment that they couldn't fail.

They had been waiting for Jorrit to give them the approval to move in and kidnap her. Two days ago they received that call and to take all the necessary steps to accomplish the task. Now they looked forward to that single magical moment that she would be alone and give them the ability to snatch her away.

What was becoming extremely frustrating was the fact that ever since they had received the approval, they hadn't been able to find Arielle without people around her. She was always with one or more of her friends. Something subtle had changed in her everyday routine, but they couldn't figure out what that something was.

The realization that they may have to take more than one hostage created a major dilemma.

After leaving Arielle's residence the night before, Vitorio decided to call Jorrit. He took his mobile out of his pocket and pressed his number on the keypad. Jorrit picked up on the first ring.

"Jorrit," he said briskly.

"Jorrit, it's Vitorio," he said hesitantly.

"Yeah, how are things in Brighton?" Jorrit asked blandly.

"Well, things are moving along, but I think we're going to need some help."

"Why is that?" Jorrit asked.

"It seems that the girl's routine has changed in the past two days, and she's never alone," Vitorio stated firmly.

"So what's the problem?" Jorrit asked impassively. Vitorio rolled his eyes in exasperation. He knew that Jorrit was the typical arrogant ass that he always was and cursed inwardly.

"The problem is," he mocked him, "that we may have to take more than one hostage."

"I still don't understand the issue," Jorrit continued, haughty once again.

Vitorio frowned at Jorrit's arrogance, but he pretended to be unruffled.

"Jorrit, we're going to need assistance. If we have to deal with more than one or two hostages, we would need extra help, wouldn't you think?" he asked flatly, trying to rein in his anger.

The silence stretched as Vitorio decided to say nothing more. Jorrit was the epitome of arrogance, but he was the boss and a son of a bitch at that. Mauritsio leaned slightly forward, staring at Vitorio intently, wanting to know what in the hell was going on. Vitorio put his index finger to his lips, motioning him to remain silent, while waiting for Jorrit to speak.

"All right, Vitorio," Jorrit finally barked into the phone. "Let me call Vasily in Belarus and ask him if he can send his boys now. They were coming down next week, so maybe they wouldn't mind leaving a couple of days earlier. I'll let you know when I have the details," he said and ended the conversation. Vitorio shut the phone and put it back in his pant pocket, letting out a loud oath.

"What did he say?" Mauritsio asked curiously.

"That son of a bitch couldn't care less as to what happens to us and how we complete this job. His arrogance makes me want to hurt him, but I know better," Vitorio said. "He would have me killed," he furthered, and lowering the power window, he spits out in pure rage.

"He didn't want to send help?" Mauritsio asked, clearly shocked.

"I'm not sure that sending help was the issue. I think being bothered was the issue. Sometimes I just hate him," Vitorio said menacingly.

"So is he going to ask for help?" Mauritsio asked again.

"He's going to talk to Vasily in Belarus and let us know," he replied, ending the discussion.

"Well, if we are given the chance to find her alone tomorrow, we have Jorrit's approval to take her. Who knows, tomorrow might be our lucky day," Mauritsio said and snorted.

Sebastian and Troy rode the elevator to the first floor in complete silence. Crossing the huge lobby, Troy noticed Sebastian's inexplicable mood and struggled to find an easy way to say the right thing, but he chose against it and remained silent. Stepping outside the revolving glass doors, he heard Sebastian taking a sharp breath and turned toward him. He wanted to help in any way he could, so he decided to break the silence.

"What's the plan?" he asked with great concern.

"I'm worried about Arielle, Troy. I don't know how to handle this. I don't know if I can keep it from her. I don't want her to worry. I am going to talk with her tonight." His jaw clenched, and he shoved his hands into his jean pockets.

"We need to go back right away." Increasing his walking pace, he didn't make another comment. Suddenly, his phone buzzed, and pulling it out of his jean pocket, he glanced at the screen. He flipped it open swiftly and answered. "Eva, what up?"

"Sebastian!" she screamed through the phone line. Sebastian came to an abrupt halt, and his muscled tensed.

"What's wrong?"

"It's Arielle."

"Is she hurt?" Sebastian flushed a glance at Troy, who was standing next to him listening to the phone conversation.

"No, she isn't hurt; she's missing."

"Missing?" he shouted, feeling the blood draining from his face.

"Yes, she's missing!"

Sebastian was horrified. "But how? When?" His voice was breaking.

"Sebastian, you need to come here right now!" she stressed.

"Where are you?"

"We are in front of the Physics building." Eva's voice was laced with panic.

Using their immortal ability, they left the car at Dylan's office and joined their friends before Eva had a chance to end the conversation. Paul, Gabrielle, and Allworth blinked in shock when they saw Troy and Sebastian appear before them instantaneously.

"What happened?" Sebastian shouted, glancing among his friends.

"Sebastian, we all watched Arielle walk into the auditorium before we went to our classes," Gabrielle shrieked hysterically, falling into Troy's arms and sobbing hard. Sebastian seemed lost. His eyes roamed from face to face, asking for some guidance.

"She's just gone," Paul whispered. The pain in his voice startled Sebastian. Turning his gaze to him, he saw Paul standing unmoved, staring at him with a blank expression, his breathe heaving. Sebastian knew that Paul truly loved Arielle. He reached over and patted him on the back warmly.

"We'll find her, Paul. We'll find her..." his voice trailed. He was powerlessly frustrated.

They all stood frozen in place, watching each other while stillness and anxiety stretched out among them.

"How could she be missing?" Sebastian murmured, utterly puzzled.

"She came to class for a very short moment. She seemed to be searching for something in her pockets, in her purse, and couldn't find it. She then suddenly turned around and ran out of the auditorium. I did wonder what happened to her," Allworth stated with a voice filled with apprehension as he ran his hand through his hair. Sebastian turned toward the voice and saw the professor standing there eyes wide open and a facial expression conveying immeasurable awareness. He wanted to help.

"Where did you all search for her?"

"I went to the parking lot to ensure that she hadn't decided to leave for some strange reason. I thought maybe she received a call from her parents or something like that," Ian said and swallowed hard. "Your car is still in the parking lot, unlocked. I found her books, her mobile phone, and the car keys shoved underneath the car, concealed from anyone's view," he continued.

"We went all over campus, but she was nowhere to be found," Loren added.

"I also found this," Ian said, and reaching out, he handed Sebastian Arielle's amulet. Sebastian's eyes shot up in shock, and the blood drained from his face. Taking the amulet from Ian, a surge of despair enveloped him. He felt the ground moving underneath his feet as if the density and the friction of his emotions set all the earth's tectonic plates into a shifting motion. His eyes lit with fire, and a loud oath escaped his lips. He pressed the hills of his palms against his temples and forced his eyes shot.

"Those bastards, they took her," Sebastian spat out. "I'll tear their hearts out." He enunciated each work; voice lined with pure venom.

"Whom are we talking about?" Eva asked.

"It's a long story, Eva, but in short, it has to do with a group in Brussels that works for the Russian Mafia. They were planning to use Arielle as a hostage to force me to surrender some critical products and designs to them," Sebastian said rigidly. "They were sending a warning note to my office, but Dylan--the head of Interpol--intercepted the delivery and had it taken to his office. That is the reason he contacted me. I didn't realize that these bastards would be acting on their threat this soon."

"Will you contact Interpol about Arielle missing?" Allworth asked.

"No, they tried to help last year, and you can see where we are today. They made a mess of the situation by letting the goons get away. This time, we're going to handle the situation the immortal way."

"Who's the top guy? Do you know?" Christian asked, holding Isabella tightly against his side.

"I'm sure the top guy is the Prime Minister himself."

"You must be joking," Eva scoffed.

"No, Eva, I'm not joking. That's why Troy, Nathan, and I were in Brussels for the past two days. Interpol had set surveillance across the street from their building, and we watched the goons at work. We saw their activities, and we identified several of their members. We followed a couple of the killers, hoping to receive more detail information, but as it worked out, we were the last people they had sawed before they met their maker." He paused for a long moment, and his eyes narrowed. "One thing is for sure. They have a lot of people involved in this attempt to extort the secret designs from my company. They are willing to hurt, and I mean hurt, those that I love by forcing me to submit to their threats and relinquish all that they demand without any reluctance or objections."

Eva gasped. "So what now?" she asked.

"We're going to destroy each and every one of them, and send the Prime Minister a strong message that he needs to stay clear of IIRL." Sebastian took a deep breath and continued. "They gave me five hours to gather the documents, but the five hours have passed. I never saw the envelope since Dylan intercepted the delivery to my office." His jaw clenched, and he pressed his mouth into a thin line. "I'm also sure that as long as they think they can make me surrender the documents, Arielle will not be harmed. They are planning on using her as the pawn in their sick game." Sebastian took a deep breath and pulverized his teeth in sheer anger.

"Sebastian, I don't want to speculate as to what your next step would be, but we need to check out all our options," Troy said firmly.

"Troy, the brutal reality is that we have no idea which way they went or where they are holding her captive. We need some mediation," he said thoughtfully, pinching the tip of his nose. Immediately, all heads swiveled toward Eva.

"What?" she asked, blowing her hair out of her face.

"Eva," Gabrielle whispered. Her eyes narrowed as she regarded her. "You're the only one with the ability to connect with Arielle's thoughts. I have witnessed the connection between the two of you. It is at a very deep level and quite amazing if I must say. Eva, this is as serious as anything can get." Her voice was coated with profound concern. "Please try and bridge your minds," Gabrielle furthered. Eva's eyes shot up, filled with anxiety.

"Can you do that, Miss Winters?" Professor Allworth asked, eyes wide open.

Eva nodded but didn't say anything. She needed a little time for the earth to stop tilting about her. Her gaze moved to Sebastian's face and her muscles tensed. If she could only feel half of the pain he was feeling, she would be able to explain the dismal expression that painted his beautiful face. The more she thought about what Sebastian said, the angrier she got. She finally turned to face Professor Allworth. "Yes, Arielle and I use streams of energy to telepathically convey our thoughts. We have successfully bridged our thoughts in the past, and I'm sure going to try this again," she said through clenched teeth.

"How can that possibly work?" Allworth was dumbfounded.

"Arielle has to be conscious. She must be aware that she dropped her amulet, and our way of communicating is the only hope she has to let us know where she is."

"That is amazing," Allworth said, utterly surprised.

Christian, Isabella, Loren, and Paul exchanged shocked glances, but remained pokerfaced and didn't say a word.

"How long has she been gone?" Sebastian asked again. Pain coated his voice.

"About an hour," said Gabrielle.

"If she was gagged and drugged, she would be most likely unconscious for the next hour or so," Sebastian said and gritted his teeth. He knew that he had to grab control of the situation. He must regain his unbreakable immortal composure and bring Arielle home safely. At this point, nothing was more important, nothing more urgent than having the love of his life back in his arms.

"Eva, can you please try?" Sebastian pleaded, watching her closely.

"Yes," Eva replied. She paused fractionally. "I'm already working on it. I'll keep at it until I connect with her thoughts."

"I think y..." Sebastian's phone rang, and he didn't finish his sentence. Flipping it open, he answered quickly without looking at the screen.

"Gaulle."

"Sebastian!" Dylan's voice boomed from the other end. "I have both bad news and some great news!"

"What is it, Dylan? I don't think I need any more bad news right now."

"You sound terrible," he said.

"What's up?" Sebastian said, ignoring his statement.

"My agents in Brussels just called. They intercepted a conversation between Jorrit and the two goons that he sent to Brighton. Unfortunately, they already have Arielle." His voice was anxious but quite cheery.

What is he so happy about? Sebastian thought to himself. "Yes, we know," Sebastian replied flatly. "Arielle has been missing for over an hour now," he continued glumly.

"Listen to me. I know that you're upset, but I have some great news!" he exclaimed.

"I don't understand," Sebastian muttered.

"Jorrit told his goons here that two assassins are flying in from Belarus to take over the situation. He asked Vitorio to pick them up at the airport," he paused and took a deep breath.

Sebastian's mind was working double time trying to figure out the best way to bring Arielle home. "How is that great news?" he asked absentmindedly.

"Sebastian! He gave Vitorio a detailed description of the two men, their flight number, and the airline. They are due to land in two and half hours at Gatwick."

Sebastian's eyes shot up. "Hey, Dylan, that's fantastic!" Sebastian couldn't hide his joy. "Can I have those details?"

"Sure, do you have a pen and paper?"

"I don't need to write it down. I'm ready; go ahead."

"They are flying in on Belarusian Airlines flight 234. The assassins are both tall and stocky with blond hair and blue eyes. They will be dressed in jeans and white shirts. Each one will be holding a brown briefcase and carrying a brown duffle bag. I know that Vitorio is tall, black hair, and green eyes so that you can keep that in mind. All those details should make them pretty easy to identify."

"Dylan, you have no idea how grateful I am."

"Sebastian, I know how eager you are to bring Arielle home. I can't keep you from going to the airport, but please be careful, and let my men do their job. They know how to tail cars inconspicuously, and they will follow them to where they are holding Arielle. I promise you that Arielle will be home today."

Sebastian couldn't contain his cheerfulness. "Thank you, Dylan. I'll be careful. I will stay out of your men's way." His beautiful face lit up with exhilaration. When he was off the phone, he took a deep breath and laughed joyfully.

Everyone around him, but for Paul and Gabrielle seemed jubilant. They had all heard the conversation between Dylan and Sebastian using their immortal ability.

"What is going on?" Gabrielle asked, glancing around, completely lost. "Why are you all so happy? Did they find Arielle?"

"No, Gabby," said Eva, "but Arielle is going to be home shortly."

"What?" She stared at Eva, with eyes wide open.

Eva rehashed the details of the phone call.

Sebastian turned his attention to Troy, Ian, and Christian. He was determined to bring all the horrid events to an end. "I would appreciate if you go with me to the airport. Everyone else, please go home, and we will keep you informed."

"But, Sebastian, I want to help," Loren whined.

Sebastian's lips quirked up at his sister's eagerness. "No, Loren, you need to go home with Paul. If I need you or Eva or Isabella, I will contact you. Keep your mobiles close."

Gabrielle glanced at Sebastian mulishly. "I want to help," she said vehemently.

"Gabrielle, please go home, baby," Troy said, taking Gabrielle in his arms and kissing her softly.

She made a face and held back the urge to roll her eyes, but didn't argue. "Can I have the keys please?" she asked.

"Oh, bloody hell!" Troy cried out and made a ghastly face. "We left the car at Dylan's office."

"Take my car," Sebastian said. He pulled the keys that Ian gave him out of his jean pocket and handed them to her. "We can't use my car anyway. It is too small."

"We can use mine," Ian jumped in.

"Isabella, can you please take Eva home?" Ian asked, and bending down; he pressed a soft kiss on Eva's forehead.

Finally, Sebastian turned fractionally and gazed at Professor Allworth. "Professor, thank you for waiting here and for your concern. I'll ring you when Arielle is home safe," Sebastian said and, reaching out, he shook his hand appreciatively.

"I'll be anxious to hear from you," he said softly. "I'm very fond of Arielle. She is quite a remarkable girl."

"Thank you, Professor," Sebastian beamed at him. "I couldn't agree more."

Once everyone dispersed, the guys piled into Ian's BMW and headed for Sebastian's home.

"What are we going to do about Dylan's men?" Ian asked.

"I wouldn't worry about them. We'll outsmart them as we did last year. When we arrive at the place they are holding Arielle, we'll enter using our immortal speed, and we'll become invisible to the human eye. We'll be in and out of there in no time at all." A strong bothersome feeling in the pit of his stomach made him swallow hard, and he scowled.

"What is it?" Ian asked, watching the expressions that lapped across Sebastian's face in a rapid pace.

"I pray that she wasn't harmed," he said severely. Everyone seemed to be at a loss for words.

"I'll tear their bodies apart piece by piece. I will make their death slow and painful." The cold in his voice sipped right through their veins and settled into the marrow of their bone. They didn't trust the goons to keep their hands off of Arielle. The good thing was this would be over in a very short time. Arriving at Sebastian's home, they all headed for the fridge in need of salve to boost their energy to the ultimate level. They put in place and discussed a short plan and, soon after that, they were in their car and on the way to the airport. Sebastian's sole thought was to bring Arielle home safely and into his arms where she belonged.

 *Chapter 6*

EARLY THE MORNING of the abduction, Vitorio and Mauritsio arrived at the campus parking lot and sat in the car, patiently waiting and planning. Suddenly Vitorio's mobile rang.

"Yeah," he answered blankly.

"Vitorio, it's Jorrit."

"Yes, sir," he said making a ghastly face.

"I called Vasily in Belarus, and he's sending two of his men. They'll be arriving in Brighton on an afternoon flight. Do you have a piece of paper? You'll have to pick them up."

"Yes, hold on for just a second."

He pulled a pen out of his shirt pocket and used the newspaper as a pad. "I'm ready; go ahead."

Jorrit gave him the flight number, the time of arrival, and a clear description of the two goons.

"I have it," Vitorio said vacuously.

"Vitorio, I gave them a description of you and Mauritsio. I'm sure you will recognize each other. Don't forget to pick them up," Jorrit's voice boomed over the phone.

"We won't," Vitorio replied and rolled his eyes in clear exasperation.

"He must think that I'm stupid," he growled after Jorrit ended the call. "I hate him," he emphasized again. Mauritsio remains silent. They sat quietly and waited, just as they did each and every morning.

A few minutes later, they saw Sebastian and Arielle pulling into a parking space. Sebastian stepped out of the car and, walking around, he opened Arielle's door and helped her out.

"He's quite the gentleman," Mauritsio snorted.

"I'd like to show him, a gentleman," Vitorio added and made a nasty gesture.

Sebastian picked up her book bag in one hand and, clasping Arielle's hand with the other; he pulled her toward the main building. They heard a digital beep as Sebastian pressed the fob key on his key chain. It was not long before they noticed the rest of their friends arrive, one couple after the other.

"I do wish our lives could be as trouble-free as their lives are," Mauritsio murmured. "Sometimes I'm sick of this life and the baggage that comes with it."

"I know," Vitorio muttered. "I have the same thoughts, quite often, but I know that it's too late to change this. There is actually no way out of this," he furthered bitterly. "It is this or the morgue." The silence stretched between them as they both shuddered at the thought. Vitorio leaned back on the headrest and closed his eyes. Now they had to wait just as they did every day. He was dozing off when Mauritsio's shocked voice snapped him out of his stupor.

"What is it?" he stammered, blinking rapidly.

"Look! Sebastian and one of his friends are leaving without the girls."

"What?" Vitorio was utterly startled. "What do you suppose this means?"

"I've no idea, but whatever it means, I like it," Mauritsio said, shaking his head in pure delight. They watched them both as they climbed into Troy's car and sped out of the parking lot with a sense of urgency.

"That's just unbelievable," Vitorio whispered astoundingly, weighing the possibilities out loud of what they just saw. "If they don't come back, the girl will be alone." There was hope in the tone of his voice.

"What do you think about that?" he asked Mauritsio, thumping him on his arm and laughing startlingly loud.

Mauritsio snorted, "This might make it very easy," he said, glancing at Vitorio. They both stared at Sebastian's blue Porsche still sitting in the parking lot, and they felt jubilation spreading across their bodies. It was exactly what they had hoped for. According to the surveillance, the Friday schedule showed Arielle leaving campus at two o'clock. Now all they had to do was wait. There was a clear possibility that Arielle might be with one of her friends, but they would have to wait and see.

"I wish we could complete this today and be done," Mauritsio said, eyes darkened, expression overwhelmed by boredom. "I'd like to go home."

"Yeah, I know what you mean," Vitorio muttered and, reaching in the back seat, he grabbed the newspaper. He decided to thumb through it and catch up on the daily news while waiting for Arielle to show up. Mauritsio's mobile beeped. Gazing at the screen, he saw a text message from his best friend Ronaldo. Sliding the arrow at the bottom to unlock it, he read the text. *Where are you, man?*

He chuckled and texted back swiftly. *I'm in Brighton on an assignment. What's up?*

His friend's next text elevated his curiosity. *Last night I thought I was going to die, and this morning for the love of God, man! —I wish I had—* ☹.

He frowned at the text message, wondering what in the world was going on. *It can't be that bad!* he texted. His best friend Ronaldo was known by all their friends to be quite mischievous. He was now intrigued, waiting to hear the latest newsflash.

Ronaldo's reply made him gasp audibly. First, he chuckled. Then he burst out into a hardy laugh, and by the end of the message, he was bent over holding his stomach.

Vitorio glanced up from the paper and stared at him in utter wonder. "What the hell is so funny?"

Mauritsio tried to explain, but he couldn't stop laughing.

"Let me see that," Vitorio said and snatched the mobile from Mauritsio's hand. The text from Ronaldo read:

I am sure happy that you were not here this morning, and I emphasize the word happy ☺ I took a laxative yesterday afternoon and forgot all about it. Last night, Franco and Bruno called to go drinking, and I was completely plastered. I don't know how I came home. Thank God I woke up this morning alone because I was horrified at the sight. I am relieved that nobody saw my bed or me this morning. Unfortunately, I did, and I immediately threw up. I'm sure you understand what happened. What a shitty mess!

Vitorio burst out into uncontrollable laughter. When he turned over at Mauritsio, he laughed even harder. Mauritsio appeared like he was at another level of consciousness, and suddenly, he went into another manic fit of laughter. By the time they stopped laughing, they were breathing hard.

"Well, that warrants a good reply," Vitorio said and laughed once again.

"You're right," Mauritsio said and coughed, clearing his throat. Hi took his mobile back from Vitorio, and holding back laughter, he texted Ronaldo. Vitorio leaned slightly closer to read Mauritsio's reply.

Hey, man, that had to be a monumental revelation! I'm overjoyed to have missed your epic event. I'm sure it was a stinky situation and a foul morning ☺!

When he hit sent, they both exploded into another round of laughter. "That was quite funny," Vitorio muttered, still chuckling, and he went back to reading his newspaper.

Mauritsio scanned across the parking lot, but there wasn't a single creature in sight. They both settled back in their seats as the silence stretched between them and boredom slipped right through their body and soul. It would be another few hours before Arielle would be finished with her last class.

Suddenly, Mauritsio let out a hard gasp. Vitorio looked up, and his jaw dropped. Arielle was running across the last quad by the parking lot. *Alone.* The book bag was dangling from one hand, and the other was stretched out toward the blue Porsche. They heard the beeping of the lock and watched dumbfounded as she reached the car and pulled the passenger door open. They were not sure as to what she was doing, but here she was, giving them the chance of a lifetime.

The parking lot was bare, not a single soul in sight. They never expected Arielle to play right into their hands in such an easy way.

They watched her vigilantly as she opened the passenger door, climbed inside the car on her hands and knees, and searched throughout the vehicle, searching frantically for something.

Quietly, they approached and stood right behind her. When she finally found what she was looking for, she straightened up and stepped back to shut the door. She never had the chance to scream. Vitorio moved fast. He wrapped one arm around her neck and yanked her firmly against his body and, with the other, he clamped a piece of cloth soaked in chloroform over her mouth and nose.

Terror surged through her body; her lungs locked as she struggled to breathe, but there was no air supply. She kicked, pushed, and tried to scream, but it came out as a stifled shriek. With all her might, she tried to escape from her attacker, but he held her hard around the neck, and soon she surrendered to a smothering sensation and finally to unconsciousness. Her body went limp, and everything in her hands dropped to the ground, scattering around them. Mauritsio used his foot and shoved everything inconspicuously underneath the car, away from curious eyes.

They carried Arielle to their car and threw her in the back seat of the black Mercedes. Taking another glance around, making sure they were not detected by anyone, they spun out of the parking lot, adrenalin working overtime. At first, they were so overwhelmed that for a long while they remained in stunned silence.

"Wow!" Vitorio finally exclaimed, unable to keep his excitement from spilling over. "That was amazing!" They both glanced at the back seat and smiled wide.

"That was a piece of cake," Mauritsio said and snorted.

"She is a real beauty, isn't she?" Vitorio added.

"Yes, she sure is," Mauritsio replied with a repulsive snort. "I hope we can have a little fun with her before this is over."

Vitorio rolled his eyes at the comment and grinned. "I think we should call Jorrit," he said joyfully. He picked up his mobile and pressed Jorrit's number.

"Jorrit here," he answered gruffly.

"Jorrit! We have the girl!" Vitorio screamed through the phone.

There was complete silence on the other end. Finally, Jorrit's voice boomed from the other end. "You do?"

"Yes, she is right here in the back seat, and we are headed to the place we've rented."

"That's great news! No—no—no, what am I saying! That's excellent news!" he screamed, unable to hold back his exuberance. "I have to call Rainer right away," he added. There was a short silence on the other end, and suddenly Jorrit's voice roared over the phone. "Vitorio! Make sure you don't touch a single hair on the girl's head. Those are the directives from the higher ups. You don't want to create any trouble for me because I'll make your lives miserable. Do you hear me?"

Vitorio was rattled in disbelief, utterly speechless. They never expected something like that. They thought that they were both in for a real good time.

"Do you hear me?" Jorrit's voice boomed from the other end, flatly.

"Yessss…yes, I hear you," Vitorio stammered.

"Good, now that we understand each other, call me when she is locked up so we can move on to the next step," he said, coarsely. He ended the conversation without waiting for a reply.

"Son of a bitch," Vitorio flipped the phone shut. Eyes pinched with anger; he cursed through clenched teeth.

"What is it?" Mauritsio asked.

"He never said good job or nice going. All he said was to keep our hands off the girl. We are not to even think about touching a hair on her head. He wants us to make sure that we bring her into the house, lock her up, and then call him."

Mauritsio made a face of disbelief. "Was he joking?"

"He didn't sound like he was joking to me."

"How would he even know?" Mauritsio asked, holding a stunned expression on his face.

"Do you want to put a wager on this?" he asked, glancing Mauritsio's way. "I thought you knew Jorrit by now. He doesn't make idle threats. You are playing with your life," he said firmly. "Jorrit isn't easy to fool, and he doesn't take well to having his directives ignored," he furthered with a stiff jaw. He recalled finding himself in a similar situation once before, and he didn't like the punishment. He was told that if this were to happen again, he would be sent to the morgue. He shuddered at the thought, and gazing out the window, he muttered fearfully. "I know that I don't want to take that chance." He was quiet for a short moment and, glancing back at his partner, he said through gritted teeth, "but if you want to do that, Mauritsio, then go ahead."

Mauritsio grimaced at the tone of Vitorio's words. "No, I suppose I don't," he murmured in a low voice, turning his attention on the road. They drove in silence for a long time. Arielle was going to be out for another hour or so. Mauritsio quickly glanced at the back seat and chuckled revoltingly. "This takes all the fun out of this job. She is very beautiful!" he complained in a sour tone.

Vitorio remained silent.

"Do we need to stop and tie her up?" Mauritsio asked.

"No, there is no need. She's not going anywhere. We'll be at the house shortly. She'll never know where she is or how she was taken there."

They drove through the streets of Brighton in high speed. They stopped in front of a small house surrounded by a six-foot brick wall. Vitorio pressed a button on the car visor and opened the gate. He pulled into the garage slowly, closing the gate and the garage door behind them.

Mauritsio stepped out of the car and moved quickly to open the door while Vitorio leaned into the car and scooped Arielle's unconscious body into his arms. The warmth of her soft body and the scent of her perfume made him shudder. His jaw muscles were locked, and his teeth clenched while trying to block his mind from accepting the appeal of this beautiful girl in his arms. Mauritsio held the door open for him, and he carried her through the door and down a long, poorly lit corridor, stopping at the top of a staircase leading to the basement.

"Turn the lights on," he yelled nervously. He needed to move away from this girl as soon as possible.

Mauritsio closed and locked the door behind him. He then flipped the corridor light switch on. Vitorio descended the stairs in a fast pace. There were three rooms in the basement. He walked toward the one in the very back and, turning to his side, he pushed the door open with his upper body.

The room was quite large with a private bath but poorly lit. There were a few cheap furnishings and a small window with iron bars on the outside. He laid her on the bed and stared at her for a long moment. Mauritsio walked right behind him and gazed down at the girl. He let a quiet whistle through his teeth.

"She's mouthwatering, wouldn't you say?" he muttered and sighed noisily. Vitorio nodded but kept his thoughts to himself. They stood there for a few more minutes, and finally, they turned around, walked out, and locked the door behind them. Climbing the stairs two at a time, they reached the front of the house, and picking up the phone; they called Jorrit.

"Okay, boss, she's locked up in the basement."

"Good job, you guys! Rainer is extremely pleased. We are almost done with our part of the job. All we have to do is send the final extortion envelope. I need some photos of her in that room showing her unconscious on this bed. Send them to me right away via text. Sit tight, and make sure nothing goes wrong. The boys from Belarus will be there soon to take over. Are you sure you were not followed?"

"Yes, we're sure. There was not a single soul in that parking lot."

"Make sure she is not harmed."

"We will," Vitorio said stiffly.

"There will be a little more money for both of you when you come back," Jorrit added.

"Thanks, boss, we'll be right here if you need us."

"Don't forget to pick up Vasily's boys this afternoon from the airport and don't forget to send me those photos."

"Mauritsio is on his way to take the photos right now," Vitorio said. "What do you want us to do after Vasily's guys arrive?" he asked meekly.

"They will take it from there, and you are free to come home. You have done good, real… good," Jorrit said joyfully. But just before he hung up, he stated again in a robust voice. "Vitorio, the photos, don't take long," and the call ended.

Vitorio rolled his eyes once again, and glancing at Mauritsio; he made a gesture toward the camera.

"He actually said some nice things, this time, around," Vitorio added thoughtfully.

"What was all that about Mauritsio is on his way?"

"Oh, I told him you were on your way to the basement to take some photos of the girl while in an unconscious state. He wants to show them to Gaulle, so he understands that we are not playing any games."

"He wants them now?"

"Yes, go and take them real quick. As soon as you come back, I'll shoot them off to him."

Mauritsio picked up the digital camera and walked out of the room. "I'm on my way. I'll be right back."

"Be sure that's all you do, and hurry back," Vitorio said, in a meaningful voice.

"Yeah…yeah…yeah…" Mauritsio called out glumly.

Vitorio took a beer from the fridge and, walking into the next room, he took a seat at a large armchair. He took a cigarette out and lit it, blowing thick smoke toward the ceiling. Wild thoughts were invading his mind. He closed his eyes and tried to wipe them out. It seemed that a century had gone by since the last relationship he had with a nice, decent girl. Nice girls didn't frequent the raunchy places he patronized and didn't fall in love with murderers like him. He wanted to find love, to feel passionate about another human being. He wanted someone to love him. He shook his head in clear frustration and, standing up, he started to pace back and forth. He wondered how many guys in his line of work had the same thoughts. He was sure that he was not the only one, but that didn't make him feel any better.

Mauritsio was back in a very short time. Taking the card out of the camera, he sat in front of the computer and transferred the images of Arielle in captivity into his file and sent them to Jorrit.

"Well, that's done. Now we wait, right?" he said out loud, snapping Vitorio out of his troubling thoughts.

"What?" he said startled and turned to face Mauritsio.

"You didn't hear me?" he asked in shocked surprise. He had come into the room whistling joyfully and kept on whistling while transferring the photos to the computer and e-mailing them to Jorrit. How could Vitorio miss all that noise? What was bothering him? "I said that I am finished with taking the photos, and I already sent them to Jorrit."

"Oh, that's great, thank you," he murmured absentmindedly

"Something is bothering you," Mauritsio insisted.

Vitorio opens his mouth ready to say something, but he closed it again deciding against it. "No...," he said, and his voice trailed. Walking back, he sank into the chair with a deep sigh. He picked up the beer and took a large swig letting out a long sigh. The cigarette was burned into the ashtray, so he lit another one and remained quiet.

"Do you want to play cards until we have to leave for the airport?" Mauritsio asked, not knowing what was eating Vitorio.

"No, we need to check on the girl and make sure she's all right."

"I just came back, and she was still out. We have over two hours before we have to be at the airport," Mauritsio said.

"All right then, go bring the cards out."

Mauritsio smiled wide and went to do what Vitorio asked. "We're playing for money," he called back and laughed.

"Yeah...Yeah... I have no problem taking your money," Vitorio replied, amused.

Chapter 7

ARIELLE OPENED HER EYES gradually. Her brain was clouded and utterly disoriented. She felt overwhelmingly fatigued and found it very difficult to keep awake. Her eyes moved sluggishly around the poorly lit room, but nothing seemed familiar. Her mind was blurry, filled with jumbled up images. She clenched her eyes shut, thinking she was dreaming, but when she opened them again, the surroundings hadn't changed. *What is happening to me?* Her brain cells seemed to be completely stripped of oxygen; she couldn't remember a thing, and she couldn't think straight. *Where am I? How did I get here? Who brought me here? Where is here?* There seemed to be no electrical impulses traveling between her brain neurons. She had all these questions but no answers. Lifting her arms, fists clenched, she rubbed her eyes back and forth, trying to amass her faculties.

Minutes seemed to tick by, and panic settled in, paralyzing every muscle in her body. Nothing made sense. The sensation deepened and she tried to block the anxiety unsuccessfully. Something was terribly wrong, but the wall between her physical body and her consciousness seemed to be temporarily impenetrable.

She lay on that bed motionless, but for how long, she wasn't sure. Muddling through her vague thoughts, she tried to make sense of her present situation. She searched around the room one more time and inhaled deeply. She couldn't gather her bearings. The silence dragged for what she thought was a century. *A century. Century.* The word seemed to be moving inside her brain and bouncing around like a Ping-Pong ball. *Why does that word seem to strike a chord?*

Her heart pounded against her chest, her brain spinning out of control. *God, what is happening to me? Where am I? Why can't I muddle through this fog in my head?* Abruptly, she was startled by a set of deep emerald eyes, intercepting her thoughts and steeling her breath away. The striking face of a man emerged from the depths of her soul and found its way through to the forefront of her vision and jolted her mind to consciousness. It was almost like throwing an enormous surge of power into an electrical device by plugging it into a wall socket.

Arielle was paralyzed by the vision. "Sebastian!" she cried out, brought back from oblivion to reality. She closed her eyes as a surge of warmth and passion for him gushed through her veins and settled deep in the pit of her stomach. *Where is he? Does he know that I am here? Is he trying to find me?* A wave of shattering pain ripped right through her body, leaving her empty, lonely, and scared. *Oh Sebastian, where are you?* She whimpered anxiously and started to sob.

Vivid memories started trickling into her brain. The last thing she remembered was fighting for breath. Someone had grabbed her while standing at the campus parking lot by the car. She recalled the frantic struggle to break free from her attacker's chokehold. She winced at the thought, and her body tensed as panic settled deep into her bones. Lifting her arm, she glanced at her wristwatch. It was 2:35 in the afternoon. It had been over an hour and a half since she had walked back to the car to retrieve her mobile phone. "Who did this?"

Supported by her elbows, she pushed against the bed and propped herself up gradually. She searched for something that appeared familiar, but nothing was coming back. A wave of anguish ripped through her, ramming her heart into her throat. *Where in bloody hell am I?*

She inhaled deeply, scrambling to distinguish between reality and a dream. She sat up, and her eyes flicked to the window. It was raining, and the sky was a dark gray. *Who could possible want to keep me a prisoner and why?*

It didn't take long and, suddenly, she gasped for breath. Icy fingers crawled slowly down her spine as a name, distorted but very familiar, flashed in front of her like a bright neon sign. Bile rose to her throat quickly, and nausea threatened. *Annabel! Annabel! Oh, God, it's Annabel.* This was the year for their wedding, and she was not going to allow her to marry Sebastian.

She fell back on the bed and threw her arm over her eyes. Tears streamed down the sides of her face and into her ears as fear raced across her body, and her hand moved swiftly to her neck. Her eyes widened in sheer shock and horror invaded every fiber of her body. Her necklace was not there. *Oh...God...,* she muttered, hopelessness taking over. Reality crashed into her skull like a thunderbolt and pressure generated a stinging pain behind her eyelids. She was trembling with fright, knowing that she was alone and helpless against an unbreakable immortal.

Forced gasps escaped her and scattered through the stillness of the room. "Why would she bring me here?" she thought out loud, scrutinizing her surroundings like a wild animal trapped in a steel cage. *And where is here?* Fear surged though her body and her muscles tensed to a painful point. Desperation and terror seeped deep into her bone marrow, and her heart pounded the walls of her chest like a sledgehammer.

She couldn't just lie here; she had to do something to escape, but how? She sprang up, swung her legs over the edge of the bed, and struggled to her feet only to almost collapse. The floor swayed beneath her feet and she grabbed on to the nightstand to steady herself.

Trembling, she tried to bring in her mind a glimpse of something to help her, something like her book bag or her mobile, but the room was sadly bare but for the furnishings. *How am I to contact anyone?* She stood in the middle of the room unmoved with a lot of undefined, perplexing, and diverse feelings. She felt isolated and desperate.

Words couldn't define the rush of emotions that surged through her body and shook her thoughts. She was trying hard to embrace the uncertainty that was enveloping her, and all she could feel was her world crumbling at her feet and disappearing into another universe. Looking through a vortex portal into this new universe, all she saw was chaos and devastation. She couldn't distinguish between reality and fantasy. Her heart was pounding her chest in a painful way. She needed

Sebastian to lean on; she needed the safe sanctuary he provided, the warmth of his embrace, and his soft voice telling her that everything was going to be fine.

Turmoil was brewing inside her mind, spreading fear and uncertainty. Carefully, she searched around once again and observed her surroundings. She could hear the rain hit against the window and took a deep breath. The room was large and furnished poorly. A ghastly bedspread covered the four poster bed where she had been lying a few moments ago. A small nightstand was right next to the bed with a glass lamp on it and a dirty lampshade. A five-drawer dresser was pushed against the opposite wall from the bed, and a window dominated the other side of the room. Two old, shabby armchairs were on either side of the window with a small square table between them.

Walked slowly toward a partly open door, and the worn-out floor squeaked painfully under her footsteps. Standing unmoved for a long moment, she finally reached up and pushed the door wide-open. The florescent fixture on the ceiling briefly blinded her when she switched it on and peered inside. The light gave her a clear view of a very small bathroom. Mold grew at the edges of the floor tiles and around the small shower area. She flinched at the sickening sight and closed the door, twisting her lips in disgust. She turned around and crept up to the door. Not sure if it would be locked, she had to try, and it was locked. Disappointment settled deep into her stomach and, putting her ear against the panel; she listened guardedly.

She caught an unclear sound of a man speaking loudly, but the sound never sharpened into real words. Perspiration seemed to seep through her skin, making her body feel damp. She rubbed her hands together and swallowed hard, trying to overcome the fear that crept into her mind. *Where in bloody hell am I? How am I ever going to leave this place?* She needed to try and connect with Eva. She was now her only source of communication. She couldn't bear the thought of never seeing Sebastian again.

Annabel was determined to destroy Sebastian, and she had promised that she would kill her, so she needed to escape from the room before Annabel made good on her threat. She had no chance at all against a strong immortal without her amulet. Thinking about it, she was baffled. She tried hard to force her attention to the earlier events. She touched her neck and grimaced. She could almost feel the warmth of the pendant against her skin but her neck was bare. *Where and how did I lose it? Maybe while I was fumbling behind the passenger seat? But how could the clasp get unfastened? I should have felt that.* Frowning, she realized with certainty that she lost it before she was taken. If she had it on, things might have turned out differently, and she might off not been in this predicament right now. *What about my mobile and my books?* She thought out loud. *Did someone find them or did my captor pick them up? Oh God!* She had so many unanswered questions.

Turning around, she walked toward the other side of the room. Her eyes drifted around. She noticed the hideous wallpaper that was covering the walls and humphed. She needed to stay strong, but how could she do that when there was not a single item around to give comfort to her nerves? Clenching her fists to her side, she stood and stared out the rain-streaked window. The sky darkened, matching the way she felt inside. Tears pooled and began to flow freely down her face. There were iron bars installed on the outside of the window. *Why? Who did that? Why? Why?...* That view appeared to seal the fate of any person held in that room. And right now, imprisonment seemed to be her fate. She blinked back the displeasure of her situation.

She was suffocating, unable to breathe, and terror crept right through her bones. Forcing air into her lungs, she stepped closer to the window. She reached up, snapped the latch upward, and pushed the window leaves wide open. Stretching her arms through the bars, she let the rain soak through her skin as she began to sob intensely.

A trembling sigh escaped her lips, and she raised her eyes toward the thick blanket of clouds in a silent prayer. She begged for the courage to find sagacity and abolish any deviation between her mind and body to face her captor with new strength. She was grateful that she was still alive, but she was frantically longing for Sebastian, her family, and her friends. She shut her eyes tightly and shuddered at the thought that this may be the end of everything. A light breeze whooshed through the open window, and a strange feeling coursed across her skin as if invisible gentle fingers stroked her pale face.

She glanced back at the sky and gasped. A small circle of clear blue sky was peeking through that thick blanket of clouds. *How could that be possible?* It was not there a second ago, almost like an answer to her silent prayer, that there was hope in sight. God was smiling at her, and she smiled back through the mist of her soggy eyes. The pounding of the rain on the window didn't promise any relief from the nasty weather.

Her head whipped around and faced the door as heavy footsteps snapped her out of her reverie. Her mouth fell open and, weighing the situation, she moved quickly. She closed the window and threw herself on the bed, shutting her eyes and remaining totally unmoving, professing unconsciousness. Her adrenalin was elevated, and her nerves were shattered.

Her ears were tuned to every sound, minor or otherwise. She heard the key turn slowly, and the lock released. The door opened, and male voices become clear and concise.

"She's still unconscious!" Mauritsio said in a stunned voice as he walked into the room.

"She should be coming around shortly," Vitorio replied. The floor creaked under the weight of the heavy footsteps as they approached the bed. Arielle heard their heavy accents, and something tried to break through her memory barrier, but it died just as fast as it came.

"*Certo lei e bella…*" Mauritsio murmured, staring down at Arielle. She had absolutely no idea what the man said, but she knew enough to understand that he spoke Italian. She wanted badly to open her eyes, but she kept her muscles still and relaxed.

"Do you think she would remember us?" Mauritsio asked Vitorio.

What? Arielle thought to herself. Her mind was in outright turmoil. She obviously had met these men before. *But when? Where?* She was listening now extra carefully to every word spoken in that room.

"If not for Jorrit, I would give this little girl something to remember me by." Mauritsio's voice was raspy filled with something sinister.

Vitorio's eyes narrowed and blew out an exasperated breath. "Yeah, I suppose you would, but unfortunately for you, that's out of the question now," he said sternly. His voice was sharp, his words strong. "She's not to be touched, and that's final."

"I don't have to be happy about it," Mauritsio added stubbornly.

Arielle didn't like the sound of that at all, but she remained still. Her confused brain locked onto the strange name. *Who was Jorrit? What did they want with her?*

"She's quite beautiful..." Vitorio said. Arielle could feel both of the men standing right before the bed, most likely staring down at her. "But orders are orders, and we don't want to take a chance to piss off Jorrit," Vitorio furthered.

"Yeah...yeah...yeah... I hear you. But a man is allowed to fantasize, Vitorio."

The blood pounded Arielle's eardrums as her anxiety increased and she was having difficulty breathing. She frantically searched the far corners of her memory to recall the names Jorrit and Vitorio, but nothing came through. Her frustration was becoming an obsession, threatening to reveal the fact that she wasn't unconscious.

She was experiencing a strong feeling of anger that was penetrating through her brain. Anger, fury, rage, and all those negative emotions bundled up into one huge ball of wrath that was nearly choking her to death. She wasn't sure if she wanted to open her eyes and see their faces or just leap out of that bed and slam herself against the man nearest to the bed and watch their reaction.

A forewarning made her pause, and she remained still, keeping her eyes shut and her mind alert. *Jorrit... Vitorio... Jorrit... Vitorio...* She kept repeating over and over again silently.

"Let's go; she is still out. We'll check on her before we leave for the airport to pick up Vasily's men from Belarus?" Vitorio said.

What? What? Arielle thought she was hallucinating. Everything she heard sounded ridiculous. She was losing her mind. There was no other explanation. *Leave for the airport? Who was Vasily? Why was he sending men to Brighton? Belarus? What in bloody hell was going on?* She just couldn't make heads or tails out of this conversation. This didn't sound like Annabel's men. Her name never came up, and all the other names and places were of no significance to her. Finally, she heard the floor squeak again as they turned and started to walk away. It sounded like they paused in the middle of the room and the next statement sent shockwaves right through her body, and reality made her flesh crawl.

"If Gaulle surrenders the documents, he will be able to have this beauty back, and we'll all go home. If not, we'll have to show him that we don't play games. So don't like her too much, if you understand what I mean," Vitorio said and chuckled repulsively. Arielle shivered trying to remain still.

"Vitorio, I just can't believe that Jorrit cares about this girl. I know for a fact that he doesn't even care about his own mother. I don't understand it," Mauritsio said, sounding very frustrated.

"Don't be an idiot," Vitorio replied. "He doesn't give a shit about this girl; he only cares about himself. The orders came all the way from the top. I'm sure that Rainer told him that his orders must be followed without any deviations," he furthered. There was a short pause, and then he continued. "I also know Rainer, and if his orders are not followed, that will guarantee Jorrit's demise. And I can assure you that Jorrit would make sure that we follow him all the way to hell." Mauritsio winced at Vitorio's words.

The silence stretched between them again, and Arielle thought she was going to die if she had to stay still for much longer.

"I should have made my move the night we met her and her pretty friend at the bar," Mauritsio snorted. "Do you remember?"

"Yes, I do. Now let's go," Vitorio snapped.

Instantaneous recognition crashed into her brain like a tsunami that slams into land with vast speed. This had nothing to do with Annabel; it was all about the issue Sebastian had with the Mafia about his company's documents. The Mafia was keeping her for ransom and not the immortals. This was a truly shocking revelation. Did it make her feel any better? Well, no. She was still locked in this room and still in danger of being hurt.

She finally heard a strong curse break the silence, and shortly after their footsteps moved farther away from the bed. Next, she heard the door slam shut, the key turn in the lock and the footsteps fade away. Arielle just stayed there totally unmoved for a few more seconds. Finally, she opened her eyes and stared at the ceiling in total shock. *Oh my God,* she finally gasped, new reality sipping deep into her very core. Mauritsio's last statement made contact with her brain cells. She inhaled sharply. She had met these guys before, but where? Deep fear sunk to the pit of her stomach. Fear was a strange thing; it could control every thought, and paralyze every muscle in your body. *So this was planned. This is undoubtedly what Sebastian was worried about, and he was refusing to tell me. He was trying to protect me. Oh my God... Where is Sebastian?*

Thinking back, she remembered that she was to meet Gabrielle outside the auditorium at two o'clock, right after her last class with Professor Allworth. She was sure that her absence alerted Gabrielle that something was terribly wrong, and she would have contacted Sebastian. Based on the conversation of her captors, Sebastian had received a demand note, using her as bait to pressure him in surrendering his secret drawings and documents in exchange for her life. They had no idea that they were dealing with a bunch of unbreakable immortals with superhuman abilities. A horrendous tornado was about to slam and abolish their dirty schemes and their miserable lives.

The thought that she would not be hurt until they heard back from Sebastian gave her strength. Sebastian's image filled her senses and warmth enveloped her like a protective shield. She missed him so very much and wanted to hold him. She needed his embrace that provided her sanctuary and put her world back on its axis. Tears filled her eyes and started to stream down her face uncontrollably.

Rising slowly once again, she swung her legs over the edge of the bed, and taking a deep breath; she stood up. The miserable and misty weather did very little to raise her mood as she gazed out the window. She approached gradually and, resting her hands on the windowsill; she pressed her nose against the glass.

She closed her eyes and tried to reach Eva's thoughts subconsciously. They had always had the ability to exchange thoughts between them by sending and receiving on the transcendent level. They were able to communicate their thoughts sagaciously without having to exchange verbal words. She kept her eyes closed and stood silently for several minutes, but she was unable to make any contact. There was complete silence coming from Eva's mind. *Why isn't Eva trying to communicate with me? Maybe Sebastian already had a rescue plan in place, and their friends had to follow that plan. Yes, that had to be it.*

She walked back slowly and sat on the bed. She was desperate for a quick solution, but she knew it was not going to be easy. She needed to think hard and develop an escape plan. They were coming back to check on her before they left for the airport; that is what they said. Bending her arms, she set her elbows on her thighs, and leaning forward; she rested her face in her hands. She closed her eyes and blew out an exasperated breath.

Where was Sebastian? Was he on the way? Why Eva didn't bother to make contact with me? She just couldn't understand any of it. It had been more than forty-five minutes since they had come into the room, and all she could do was sit and wait until they decided to come back. Maybe she could talk her way out of it. She pursed her lips, flicked her eyes at the locked door, and her face tightened. A sudden thought made her stand up and walk to the door. Maybe they forgot to lock it; she had to try.

Her fingers traced over the door handle, gripped it tightly and pulled as hard as she good. Nothing happened. The door wouldn't budge. She stood there gazing at the door as hopelessness closed and stinging stirred behind her eyelids. Tears pooled in her burning eyes and started to stream down her face once again. She was losing hope. There was no way that Sebastian would find her if Eva didn't try to communicate with her.

 *Chapter 8*

SHE TURNED to face the window and froze in place. The sound of the door handle was turning drove a cold chill down her spine. She was so lost in her thoughts she never heard footsteps approaching. The door opened behind her, and someone stepped inside. Arielle spun around and came face to face with Mauritsio. He was alone. Surprise flickered in his eyes and shock crept over his face.

"What the fuck!" he exclaimed. He didn't expect her to be standing right inside the door. Arielle's eyes widened, and her mouth dropped as she gasped in disbelief. Recognition crashed into her memory the moment she saw his face. He was one of the two Italian men she and Gabrielle met and talked with while Troy and Sebastian were in Brussels. She opened her mouth to say something but closed it back again. Words stuck in her throat, and the silence stretched for a few moments.

Mauritsio was still staring at her. He remembered the effect she had on him up close. She was quite beautiful. A lot more beautiful than he remembered from the very first time they met. He couldn't think beyond the sensation of those deep blue eyes. Her voice snapped him out of his crazy reverie.

"You...you... you're Mauritsio," she stammered, and her voice fell to a measly whisper.

"You remember my name?" he huffed in clear disbelief.

She rolled her eyes. "Why are you surprised about that?" she said blankly. "But what are you doing here? Better, what am I doing here?" she furthered.

He shrugged. "Hum… it is a long story," he said unemotionally.

She laughed a throaty laugh. "As you can see, I'm not going anywhere." Peering around the room, she made a circular motion with her hands. "I've had all the time in the world, so what am I doing here?"

He laughed a low scathing sound and shook his head. "I can't discuss this with you," he said.

She paused for a short moment, pondering his words. "You can't discuss this with me? I am your hostage; I have the right to know. Why are you doing this? What do you want from me?" she breathed quietly.

"There are many things I want from you, but now is not the time," he said wickedly.

"I don't understand," she said irritably.

"Let's just say that if you just cooperate, you will make this a lot easier for all of us."

"Who is all of us? What do you want from me?" she asked once again.

"No more talk," he said. "Go and sit down," he ordered, pointing to the bed at the other side of the room. Lifting his hand, he traced his finger down the side of her face. Arielle recoiled and gave him an icy stare. A furious flush crossed his eyes, noticing her repulsion.

"You do think you are too good for me, don't you?" he said, spitting out the words with clenched teeth.

"I thought you and your friend were nice guys and to think you're nothing but scum," she said disgustingly and spat on him.

"You better shut the fuck up," he said with a furious growl. "It's not my fault you're here. You're here because that bastard of a boyfriend you have is refusing to go along with the program."

"Wh—Wh—What?" she mumbled. "The program? What program are you talking about?"

"Don't play dumb. I'm sure you know that he is refusing to turn over the documents we want. If he doesn't comply, I can assure you that it's not going to be good for him, and it will even be worse for you," he said and cursed, never taking his eyes off of her.

"You're nothing but thugs," she said. "You have no idea who

you are messing with."

"Oh...please enlighten me," he said and laughed out loud.

Arielle decided to keep quiet and say nothing more.

"I would like nothing more than to teach you a lesson. To show you what it means to be with a real man."

"I suppose you think you are a real man," she snorted.

Mauritsio's mouth dropped open, and his eyes narrowed to slits.

"I told you to shut the fuck up," he said, fire spitting out of his eyes.

"Or what?" Arielle snorted, not understanding where all that nerve came from.

He suddenly reached over and grabbed her throat tightly, giving her a meaningful glare. "I'll throw you on that bed, and I'll show you what a real man can do, you fucking bitch," he said through clenched teeth. She raised her arm and slapped his hand away from her throat. Fury flickered in his eyes and, lifting his hand, he backhanded her hard. The stone from his pinky ring tore her cheek and pain shot right through her bones.

"Bitch!" he growls again as he watched Arielle staggered backward and, losing her balance, she dropped to the floor. Lifting her hand, she touched her cheek and felt something warm and wet. She knew she was bleeding. She pressed her lips together as wrath pooled deep in her stomach and the sound of the blood rushing through her veins pounded in her ears. She had to make her move now. She had to try and help herself out of this situation.

Blocking the excruciating pain out of her mind, she leaped up and threw herself on him. One balled hand caught him by surprise right between the eyes and her knee connected perfectly with Mauritsio's groin. The reaction to Arielle's attack on Mauritsio came both fast and furious. He doubled over in excruciating pain, holding his groin and gasping for air. His lips moved, but no sound came out. Arielle released the breath she was holding and just stared at him with rebellion as he crumbled to the floor.

"A real man," she humphed, amassing all the courage she could find, and darted out, shutting the door behind her. She turned the key, locking the door, and taking a few steps back, she stared at the closed panels. She knew that she had a short amount of time before he would recover and start to pound on the door.

Sweat dripped down her back and blood down her cheek. She swallowed hard. Swiftly turning on her heels, she vaulted toward the staircase.

She scaled them two at a time. Reaching the landing, she bolted right into a wall of muscles. She stumbled backward, lost her balance, and fell down a staircase. Her body bounced painfully off of each step and finally landed on the basement floor with a loud thump. She groaned in sheer pain. *Oh, God, I hope I didn't break any bones,* she thought anxiously. Opening her eyes, she stared up at the landing and saw a man standing there watching her, utterly astonished. She couldn't make out his face in the poorly-lit corridor, but he did seem familiar. She put her hands on the floor and pushed herself up slowly, trying to rise to her feet. The floor swayed beneath her, and she crumpled back down to the ground.

The small spark of hope that slipped through her veins after she left the room was now gone before she had time to decipher it. An expression of wretchedness flashed across her face. She was doomed. The pain was excruciating. She couldn't feel her limbs; her face burned and her eye felt swollen. She closed her eyes, feeling trapped and discouraged. She wanted to run, but her legs wouldn't respond, and even if they did, where could she go? Her lungs seared, and she couldn't contemplate anything but how to escape. Her heart thudded so loud she could hear it pounding her chest. She heard the man descending the steps unhurriedly. With a few short strides, he was standing right over her, and she swallowed nervously.

"What do we have here?" he said, his voice stunned. Reaching down, he grabbed her by her shirt and lifted her as if she weighed nothing at all.

Mustering all the courage she had, she opened her eyes. Their faces were barely a few inches apart. His lips were curved upward in an aggravating half-smile. Arielle stared at him in shock and gasped in surprise. This was the other man she and Gabrielle had met before.

"You...you are...Vitorio!" she muttered, eyes wide-open, voice barely audible.

"Yes, that's me," he said laughing unevenly. "Good memory, Arielle," he scoffed. He then moved his gaze behind her in sheer wonder, scanning the hallway for Mauritsio.

"Wh...where," he started to say and stopped mid-sentence when loud pounding came from somewhere at the end of the hallway. Vitorio stiffened, and his eyes flicked toward the pounding sound and then swiftly returned to her. Astonishment filled his eyes, and he let out a low, throaty grunt. Fury seethed as awareness settled deep into his mind. Pinning her with an icy stare, he slammed her twice against the wall indignantly, discarding her like unwanted trash.

Arielle crashed to the floor once again, and an agonized groan escaped her lips. Something warm and coppery cascaded over her mouth, down her chin, and soaked the front of her shirt. *Oh God! Please help me,* she thought. Her face was on fire, her body ached badly, and her throat felt dry. Vitorio stomped past her and headed down the hallway toward the room the desultory pounding originated from without looking back. Arielle's heart sank and hopelessness spread across every muscle in her body. Her plan of escape had skidded to a dreadful halt.

Tears streamed down her face, burning the deep laceration on her cheek, creating a penetrating bite. The pain was excruciating, but she couldn't stop crying. Her thoughts were revolving uncontrollably, unable to find the power to slow down long enough to figure out her next move. Did she have the next move? Her victory had been short lived and rather discouraging. Her mouth set into a straight line and she tried to lift her hand to wipe her face, but the pain was unbearable. She drew in a deep breath and her chest muscles screamed in discomfort. She concentrated on the pain, and her brain ordered her to stay still. Where was Sebastian? Why was he taking so long to come to her rescue?

A loud voice from the room down the hall snapped her out of her stupor. "What the fuck happened in here?" Vitorio's voice boomed. "Why are you on the floor? Did you let a little girl make a joke out of you?"

"That fucking bitch! Where is she?" Mauritsio growled.

"She's still here, no thanks to you!" Vitorio scoffed. There was a short pause. "Get off the floor. What's wrong with you?" Vitorio spat out. Mauritsio was still holding his crotch. Agony and Sweat covered his face as he tried to straighten up and failed. His eyes focused on Vitorio.

Vitorio scrutinized every move Mauritsio made carefully, eyes wide-open, lips curling up into a smirking grin. "Oh! The old trick, perfect blow right into the groin," Vitorio furthered, unable to hide the amusement from his voice.

"Damn it! It's not funny, Vitorio. It hurts like a bitch," Mauritsio growled and frowned, cursing out loud. "Where is that bitch? I'll give her what she deserves," he said, looking around wildly and making a huge effort to stand.

"I don't think you're in a position to give her anything right now," Vitorio said, and leaning down, he helped him to his feet. He watched him take a couple of steps, moaning painfully. Mauritsio's dark gaze flicked to Vitorio and scowled; he was unable to suppress his embarrassment.

"How in the hell did you let her come so close?" Vitorio muttered quizzically.

"It happened so fast I can't even remember," Mauritsio murmured awkwardly.

"You have to admire her for trying to escape," Vitorio said now, teasingly.

"What? You've got to be joking," Mauritsio exclaimed.

"Just kidding man; I was only kidding." Vitorio snorted, and giving him a soft push; they headed out of the room.

"Well, where is she?" Mauritsio asked again.

"Don't worry about her," Vitorio said. "She'll not be able to walk anywhere for a while.

"What do you mean?"

"She fell down the staircase trying to escape, and she is in bad shape."

"Oh!" Mauritsio walked slowly out of the room still holding his crotch and, turning to his left, he stared down the hallway. All he could see was a coiled body on the floor, not moving at all.

"I wanted to kill her," Mauritsio hissed.

"Well, I'm glad you didn't. That would make a few people quite angry at you if you know what I mean."

"How bad is she hurt?"

"She is a bloody mess," Vitorio continued.

"Well, Jorrit is not going to like this either," Mauritsio murmured thoughtfully.

"Um...what happened isn't our fault," Vitorio mattered. "She tried to escape and fell down the staircase. He'll understand that," he furthered.

Standing over Arielle, they stared down at her. She angled her head upward and gave them a flat stare; she wasn't going to give them the satisfaction of knowing how badly she was injured. She was afraid that her irregular gasping would reveal her state of mind. Gathering all the strength she could muster, she lifted her leg and kicked Mauritsio blindly right between his legs. It was a perfect blow to his groin once again.

Mauritsio shot her a disbelieving glance and let out an unnerving sound. Arielle stared at him wide-eyed. There was a gasping sound as he finally took a mouthful of air. "Fuck!!" He shrieked and his body doubled from pain. He grabbed his growing with a loud grunt. There was a shocking moment of silence, and then he let his right hand fly as hard as he could and backhanded Arielle on the side of her face. Her head jerked backward and hit the wall with a loud thud. Blood shot from the deep laceration on her face and sprayed the front of Mauritsio's shirt. She groaned severely and closed her eyes. Mauritsio grabbed the corner of his white shirt and stared at the bloodstains with utter revulsion. Fury emanated from his eyes, and a deep growl escaped his mouth.

"I'll kill you," he hissed wrathfully and, pulling his hand back, he prepared to strike her once again. She shut her eyes and prepared for the next blow. Stand silence fell, and darkness moved in. She had lost consciousness.

Vitorio grabbed Mauritsio's hand in the air, just before it made contact with Arielle's face once again.

"She's passed out, man!" he snapped. Staring down at the bloody mess on the girl's small frame, Vitorio sensed a flash of sadness surging through his veins, making him quiver, but it vanished just as fast as it came.

Mauritsio stared at him in shock. "Why do you give a fuck about her?" he hissed angrily.

"We need to leave," Vitorio replied blankly. "Change your shirt while I take care of her." Without another word, he bent down and, with ease, he lifted Arielle into his arms and carried her back into the room. He laid her on the bed and stared down at her for a short moment. He shut his eyes at the unpleasant sight in front of him. The cut on her cheek was pretty deep and bloody, her lips were swollen, and her left eye was black and blue. The exposed parts of her body were badly bruised from the fall, and her clothes were stained with blood. "Holy shit!" he thought to himself.

"Vitorio, come on! We have to go," Mauritsio called from upstairs.

Giving her a last glance, he turned around and left the room, locking the door behind him. He gave the handle a hard jiggle to make sure it was locked. He now knew that this girl was going to try everything she could to escape out of there, and he couldn't allow that. He stared at the door panels thoughtfully. He couldn't explain why this situation was becoming so personal and so bothersome. He had a job to do, and he couldn't afford to think about anything else. Turning slowly, he saw Mauritsio waiting at the top of the staircase, acting quite awkward. He closed the distance between them with a few short strides and climbed the stairs quickly.

"How are you feeling?" he asked Mauritsio.

He shrugged. "I'm fine," he said in a dry tone, recognizing mockery in Vitorio's question.

They left the house, making sure all the locks were securely in place and headed for the airport. It was now after 3:45. The rain had let out a bit, but the sky was still dark and cloudy. A heavy mist in the air was making the pedestrian faces that moved quickly on the sidewalks appear slightly out of focus.

"This is not where I'd like to be during a rainy afternoon," Vitorio muttered gloomily.

Mauritsio glanced his direction. "Me neither," he added irritably, and turning, he stared out the window.

Vitorio pressed lightly on the gas and mumbled a few cuss words under his breath. "We're never going to get there in this horrible traffic," he said, utterly frustrated. The heavy rain had caused problems for the traffic as the afternoon commuters were heading home.

"This is a miserable day," Vitorio hissed again, and Mauritsio nodded in agreement as he watches the water rush into the storm drains.

The silence stretched, and they both kept their own thoughts. After a long, exasperating fifteen minutes, the traffic toward the airport thinned out, giving a little solace to their frustration, and Vitorio slammed the pedal to the floor.

 *Chapter 9*

AT THE LGW international terminal, Sebastian, and his friends chose to stand against the back wall of the huge waiting area. They were obscured by a vast number of travelers moving to and from the terminals, and a huge crowd gathered to welcome their family members or friends.

Their immortal skills gave them the ability to watch effortlessly from a distance and hear people's conversations clearly.

The arriving international flights had a designated exit area, making it a lot easier for the immortal group to have a clear view of each passenger that came into the waiting area.

The wall monitor showed the flight from Belarus being in route and landing on time. Sebastian glanced at his watch, noticing that there were twenty minutes left before landing.

Scanning carefully over the huge crowd, he picked out four men standing quite close to each other at the opposite end of the room, exchanging glances and whispering to each other. Their barely audible voices reached Sebastian's ears clear as church bells on a Sunday morning.

They were Dylan's detectives, observing the arrival flights on the huge wall monitor anxiously.

"I see Dylan's detectives," Sebastian murmured. Troy, Ian, and Christian turned simultaneously and followed the line of Sebastian's gaze. Sebastian smiled thoughtfully and gave them a measured stare. He then skipped over them and continued to scan the people that were waiting for the arrivals. According to Dylan, Arielle's abductors were picking up their co-conspirators upon arrival, so they had to be somewhere among this large crowd.

Sebastian glanced furtively around and, finally, his eyes rested on his friends' expressionless faces, and they read his anguish.

Suddenly, a low-key statement from one of the detectives reached them and grabbed their undivided attention.

"Marc, I see Mauritsio and Vitorio," the young detective whispered to the guy standing next to him.

"Where?" Marc looked anxious.

"They're standing over there by the information booth," he said and motioned with his eyes.

Sebastian followed the detective's gaze and zeroed on Vitorio and Mauritsio's faces. A sick feeling settled in the pit of his stomach. Rage seized his throat and his jaw muscles locked.

Troy noticed. "Sebastian," he murmured, placing his hand on his friend's shoulder. "Fortitude, ol' chap."

Sebastian's mouth was set in a grim line. His eyes emanated pure anger, fury, and anguish. The blend of emotions was a deadly potion for anyone that would have to face an immortal.

"Don't take your eyes off of them, Jonathan," Marc ordered. He seemed to be the lead detective.

He then turned his glance at the other two detectives. "Scott, Daniel, did you place the tracking device under their car?" he asked enquiringly.

"Yes," they both replied simultaneously.

"Good job," Marc said again and thumped both of them spiritedly in the arm. "Dylan will have our ass if we mess this up."

"Don't worry; nothing is going to go wrong," Jonathan added supportively.

"We'll follow them to the house, set up surveillance, and make sure none of them leave the premises without us knowing."

"That's the entire plan?" Scott asked curiously.

"No, Dylan said to wait for his orders once we reach the place. When Jorrit contacts Gaulle to arrange for the meeting, we'll raid the house and rescue the girl. We have to take away all the negotiation power in their possession right now, and that means the girl," he said confidently.

"Are we to make arrests or shoot to kill?" Daniel asked pointedly.

"Whatever it takes to bring the girl home safe," Marc replied.

"Is that what Dylan said? Or…"

Marc holds up his hand in a firm gesture, to stop him from saying another word. "Those were Dylan's last words," Marc said categorically.

Silence dropped between the four friends and stretched while they turned their probing gaze toward the information booth.

"Their plan falls perfectly within our plans," Troy murmured. "We'll have plenty of time to take Arielle away from that house and finish our business with the goons before the detectives storm the house."

"Yes, that's a perfect scenario," Ian said agreeably.

Sebastian stared across the room as if seeing something that wasn't visible to anyone else. "I need to find Arielle," he insisted indignantly, his voice trembling. "I'm going out of my mind. I can't envision my life without her." He was now gasping anxiously. "What if she is hurt?"

"Sebastian, you can't let your anger control you at this moment," Christian said with unbelievable calm. "We are going to bring Arielle home, and these guys have absolutely no chance in hell of surviving this encounter."

Sebastian smiled ruefully, and he nodded in agreement. His burning gaze turned back on Vitorio and Mauritsio. He noticed that one of them was glancing between the wall monitor, his wristwatch, and the people around them. The other was completely disengaged from his partner. He was on his mobile phone, chatting casually with someone and smiling cheerily.

Sebastian clenched his teeth once again and tightened his fits. He wanted to wipe that smile right off the guy's face. He was going to bring them to their knees and make them feel fear like they never had before. If they had touched a hair on her head, he would shred them apart piece-by-piece. He would spread excruciating pain through every fiber of their body and torture them until they took their last breath. The thoughts made him scowl and stifled an explicit oath threatening to escape his lips.

He yanked his eyes away from the two goons and glanced at his friends. "Don't let those two out of your sight."

He didn't have to ask that, because the guys were already watching them, waiting for the next phase of the plan. Pushing the sullen thoughts out of his head, Sebastian searched around quietly and winced at the sight of couples who were hugging lovingly, happy to be reunited. He watched the blissfulness that spread across their faces, and he almost felt the eagerness of their kiss, the warm expression of their love. He was standing among hundreds of people, but he felt completely alone. He needed to set his eyes on Arielle's beautiful face and the smile that made the sun rise in his universe each and every day. His arms ached for her. He needed her back where she belonged. *With him.*

Her image filled his thoughts, and a twinge of hurt ripped right through his already aching chest. He wanted to hear her soft voice and feel the joy her presence sent straight to his very core. He paled at the thought of the possibility that someone wanted to hurt her. "I wonder if they left Arielle alone in that house?" Sebastian muttered despondently, as though talking to himself.

"Maybe they sent more than two thugs to do the job, and they have left someone behind to guard Arielle while they are here," Troy replied.

Sebastian didn't acknowledge Troy's statement; he seemed to be lost in his thoughts. His friends could see his hands clenched into tight fists and his eyes burning with scorching fire. He appeared dangerous. Troy put his hand on Sebastian's shoulder once again and gave him a friendly pad.

"She's fine, Sebastian. They can't afford to hurt her. They need to keep her for ransom. At this point, they know that you are to be contacted to meet them for the exchange. They need her safe and sound at least until then. Arielle will be back home way before the time is up. These guys will be all dead by then," he said scoffing outwardly.

Sebastian nodded, but he didn't relax. "I don't trust them, Troy," he said nervously. "I'm worried about her. I know she's scared and alone, and it is all because of me," he muttered and shuddered at the thought. "If anything happens to her, I will never forgive myself. She is my life, the air I breathe." Anguish strained his beautiful face, and he let out a long, tremulous sigh. He glanced at his watch once again and inwardly cursed.

Time was creeping along at an agonizingly slow pace. Fifteen more minutes for the flight to land, and getting closer to the moment he was to hold Arielle in his arms. *Oh God! Why does it hurt so badly?* He thought worriedly. The feeling was excruciating.

His life had been a wonderful dream since the first moment he had laid eyes on Arielle. She had become the love of his life, the air he breathed, the core of his universe. He didn't want to be anywhere without her. He was now ready to give up everything to just set his eyes on her beautiful face once again, to get lost in her sapphire gaze, to bathe in the glow of her smile, and to hold her tightly in his arms for eternity. He was thirsty for her soft lips and starving for her company. He was deeply in love with her; there was never going to be another. She made him complete; she fulfilled his hopes and desires more than any person had ever done before. She brought out feelings in him that he never knew he had. He was lost in her thoughts and a smiled touched his lips. He yearned for her.

"Sebastian," Troy's voice broke him out of his reverie. He glanced over and gave Troy a quizzical look.

"The plane landed," Troy stated, pointing to the large monitor.

Sebastian's face grew paler, and the smile faded. Reality crashed right back into his brain, and the pain he was feeling was infinitely worse than any other hurt that he ever had over his long life on this earth. How was he going to find Arielle? Would she be all right? He pressed his lips together and shook his head, trying to shake the surreal thoughts invading his mind.

They locked their gaze on Mauritsio and Vitorio and listened carefully to their conversation.

Vitorio tapped Mauritsio on the shoulder. "Get off the phone; I see them," he said. Mauritsio put his phone away, and they pushed their way ahead of the other people waiting, ignoring the dirty stares and obscenities thrown their way.

"Where?" Mauritsio asked, stretching and searching over the arriving passengers that were approaching the exit. "Oh, never mind, I see them," he said and gave a wave in the direction of two tall, well-built, and blond haired men heading their way.

The newcomers were dressed in jeans and white shirts just as Dylan described them. They each carried a brown duffle bag over their shoulder and clasped a brown briefcase in their hands.

"There're our guys," Sebastian muttered.

The men moved toward Vitorio and Mauritsio and shook hands.

"We're glad to see you," Vitorio said. "I'm Vitorio, and this is Mauritsio," he added pointing toward Mauritsio.

"I'm Aiden," the taller guy said, "and this is Colton."

"Where is the girl?" Colton asked.

"She's locked up at the house we have rented."

"Alone?" Colton asked again.

"Yeah…yeah…she's locked in the basement and not in great shape right now. She doesn't have a prayer of escaping."

Not in great shape? Sebastian thought, clenching his teeth.

They strolled toward the airport exit. The guys noticed that Dylan's agents also had them on their radar. They let the agents follow the four criminals, and they walked slowly behind the agents, keeping all of them in their scope. Aiden's next question made Sebastian's skin crawl.

"What do you mean she is not in great shape right now?"

"Well, there was a small accident before we left for the airport," Vitorio mumbled.

Sebastian's blood ran cold, and his lips pressed into a hard line. Troy, Ian, and Christian turned toward Sebastian. He appeared devastated. A shadow draped over his soul, and his world stopped for a long moment. Ian reached over and grabbed Sebastian's arm in support.

"She'll be all right, Sebastian; hang in there friend." All three kept tuned to the goons' conversation, listening to every word and trying to keep Sebastian from doing something irrational.

"She tried to escape," Vitorio whispered, "and she fell down the stairs and was hurt."

Sebastian grew paler and shuddered inwardly, letting out a low growl.

"Vasily said the orders were—the girl is not to be touched. This is not going to sit well with Rainer," Colton insisted harshly.

"It wasn't our fault," Vitorio hurried to explain. "She was running up the stairs, and I was at the top of the landing. She ran right into me and bounced back, losing her step and tumbling down the stairs."

"I don't like that," Colton stated. "I don't like it at all..." His voice trailed.

Sebastian swallowed hard and let out a low growl again. He could barely hold himself from vaulting at them and hurting them, but that would jeopardize the reason they were here. He needed the goons to lead them to Arielle.

"Let's go to the car," Aiden roared gloomily.

Vitorio didn't like his tone of voice, but he decided to keep quiet. He led them to the parking deck, and they piled into the black Mercedes.

"That's the car that they used to follow Arielle," Sebastian said and scowled.

Dylan's detectives followed discretely, walking along behind many other people heading for their cars. This was an easy place to blend among the crowd and follow someone without being detected. They climbed into a gray van and waited for the black Mercedes to pull out of the parking space.

Sebastian and his friends, moving with immortal speed, were already in their car and heading to the toll both before the other two cars had a chance to even start their engines. They handed their ticket and exact change to the parking attendant and drove out, keeping their eyes on the black Mercedes waiting in line to pay toll behind three other cars. They couldn't see the van with the detectives, but they were sure they weren't far behind. They drove slowly, letting the Mercedes catch up, drive by them, and get in front of them. Now they had them exactly where they wanted them to be.

Troy was driving, and Sebastian's gaze was glued to the back of the black car. His emotions were engaging a wild war, and his body was on high alert. He could hardly wait to reach the final destination.

"I think we've lost the gray van," Ian said from the back seat. Troy looked in the rear view mirror, and he couldn't see the van either.

"It doesn't matter," Sebastian said slowly, intensely. "They placed a tracking device on the Mercedes, so they are not worried. We don't need anyone right now. We will take care of this swiftly." His mouth pressed again in a hard line.

Chapter 10

THE ROADS WERE BUSY and the traffic was moving at a painfully slow crawl. Sebastian drummed his fingers on the door panel peevishly. They were not driving any longer; they were creeping along the asphalt inch by inch, and Sebastian's patience was fading away slowly but surely. After a very long, agonizing amount of time, the traffic thinned, and they started to move again. Troy hung back at a discreet distance and followed them as they took the on-ramp to the interstate. The assassins were clueless at the tail they had picked up at the airport.

Troy glanced at the rear view mirror and said gingerly, "Oh, here come the detectives!" Christian and Ian turned toward the back window, but Sebastian remained glued to the Mercedes in front of them. This was his major interest and the only thing in his horizon right now.

The van was a couple of miles behind, but they were following the black Mercedes steadily.

Sebastian's voice broke Troy's thoughts. "When you see the car slowing down, pull into the closest side street and stop."

Troy nodded in agreement.

"How are we going to do this?" Ian asked.

"We'll move by foot using our speed. We'll enter the premises and take Arielle out safe before we deal with the thugs."

"That sounds like a plan," Christian muttered.

It wasn't long before the Mercedes turned off the interstate. They drove past a couple of shopping malls and after another fifteen minutes, they entered a nice subdivision with fairly large homes surrounded by tall walls and private gates. It made a lot of sense that they would rent a residence with this type of privacy for their sinister motives. The black Mercedes turned right on Fern Street. Troy drove past them and glanced over. He noticed that it was a dead end street. He parked the car in the next lane over, and they stepped out quickly.

They darted down the street and reached Fern Street in a few large strides. Peering around the corner, they saw the black car stopped in front of a two-story home at the end of the cul-de-sac. A six-foot wall was erected around it, preventing the view of the first floor from the street. A huge iron gate with an electric device and cameras on either side provided extra security for the occupants.

The car was sitting idle, waiting for the gate to open. As soon as the car started to move, so did the four immortals. They were inside the garden before the car even cleared the gate, moving at high velocity, totally invisible to the car's occupants. Huge hedges surrounded the house walls, and that is where the guys found concealment when they stopped moving. They watched the garage door pull up and give access to the black car. As soon as the garage door came down, the guys moved again like lightning.

Sebastian and Ian went around the back while Troy and Christian scaled the wall with one jump and accessed the house through the window on the second floor. They were to wait upstairs hidden from the goons until Sebastian and Ian made their appearance. Their mobiles were set on vibrate and Sebastian was going to notify them via text as soon as they had Arielle.

Sebastian and Ian walked around the right side of the house and noticed steps leading downward to a huge back yard. This house had a full light basement, but no doors that would provide access to the house. Three midsize windows in the back had iron bars on the outside, making it very difficult for a burglar to break in. There was nothing behind the house but empty fields, making the house quite private from curious neighborly eyes.

They crept along the wall and peered inside the first window. The room was dark, and the cloudy skies made the inside view even darker, but their immortal eyes could see perfectly each and every detail inside. It appeared abandoned. Moving to the next window, the results were not much different but for the fact that they could see numerous huge boxes piled up in the middle of that room. Creeping along the wall, they reached the last window and carefully peered inside.

Sebastian skimmed over the contents of the room in disgust. Two chairs with scruffy covers, a tall cracked chest against the wall, and four old pictures that hang lopsided on the walls. Dirty brown wallpaper covered the walls, making the room seem even more depressing. His eyes finally rested on the half broken bed with the small nightstand and a half broken lampshade on top of it. His eyes zeroed on the small body coiled up on top of it. He stared in shocked horror, recognizing the shirt and the jeans Arielle wore that morning. He opened his mouth to say something, but the words choked in his throat, and he closed it again as he allowed these ugly visions to bleed into his brain one after the other.

"I think it's Arielle," Ian whispered.

Sebastian nodded his head in clear wretchedness. He grabbed the iron bars with both hands, ready to bend them open when they heard the lock on the door click. They pulled back out of view. Voices filled the room as heavy footsteps crossed the old broken floor that cried out in agony with every footstep that landed on it.

The conversation that followed had Sebastian growling and seething in fury. If not for Ian to keep him under control, he would have leaped into that room before the next word was uttered.

"She's here," Vitorio said, pointing at the bed.

A shocked voice was heard a few minutes later.

"Good God! What happened to this girl?" Colton asked as he put his hand on Arielle's shoulder and turned her over to her back.

"What do you mean?" Vitorio muttered.

"The girl's face is swollen and bloody, and her body badly bruised," Colton hissed, utterly disgusted. He noticed the thick layer of dried blood on Arielle's cheek and down the side of her neck. Her shirt and the worn out bed comforter were soaked in blood. "The girl is barely breathing!" he bellowed in disbelief. "Did you even check?"

"I told you she felt down the stairs," Vitorio protested through clenched teeth. He didn't like the attitude thrown at him from the Belarus boys.

"This is not just falling down the stairs," Aiden added angrily, standing next to Colton and looking down at Arielle. "What the fuck happened in here? If something happens to this girl, Rainer will have your ass."

"The bitch hit me," Mauritsio jumped in, defending the situation.

"The girl hit you?" Colton asked appalled.

"Yes, she kneed me in the crotch, and I backhanded her. She then came after me, and I hit her again. My ring ripped her cheek open. I was not going to sit and take it. She asked for it, and I let her have it," Mauritsio spat out in clear anger.

"You idiot, don't you understand that you might compromise the whole assignment? You need your hostage in good condition to be able to negotiate successfully. What if Gaulle wants to see her before he provides the secret documents? What then?" he shrieked.

"Fuck him. I don't give a shit what he wants. I thought you guys were here to handle this. Things don't always work out perfectly. If they did, we wouldn't need you," Mauritsio said, menacingly.

"Well, now I'm convinced that you are an idiot," Aiden said and shook his head.

"Is she still unconscious?" Vitorio asked.

"I'm going to ignore your question because it frankly makes me mad," Aiden said.

"It. Was. Not. Our. Fault." Vitorio enunciated each word separately, angrily glaring at Aiden. He tried to cover his poor judgment about Mauritsio's outrageous performance as well as his own. He was the one that pounded the girl's small bruised body against the wall right after she plummeted down the stairs and allowed Mauritsio to hit her again.

"I don't give a fuck whose fault it is right now. It happened during your watch; that's all that matters," Colton screamed, glaring back at Vitorio.

"How bad is the girl?" Aiden asked Colton.

"She seems to have lost quite a bit of blood from the cut on her face and her breathing is frail. She is unconscious, but she's still alive... no thanks to you!" he yelled, staring at Vitorio and Mauritsio threateningly. "I'm going to put a call through to Vasily and attempt to repair this horrible situation. In the meantime, I think you two should pack your shit and get the hell out. Just leave! You've done enough damage," Aiden screamed sharply.

Vitorio frowned contemptuously and, turning around, he motioned to Mauritsio and they left the room.

"Colton, come with me, and help me find something to clean up the girl's face," Aiden suggested, eyes burning with fury. Footsteps pounded the crackling floor once again, and the door slumped closed.

Sebastian peered inside once again, and the room was empty. He grabbed the bars and pulled them apart. With one movement, he had the window wide open. He didn't hesitate. He leaped, catching the edge of the windowsill, and propelled himself inside the room. Ian followed in his heels.

They ran to Arielle's bedside and stared down at her bloody face and bruised body in stunned disbelief. Sebastian's world crumpled, his mind frozen in place and the pain in his chest expending. His eyes widened in complete shock. He inhaled sharply, and for a short moment, he thought the floor swayed beneath his feet. His joy of finding her suddenly faded into horror. The most astonishingly beautiful image in his head had become the most gruesome.

Sebastian bent down and set his hands flat on the bed to take a closer look. The bed springs creaked under his weight. He then slipped his hands under Arielle's body and, lifting her into his arms, he held her against his chest protectively. How could it be possible that he felt his heart breaking into a million shards if his heart had been dead for over five hundred years? And how could it be possible that he felt tears flowing if he couldn't cry? His eyes drifted over her face and down her broken body, and relentless pain spread across every fiber of his body. The blood was pounding his veins like a sledgehammer. He bent down and pressed a soft kiss on her forehead.

"Hey, baby, I'm here...I'm here...you're safe now," he murmured. "Baby, can you hear me?"

Arielle was not responding. He pressed another soft kiss to her forehead. "Oh God! Arielle, please wake up, baby. I love you," he muttered despondently. The anguish that spread across every nerve in his body was tormenting. He was too worried about her condition to think straight.

Ian instinctively raised his hand and gripped Sebastian's elbow, interrupting his tremulous thoughts. "Sebastian, come on, man. We need to take her out of here before they come back." His voice was supportive.

Sebastian turned to face Ian and took a short minute to process his request. He finally nodded in agreement. His eyes narrowed, and his expression changed to that of a man in control of his faculties.

"Take her to the hospital," he murmured. "Troy, Christian, and I will finish the job. Please call the others." His anxiety was fading away slowly, and it was being replaced by fury.

"What about her parents?"

"Let's wait on that," Sebastian said thoughtfully.

"Why?"

"Ian, we need to have a good story as to how this happened. Where was everyone? How did we find her? All these questions will come up, and we need to have good answers."

"You're right. I'll take her to the Royal Sussex County Hospital, and I'll wait for your call to give me the details on the story before her parents arrive," Ian said.

Sebastian's face crumpled at the thought of Arielle's parents. This was becoming a redundant thing. He had met them at the hospital over their daughter more often that he wanted to remember. He forced a smile and nodded, eyes distraught. "Yes, I'll call you as soon as we're done here."

Ian moved promptly toward the window. The rain had stopped, and a cool breeze caressed Ian's face as he scaled the windowsill and landed softly outside. He then turned to face Sebastian. "Let me have her," he said, stretching his arms to take Arielle.

Sebastian looked over his shoulder, reached through the window, and placed her carefully into Ian's arms. "Please take care of her," he murmured, anxiously.

"Sebastian, she's safe now," Ian said and gave his friend a reassuring smile.

"Take the car. We don't want to raise any questions about you showing up at the hospital without a vehicle. We'll be there as soon as we're done here."

Ian tucked Arielle snugly in his arms and took off, disappearing into the thin air.

Sebastian fished his mobile from his jean pocket and texted Troy. *Arielle is safe. She's on the way to the hospital with Ian.*

Where are you? Troy texted back.

I'm in the basement, ready to come upstairs. And you?

We're on the second floor. We can hear the goons somewhere on the main floor.

Let's meet on the main floor. Sebastian responded.

He put the phone back in his pocket and left the room. He walked down the corridor and mounted the steps soundlessly. Reaching the top of the landing, he crept up to the door on his right. Colton was on the phone, facing the other way. Aiden was on the computer, checking through some information on the screen. Mauritsio and Vitorio were gathering pieces of equipment scattered all over the room and placing them in their cases.

"Vasily, the girl, is in horrible condition," Colton said, quite agitated

"What do you mean in horrible condition? What happened?" Vasily asked.

"She had an accident, according to Jorrit's men and on top of that, they beat her up," he continued, glancing at Vitorio and Mauritsio, but they completely ignored him.

"Those sons of bitches! I thought they were professionals," Vasily's voice boomed from the other end of the phone.

"Well, all I can say is that I hope Gaulle doesn't ask to see her before he surrenders the documents," Colton said darkly.

"Tell them to get the hell out of there and go back to Brussels. I'll call Jorrit, and he will prepare the welcome committee for them," he said venomously.

"I already asked them to pack their stuff, and that is exactly what they are doing right now. Aiden and I will try to clean up the girl and make her comfortable. We want her to be able to talk if Gaulle wants to hear her voice."

"I know you guys will do a good job," Vasily said. There was a short pause. "When are you calling Gaulle for the meeting? And has Jorrit send the last photos to Gaulle?" Colton asked

"One hour from now? And yes, he already sent the photos to his office."

"Good… One hour will give us time to take care of the situation here." There was another long pause. "Call me when the girl is in better shape," Vasily said.

"All right, I will," Colton replied and ended the call.

Sebastian moved to the opening of the door, but he was still totally unnoticed. It seemed that Troy and Christian had captured their attention as they now stood at the bottom of the staircase that led to the upstairs floor.

"What the fuck?" Colton yelped. He could not believe what his eyes were seeing. His brain could not process the sight of the two men. Their sudden appearance didn't accurately register. After a short pause, he collected his thoughts. "Who the hell are you?" his voice boomed.

Troy smiled wide and took two steps into the room.

For the next second, Colton sat reluctantly in silence, unsure if he was going to have his question answered. Troy let out a heavy sigh and rolled his eyes impatiently, but kept his mouth shut. Colton's eyes lingered over Troy uneasily.

"Who…," he began to ask again, but Troy cut him off with a sharp move of his hand.

"You don't need to know," Troy said firmly.

Sebastian moved inside the room and stood right behind them. All four thugs whirled around to face him. Sebastian's arctic look drove terror into their minds. Troy and Christian walked farther into the room and closed the distance between the goons and Sebastian. The air in the room turned icy in a matter of seconds. The four goons sidestepped and placed themselves against the wall, facing three very angry immortals.

Colton took a deep breath, willing bravery. "What in the hell is going on here? Who are you? What do you want?" he muttered and swore audibly.

"Where did you come from?" Vitorio interjected, sounding genuinely surprised.

A slow smile crept up and lit Sebastian's face, but it didn't touch his eyes. "We came from hell with the orders to bring you back with us," Sebastian replied, venomously. His frigid voice was arctic enough to freeze the blood in their veins.

"What the hell are you talking about?" Mauritsio mouthed, completely baffled by Sebastian's statement.

"If you broke in here to rob the place, take what you want and leave," Colton interrupted, hoping to rid of the three unwelcome males that were now standing in the middle of the room glaring at them. "This is beyond belief," he muttered under his breath. Then darting his angry gaze between them, he shouted once again, "Take what you want and get the hell out of here; we're not going to stop you." He didn't have time to deal with some measly thieves or their motives. Time was of the essence, and they needed to move on with the assignment, but surprisingly, nobody moved.

"So what are you waiting for?" Colton hissed, glancing between the intruders impatiently.

The image of Arielle's wounded body clouded once again Sebastian's thoughts. He struggled to remove the physical pain that was outpouring from every single muscle in his body and embrace calmly the present situation in hand.

 *Chapter 11*

SILENCE HAD STRETCHED beyond terribly uncomfortable. Sebastian remained entirely still, and an unnerving smile painted his angry face. "We're going to kill you, slowly and painfully," he hissed. "Especially you," he furthered, pinning Mauritsio's stunned face with an icy stare, allowing coldness to creep into his voice.

Colton drew a sharp breath and exhaled deeply. "Un…unbelievable," he mumbled and glanced around in stupefied surprise.

He stared spitefully at Sebastian. Rage boiled inside at the thought that Sebastian was mocking him.

The silence stretched again for a long moment, and finally, Colton started to laugh uncontrollably. Mauritsio, Vitorio, and Aiden turned and stared at Colton, not understanding the humor in the situation. Eventually, Colton stopped laughing and coughed trying to clear his throat. He formed a serious look and let his gaze sweep over the three intruders. His lips lifted in a sarcastic smile. "So… you are going to kill us?" he scoffed. "Who is going to do that? He asked and grinned wide. "You three?" his hand made a motion in the air between Troy, Christina, and Sebastian. "Where are the rest of your playmates?" he mocked. He then broke out into laughter once again, trying to keep the atmosphere as smug as possible. Aiden, Vitorio, and Mauritsio joined Colton in his bizarre hilarity.

Sebastian, Troy, and Christian remained unmoved, stone-faced. They didn't share in the assassins' enthusiasm and cheerfulness. Fire flashed through their immortal eyes, scorching the laughter right out of the assassins' throats.

Vitorio moved first. Sprinting forward, he pulled his right arm back, suspending his balled fist next to his ear, and with all the force he possessed; he sent it toward Christian's face. Christian dodged quickly, avoiding the blow. Missing his target, Vitorio tried to resist the forward force, but lost his balance and flew headfirst past Christian, bouncing off the opposite wall and collapsed onto the floor.

Colton, Aiden, and Mauritsio were watching in stunned silence. Totally humiliated, Vitorio bounced right back up, cursed out loud, and threw his body weight as hard as he could against Christian. His breath came in frayed gasps, and his eyes glazed with rage. Christian's fist moved fast and caught Vitorio in the middle of his chest. Silence fell in the room like a death screen as everyone heard the horrible noise of Vitorio's body bones shattering. Vitorio's breath hissed, and blood spattered out of his mouth. Christian lifted his other hand and, grabbing Vitorio around his throat; he lifted him off the ground as if he were completely weightless. His fingers squeezed tightly. Vitorio tried to free himself by thrashing wildly, desperately. Christian's grip was deadly; he didn't budge. Vitorio's eyes widened. Then they rolled back in his head, and he stopped moving. Christian released him, and he dropped to the floor with a loud thud.

Shockwaves tore across Colton, Aiden, and Mauritsio's faces as they watched the death of Vitorio like a short film playing in front of their appalled brains.

"Wh…what," Colton started to say but stopped mid-sentenced when the realization of Vitorio's death resonated through his mind. His thoughts shattered as if a grenade detonated inside his head. He blinked, and quickly, he pulled his gun from the back of his belt and, without thinking, he fired. The bullet slammed right into Troy's chest, and he staggered backward but didn't fall. A small bloodstain appeared on the front of his shirt, and slowly, it spread wider. Troy's lips quirked into a devilish smile, and he took a step forward. Colton stepped back, not believing his eyes. He pointed the gun once again at Troy and started to squeeze the trigger, but Sebastian leaped forward and snatched the gun away from Colton. Folding his fingers around it, he squeezed effortlessly, crushing it into scrap metal.

"What the hell!" Colton shrieked. "Who the hell are you?" he shouted, not believing his eyes. "What the hell are you?"

Sebastian smiled, totally unruffled. "I'm the last person you'll see before you meet your maker," he hissed.

Colton's eyes moved around wildly. He knew something was different and extraordinary about these guys, but he had no idea what he was up against. Looking behind Sebastian, he noticed that Troy was now on the floor on his knees and was holding his chest. He breathed a short relief, thinking he rid of one of them. The shot was a temporary hindrance to Troy's abilities. He glanced between Aiden and Mauritsio, and turning to Sebastian, he said firmly. "As you can see, your friend is out of commission," he snorted arrogantly, pointing at Troy. "That leaves the two of you against us three. These aren't very good odds for you and your friend. Your magic tricks will not work with me," Colton said, tilting his chin up and pinning Sebastian with his livid gaze.

The assassin scowled. He was mentally frustrated and exasperated. He was now hoping that Sebastian and Christian would decide to leave without any further incident. They each lost a guy. He had no emotional ties to Vitorio, and he was sure that a couple of thieves didn't have any emotional ties with the guy who was shot.

Time was of the essence. Colton needed to check on the girl and then report back to Vasily on her condition. He was to be informed of the time and place to meet with Gaulle and make the exchange. There were three things he couldn't allow to occur. He couldn't allow Gaulle to see the girl before the exchange took place, he couldn't allow Vitorio's death become an issue, and he couldn't allow a couple of thieves to jeopardize this assignment.

Time was ticking away, and he was becoming anxious. "This is your last chance," he screamed at Sebastian. "Are you going to leave?"

"Oh, I wouldn't think of depriving you of the pleasure of killing us," Sebastian said and smiled wide.

Confusion showed on Colton's face. *What the hell is wrong with these guys? Why don't they leave?* He thought to himself, clenching his fists. "Don't say we didn't give you a chance," Colton continued, narrowing his eyes in warning.

Christian moved right behind Aiden, using his immortal speed. Raising his hands, he closed his fingers tight around Aiden's neck and lifted him off the ground. He then proceeded to squeeze slowly and firmly. Aiden tried to jerk free from Christian's steel vise but to no avail. Colton and Mauritsio went rigid. They never saw Christina move, so how could he be standing behind Aiden? They heard Aiden gasp for air, moving his hands in sheer desperation. He tried to scream, but no air exited his lungs. Soon the shroud of death wrapped around him, and he stopped breathing. Christian let go of Aiden's neck and his body hit the floor like a rock. He then turned around to face Colton and Mauritsio, who were still in shocked motionless. His loud voice snapped them out of their frozen state of mind.

"Well...this evens the odds, don't you think?" he hissed.

Sebastian looked at Christian and smiled. "I'll take Mauritsio," he said evenly. "He's the one that hurt Arielle."

"Who are you? What are you?" Mauritsio mouthed, demanding to understand what the fuck was going on.

"I'm Sebastian Gaulle, and the little girl you banged up is my fiancée. Now you will pay. You will die slowly. Your scummy friends died swiftly; you, however, aren't going to be that lucky."

Mauritsio flinched at his words, but he glared stubbornly at Sebastian. "Your fiancée is a bitch. If I had had my way, I would have given her something to remember me by. I would have shown her what a real man could do." There was no filter between his brain and his mouth. He just watched Sebastian kill his friend and he kept on.

Sebastian's eyes burned with fury, but he kept his composure and just smiled.

"I have plans for your ugly face..." Sebastian hissed.

"You are not scaring me with a couple of cheap magic tricks," Mauritsio hissed right back.

Christian was absorbed and enjoying the heated conversation between Sebastian and Mauritsio. Colton's attack startled Christian.

He saw him just as he leaped and landed a hard blow right between Christian's eyes. Christian staggered backward, but didn't fall. He lifted his hand, striking Colton in the chest and sending him flying across the room. Colton's body bounced off the hideous wallpaper, and his head jerked backward, hitting the wall hard with a crashing noise. He slid to the floor, and his breath came out in a tense shriek. Christian watched him lift his hand and touch the back of his head. His face twisted, and his body shuddered. To Christian's surprise, Colton was not out for the count. He pressed his lips together in agony and pushed himself up, glaring at Christian's unruffled face with fury.

"You bastard!" he screamed and, pushing away from the wall, he threw himself against Christian. His forward momentum halted as though he'd hit a concrete barrier. Making contact with Christian's body was an experience he never had and never expected to have. Being hit by a speeding train would have been a lot easier.

The gruesome sound of bones breaking held Mauritsio in his tracks. *What the hell is going on?* He thought to himself. Before another thought could cross his already confused brain, he watched in horror as Christian's body loomed over Colton's, a hard smile curving his lips. He appeared like a bomb ready to explode. Colton snapped, his eyes searched Christian's face in complete astonishment. "What the fuck are you?"

Christian's fist smashed into Colton's face in reply. A bloody curdling howl escaped Colton's lips as blood spattered everywhere and his body bowed backward. Blood oozed out of his face and soaked the front of his shirt. Christian bent down and, hauling him upright; he threw him swiftly across the room. Colton's body passed in front of Mauritsio's shocked eyes like a flare, and this time, the assassin went right through the wall, disappearing behind a mixture of drywall, paneling, studs, and insulation that crumbled to the floor, leaving a huge hole in the dividing wall.

He listened vigilantly, but no sounds came from the other side, no movement at all. He swallowed down nausea that was climbing his throat quickly and his eyes moved wildly around the room. Troy was up on his feet and walking slowly to stand between Christian and Sebastian, facing Mauritsio. He had a wide smile on his face that didn't touch his eyes.

Mauritsio's expression was that of a stunned shock. *How could that be?* He was shot in the chest; he was bleeding all over the place, and he had been on his knees on the floor. Mauritsio blinked again. This had to be a nightmare; it couldn't be happening. He shut his eyes tightly, hoping that when he opened them again, everything would be the same as when they first walked into the room. He waited a few long moments and finally opened his eyes slowly. Nothing had changed. His three conspirators were dead, the wall was damaged, and he was standing all alone facing three very angry men.

"You don't have to do this," he murmured in a barely audible voice. "The girl is fine; she is downstairs. You can take her and leave." He was seriously trembling, and he had to reach and grab the back of a chair to be able to stand up.

"I don't think so," Sebastian hissed.

A noise came from behind the wall, and they all turned in astonished surprise. Silence threw a creepy realization over the room. They watched Colton's broken body trying to climb over the broken wall. His face was distorted, covered in blood, and his body awkwardly dismantled. An unnatural noise came from the back of his throat and, closing his eyes; he felt life fading from his body. He slowly disappeared once again behind the pile of crumbled drywall. Mauritsio gasped in horror. He wanted to run and disappear, but his legs felt like they were glued to the floor. He couldn't move. Fear was taking over every pore in his body and slipping deep into his bones, like rainwater in the dessert. He jerked his head back and glared at the three unforgiving men.

"Three against one?" he hissed. "That's a coward's way to fight one man," he continued menacingly.

Sebastian glanced at Christian and Troy, and his lips moved. Mauritsio didn't hear a sound and didn't grasp what was said. His lip reading skills were nonexistent. Astounded, he watched Christian and Troy stroll unhurriedly toward the other side of the room. They leaned against the wall, crossed one leg over the other, and folded their arms against their chest. They pinned Mauritsio with their cold gaze, and a sarcastic smile painted their sculptured lips.

Mauritsio was startled to realize suddenly that all three looked extraordinarily alike, but for the color of their eyes and hair. *That is just too eerie,* he thought. Sebastian's voice brought him back to reality.

"Well, it's just you and me again," Sebastian murmured through clenched teeth. "Do you want to show me a real man?" He was using Mauritsio's words, his voice was calm, the tone icy cold.

Mauritsio turned and stared right into a pair of eyes that drove a chilling sensation right down his spine. Sebastian moved closer, and he was now standing right in front of him.

"Well?" Sebastian snapped. "Are you going to show me a real man? Or are you just keeping that for the women you abuse?" He spat in clear disgust.

"Fuck you," Mauritsio screamed, and with a quick movement, he slid a knife he had palmed right into Sebastian's gut. Surprise crossed Sebastian's eyes, but it disappeared just as fast as it came. Reaching up, he pulled the knife out, and grabbing Mauritsio's arm; he broke it in two. A wild scream left Mauritsio's lips and moved his right hand to shield his face. A steel vise wrapped around his right wrist and twisted hard. The sound of broken bones filled the silence. The pain was unbearable. Mauritsio screamed between the endless chain of oaths. Sebastian tore a piece from his shirt and gagged him. He smashed his fist into the goon's chest like lighting. Mauritsio's feet lost touch with the floor, flew across the room and bounced against the wall. The earth quaked beneath his feet just before he crashed to the ground. Sebastian walked over, and lifting his foot, he smashed Mauritsio's left knee first and then the other. Loud noises of broken bones mixed with the gagged groans of pain filled the room. Mauritsio's face was distorted and thick sweat mixed with blood pour down his face.

"This is for Arielle," he hissed and smashed his fist once again in Mauritsio's face. Blood spattered out of his nose, and the gag in his mouth was now soaked in blood. Mauritsio's body was awkwardly sprawled on the floor with broken arms, legs, and now a broken face. Sebastian bent down and punched him a few more times with an unforgiving anger. Mauritsio's body convulsed wildly, and after a few more hits, blood started to pour out of his mouth, ears, and nose. He stopped moving. Sebastian was ready to hit him again when Troy's hand grabbed his arm mid-air.

"Sebastian, stop! He's dead, man! No more."

Sebastian pulled himself up, still staring at Mauritsio's broken body. Anger boiled inside his mind. The sight of Arielle's bloody and bruised body blinded his good judgment.

Christian pulled away from the wall and walked over to Sebastian.

"We need to clean up the mess and rid of their bodies," Troy said quietly, "before Dylan's men decide to come in."

"Yes, you're right." Sebastian agreed. They moved in their immortal speed, and soon the place appeared like nobody had been there, but for the crumbled interior wall.

"We need to take the back stairs," Sebastian said.

"The detectives are here ready to set up surveillance on the house."

Satisfied with the outcome, they moved quickly down the steps to the basement, crossed the long corridor, ran through the bedroom, hurdled over the windowsill, and landed in the backyard.

"The car is not here," Sebastian said. "Ian used it to take Arielle to the hospital."

Troy and Christian exchanged glances hesitantly. They were not sure if Sebastian was ready to talk about Arielle. He was troubled, his eyes hard, his facial expression rigid.

They wanted to deflect the uncomfortable topic, but they needed to know. "How is Arielle?" Troy finally asked.

Sebastian gasped at the sound of her name. His face paled, and he took a long shaky breath before he replied. "She is hurt."

"Sorry," they both said simultaneously. Sadness coated their voices.

Sebastian gave them a quick glance. "It's not your fault. It's nobody's fault, but mine." He came to an abrupt halt, and facing his friends; he shook his face in disgust. "It is all my fault. There are people out there that want to kill her. I have brought nothing, but pain into her life. I wish I had the strength to walk away and let her live a normal, happy life." He raked both hands through his hair. "I don't know what to do anymore. I hate to see her in pain."

"Sebastian, you need to stop thinking this way. You can't let her see you like this," Troy said firmly.

He managed to flip the switch to reality, and he nodded in agreement. "We need to come up with a good story that will sound believable to her parents and the police," Sebastian said.

"The police?" Christian exclaimed.

"Yes, any time they admit someone in Arielle's condition, the doctors call the authorities to investigate. That's just normal procedure."

"So what's the story that we are going to use?" Troy asked.

They all fell silent, thoughts of Arielle and the situation at hand weighing them down. "I'm thinking," Sebastian said quietly. "I've got it!" he said interrupting their thoughts.

"And that is... what?" Troy said watching him carefully.

"I thought that we might say that Arielle was taken from school to ransom for important documents that the Mafia needed from me. Interpol was on to them, but they were too late. Arielle used her cell and texted Eva to tell her that someone kidnapped her. She was badly hurt and locked into a room, but she had no idea where she was. Ian tracked her phone and located her while we were in a meeting with Dylan. He rescued her and called us, just as we were leaving Interpol. We are now on the way to the hospital."

Troy and Christian appeared to seriously ponder Sebastian's story.

"I think I would believe something like that," Christian snorted.

"Yes, it sounds quite believable," Troy, added.

Sebastian glanced between them. "Well, we'll have to go with that, because I can't think of anything else. If you can think of something better, let me know."

"I don't think I can make up anything better," Christian replied. And Troy just shrugged. "It is a good story," Christian said again, grinning.

"It is what it is," Sebastian added dismissively. They agreed and started to walk away from the home.

"I would like to be a fly on the wall when Rainer gets the news," Christian whispered.

"This will be a great wake up call for Rainer and his organization," Sebastian said flatly, a grim smile tightening his face.

"Christian, I think you should go to the hospital first since you're supposed to be with Ian. Troy and I will wait for a short period, to make the story fit."

Christian nodded. "I'll see you soon," he said and took off.

Sebastian and Troy used their immortal speed and left the location. They waited for about a half an hour, and then Sebastian picked up the phone and called Dylan. He needed to clear the situation with Dylan before they moved on.

"Jamison here," Dylan answered flatly.

"Dylan, it's Sebastian."

"Oh, Sebastian, I'm glad you called. I was getting ready to call you." His voice changed to that of great concern. "Well, my detectives followed the goons from the airport to a location on the North East part of town and parked a couple of blocks away. The bizarre thing is that they waited for a long time and nobody ever came out."

"I don't understand. Did they go inside to investigate?"

"Yes...yes, they did. The house was empty, and there were no traces of anyone ever being there. It was as if they all vanished into thin air."

Sebastian tried to keep his words measured. "That is very peculiar."

"Yes, I thought so, but now I am worried about Arielle."

"But that is what I wanted to talk to you about. While we were leaving your office, Ian called and said that he had tracked her phone to an abandoned house and took her to the hospital. She is badly hurt, but she is safe. We are on the way there now."

"Arielle is in the hospital?" Dylan's voice was that of utter shock.

"Yes."

"Oh, I'm really happy to hear that. I don't mean I am happy that she is in the hospital, but I am happy she was rescued. I can't understand how my detectives missed seeing Ian leaving the house."

"Ian used the back of the house to enter and left the same way after taking Arielle with him, trying to stay undetectable. Maybe your guys were waiting for the goons to come out the front door."

"Well, that could be the case, but what in the world happened to Jorrit's man? They were not in the house. There was no trace of anyone being there at all." Dylan sounded confused.

"I don't know, Dylan; I wish I did. All I know is that Arielle is safe under doctor's supervision."

"Yes...Yes... I am happy about that as well." Perplexity still coated his voice.

"I am just curious," Dylan said suddenly. "Did you end up going to the airport?"

"No, once I found out that Arielle was safe, I didn't bother. Are you sure that your detectives were at the correct location?"

"Absolutely. They watched them drive inside the garage and close the door behind them," Dylan said, his tone of voice confused. "The car was still there but nothing else."

"You must be joking," Sebastian said, professing to be totally shocked.

"No, I'm dead serious," Dylan said powerfully.

"Have you heard anything from the surveillance team in Brussels?" Sebastian asked again, trying to show interest.

"Well, that's what has my whole team in dismay. Jorrit and the goons seem to be very distraught and very baffled."

"About what?" Sebastian insisted.

"Jorrit can't locate his two guys and the big goon in Belarus has not heard back from the men he sent to Brighton to help with the extortion. They can't understand how they can all just disappear from the face of the earth."

"That does sound crazy," Sebastian added.

"I'm telling you, Sebastian, this is the weirdest thing that has ever happened in my twenty-five-year career," he said totally frustrated.

"Well, if I hear something, I'll give you a ring," Sebastian furthered.

"Okay, Sebastian. I'm happy that Arielle is safe. If I find out what in the world happened, I'll let you know."

"Thanks, Dylan, I appreciate your support on this issue."

"Later," Dylan said and ended the call.

 *Chapter 12*

BATTLING ANGER about Arielle's condition, Ian focused on getting her swiftly into the hospital. As soon as he arrived at the emergency entrance, he jerked the door open and stormed inside. He carried her past curious onlookers and surrendered her to the emergency room staff that ran to assist him. They eased Arielle onto a gurney, gently, and wheeled her immediately into the emergency room.

Ian stood there in silence for a short moment, watching them disappear quickly behind the swivel door of ER room. He drew in a breath and tried to absorb the significance of what had just taken place. He was too worried about Arielle to think straight and too drained to try and grasp how much of a recollection Arielle would have...Surely she wouldn't remember most of it. She was unconscious when they found her at that dreadful home.

He moved slowly toward the glass doors, and his eyes drifted outside, wondering what Sebastian, Christian, and Troy were doing. He thought about Eva and how devastated he would have been if she were human and in Arielle's place. He certainly never envisioned the day to turn out the way it did. He liked Sebastian from the first moment they met. He had become a great friend and, along with Troy, a great mentor during his and Eva's transition to immortality.

He knew that Sebastian was crushed about Arielle's condition, and he wanted to do everything he could to help. Sebastian had asked him to stay at the hospital and make the necessary calls to their friends and family. However, he didn't want him to discuss details with her parents until Sebastian gave him a scenario that they could use as a story.

He tried to reject the sting of pain he felt for his great friend and stay strong for him and for Arielle, who was lying unconscious and bruised up in the emergency room. A surge of anger crushed through his body and he cursed inwardly.

A small voice startled him, interrupting his reverie, and turning around, he saw a young woman standing right behind him, watching him carefully. They regarded each other curiously. Ian unclenched his jaw, and his eyes swept over her, studying her for a short second. "Can I help you?" he asked briskly.

Her eyes widened at the tone of his voice, and she took a step back. She cleared her throat as if she weighing her words. She met his gaze with narrowed eyes, ready to snap at him, but she held her tongue. She seemed to understand that he was probably worried about the new patient he had just brought in. "Yes, sir," she replied calmly. "Did you bring the young lady that they took into the emergency room?"

"Yes," he replied. Stress was evident in his voice.

"I will need for you to come with me at the admitting desk to provide some information on the patient," she said kindly.

Ian shook his head. "I'm just a friend," he said. "I'm in the process of ringing her parents. Upon their arrival, they will be able to provide you with all the essential information and documentation that you require about their daughter," he replied.

"I also want you to know that it is hospital policy to notify the authorities in cases like this one," she said, firmly.

His eyes flickered over her shoulder to the emergency room door, and he sighed, wondering how Arielle was doing. Anger rushed through him like blazing waves of the fire sipping deep through every immortal vein and consumed him. A low sound of discomfort emanated from deep in his throat, at the thought of the assassins and the beating the inflicted on Arielle.

"That's fine," he replied, inattentively.

"All right then," she added. "Please make sure that her parents come to see me as soon as they arrive." She then turned and walked away.

Ian watched her disappearing around the corner and, fishing out his phone from his jean pocket; he called Arielle's parents. In a few words, he told them where he was and that he would be waiting for them outside the emergency entrance to give them more details. He wanted to talk with Sebastian first to make sure that they have the same story. He then called Eva. At the sound of her voice, his anger diminished.

"Hey, baby."

"Ian!" She called out. "Did you find Arielle?"

"Yes, but she's in bad shape. Sebastian asked me to bring her to the Royal Essex County Hospital while he, along with Christian and Troy, finish up with the thugs.

"Where are you now?"

"I'm at the hospital."

"Are the guys there yet?"

"No, but they should be coming shortly."

"Oh my God! What did they do to her?" Eva's voice was filled with anguish.

"She is beaten up pretty badly."

"Oh no..." Eva's voice trailed. "But...but I thought they were not going to touch her until they had Sebastian's documents."

"So we thought," he said disgustingly.

"What do you want me to do?"

"Please ring Gabby, Isabella, Paul, and Loren. I'm going to wait for Sebastian and hopefully he will be here before Arielle's parents do."

"Okay, love. I'll be there shortly. I love you, Ian."

"I love you, too, baby."

Unfortunately, Arielle's parents arrived at the hospital shortly after receiving Ian's call. They were in a complete panic.

"Wh—why is Arielle here? Where is she?" Danielle Lloyd asked anxiously.

"She's in the emergency room," Ian replied.

Their eyes widened in sheer horror. "What happened?" James

Lloyd asked apprehensively.

"She was taken from campus this morning, and we didn't know where she was until later this afternoon."

"Taken—? What do you mean by taken, taken by whom?" her father asked swallowing hard.

"We don't know," Ian said thoughtfully.

"But... but you were all on campus together. I don't understand. How could she be taken?" her mother cried, utterly confused.

"I'm not sure," Ian replied. "I don't think anyone of us knows exactly what happened." He heard James Lloyd gasp out loud.

"She just disappeared from class?" her father repeated, staring at Ian potently, his voice hitting a high sharp tone.

Ian's eyebrows rose to the sharp tone of his voice.

James Lloyd missed Ian's reaction; his attention turned to his wife. His arm was wrapped around her, trying to support her weight. She was trembling uncontrollably.

Ian understood the turmoil that was ripping through them and kept his voice calm. "Arielle had chemistry this morning, and she was to meet Gabrielle after class, but she never showed up. Professor Allworth said that she did go inside the auditorium, but for just a short moment. She then turned around and ran out again. She had seemed as if she had forgotten something, but she never returned to class."

Arielle's parents appeared bewildered. There was a long silence, and it grew heavier and heavier. "How did you find her?" James Lloyd asked finally. He remained quiet, waiting for Ian to say something. It seemed like an eternity before he decided to answer his question.

"Well, when she didn't show up, we spread out to search for her, but she was nowhere to be found. Her car was still in the parking lot, so we didn't know where to start. We tried to phone her, but she didn't answer the call."

"This is insane," Arielle's mother muttered. It was becoming a very complex puzzle. Trying to put the pieces together would turn out to become a mammoth task for the Lloyds.

"So how did you find her?" Mr. Lloyd asked incredulously, further probing for more information.

"I will tell you as much as I know, but first, you need to go to the admitting desk. The lady has asked me twice to tell you that she needs to see you as soon as you arrive. You must complete some paperwork before they can move Arielle from ER to a room. Her desk is right around that corner," he said and gestured toward the admissions office. To his relief, they nodded with grim reluctance and headed that direction.

They found the admissions clerk waiting for them. They introduced themselves politely. "We are Arielle Lloyd's parents. She was brought into the emergency a short time ago," James Lloyd stated. "We understand that you need some information from us."

"Yes, sir, I would like for you to fill out these forms about your daughter. I will also need insurance information and identification card," she said and handed them two forms and a pen. "The second sheet is for you to list if she has any allergies and if she is taking any medications right now," she added.

James Lloyd pulled his wallet out of his back pocket and gave the clerk his insurance identification card. "Can you please find out how she is doing while we are completing these forms?"

Their expression was that of worry and wretchedness. The girls felt bad for them. "Just a moment, please, sir. I will check for you," she replied kindly. She stepped away from her desk and disappeared behind a closed door. She returned shortly. "The attending physician will be sent to the waiting room to give you status as soon as they are finished."

"Thank you," they both mumbled and started filling in the forms and answering her questions.

Ian disappeared around the corner and walked back into the lobby. He pulled his mobile out and rang Sebastian. He picked up on the first ring.

"Everything okay, Ian?"

"Yes, Arielle is being taken care off, but her parents are here. They are busy filling some forms, but as soon as they come back, they'll be asking questions. I need to know what I should say."

"Is Christian there?"

"I have not seen him as of yet. He may be here somewhere."

Sebastian in a few words explained to Ian the scenario he came up with. "Don't worry; we are on our way. We should be there shortly."

"Okay. No worries; at least I know what to say now. I'll see you soon." He shut his phone and slipped it into his pocket.

Suddenly, the door opened, and Arielle's friends burst inside, expressions anxious and extremely worried. Eva fell into his arms, and he held her tight.

"How is she?" Gabrielle and Eva asked in unison.

"We don't know yet," Ian replied, placing a soft kiss on Eva's lips. "We're waiting for one of the attending physicians to give us some information. Let's go to the waiting room." He kept his arm around Eva, happy that she was by his side.

"Have you called her parents?" Eva asked.

"Yes, they are here; they are filling out some paperwork. They should be here shortly." Soon Christian showed up, and Isabella was happy to see him. They all agreed to let Ian talk if there were questions asked to keep the story straight until Sebastian and Troy arrived.

It wasn't long before the Lloyds walked in, looking apprehensive and nervous.

They all took turns in expressing their sadness about Arielle's situation. After chatting with them for a few minutes, they moved to take a seat and lost themselves in their own thoughts.

James Lloyd turned to Ian. "Have you contacted the authorities?"

"The authorities?" Ian asked, startled.

"Yes."

He wasn't prepared for that question, but he recovered quickly. "I didn't," he replied. "But the hospital did. It's a hospital policy I was told. There is nothing more that I could tell them, but for what I have already said to you," he furthered. "They will have to wait for Arielle to come around and tell them what happened. She's the only one that has the facts," he said tightly.

"But...but how did you find her?"

Everyone's gaze landed on Ian. He took a deep breath and went with the story Sebastian gave him.

"A couple of hours after we found out she was missing, Arielle sent a text to Eva, telling her that she needed help. She had no idea where she was, so we used the phone locator to find her. She said that she was hurt, so Christian and I decided to go and bring her back. I contacted Sebastian and Troy at once. They were in a meeting with Dylan Jamison, the head of intelligence with Interpol, and they should be here shortly. We found her in an empty home badly beaten, and by the time we arrived, she was unconscious. There was no one around, so we had no idea what happened or who was involved. She was in bad shape, so we thought the best thing would be to bring her here as fast as we could. That is pretty much all I know."

Her parents looked shocked. Their apprehension grew quickly to a fearful level. Who could want their daughter hurt? What do they want from her? Stony silence fell in the waiting room and grew thicker and thicker.

James Lloyd broke the awkward silence. "Thank you, Ian, Thank you, Christian, for saving our daughter." His voice was breaking.

It was not long before Loren and Sebastian's parents came in, taking a seat next to the Lloyds. Christian Dillon shook hands with James Lloyd, and Olivia took Danielle's hands in hers and pressed them softly.

"How is Arielle?" Olivia asked.

"We should know shortly," Danielle replied.

"I understand that Sebastian was in a meeting. Has someone notified him?" Olivia asked.

"Yes, Ian just told us that he is on his way."

"Good," Olivia whispered as if she was talking to herself.

It was a very difficult time for everyone as the time ticked away in a very slow pace. It had been a while before a man in scrubs appeared at the door of the waiting room and asked for Arielle's immediate family. He then introduced himself.

"I'm Doctor Slater," he said with a kind smile on his face.

"How is she, Doctor?" her father asked anxiously

"Your daughter suffered numerous injuries on her body and face.

She has several lacerations that needed stitches and took a dreadful blow to the head. Our concern is mainly the mild swelling on her brain. But she is unconscious, and that will help in keeping her still."

"Swelling on her brain?" her mother shrieked.

"It is very mild and nothing to worry about. She is a strong young lady, and she will come out of it just fine," the doctor said. "She will be wheeled into a private room shortly. She's not to have any visitors but family," he added glancing around at the group of friends in the waiting room. "Dr. McKenna will come to see her later on. Don't worry; she'll do just fine," he said encouragingly.

They both thanked him as he turned and left the waiting room.

It wasn't long before they were notified that Arielle had been brought into a private room.

The Lloyds stood up, and glancing around the room; they thanked everyone for coming to the hospital.

"Let us know how she is doing," Olivia said. "We will wait here for Sebastian."

James put his arm around his wife, and they left the room.

Overwhelming numbness took over the Lloyds as they approached their daughter's bed. The color drained from Danielle Lloyd's face, and rage vibrated through James Lloyd's body. Arielle appearance was ghastly. Her beautiful face was completely distorted. The upper part of her face was black and blue. Her eyes were swollen shut, and small sutures covered a six-inch laceration on her right cheek. There were IV's in both arms, and she was connected to a monitor that produced a steady beep.

Danielle Lloyd sighed deeply and tears pooled in her eyes. Her husband reached over and clasped her hand pressing it softly.

"She'll be fine, Dani," he whispered, but his face didn't hide his deep concern. They had no idea how long they sat quietly at her bedside, waiting for their daughter to wake up.

Chapter 13

TAPPING OF LIGHT FOOTSTEPS and distant murmurs grabbed Arielle's attention. A pounding throb started in her head. Someone was approaching, the sound echoing off the floor. *Who? God, where am I?* Fear surged though her body and tears stung the back of her eyelids. A robust pain surged through her brain and spread across her body like fire, and darkness consumed her.

She found herself standing on the top of a mountain, gazing over the green blanket of the treetops. She kept her eyes across the expanse of the deep blue ocean that stretched out into the distance and fused with the horizon. The sun dipped slowly into the ocean, spurting a mixture of red and orange hues across the patterns of the gray and white clouds, turning the water to a simply breathtaking sight. The experience offered something special beyond the power of words to describe; perhaps it was just a dream.

She stood in complete stillness, draped in silence, as the light of the day started to turn dark. Why was she alone? What was she doing alone on the top of a mountain? Why was everything so quiet? Where was everyone? She tried to process and discharge the images that were passing through her hazed mind.

Time seemed to fly, and suddenly, it was dark, very dark, and she was still standing on the top of this mountain— alone. What was she to make of the shadows? Could the shadow's end carry the answers to her questions? She started to panic, a blistering rush of adrenaline spreading through her veins, and she could hear the steady thud of the blood thrashing into her ears. Panic turned to fright, and a voice in the back of her mind was telling her to run, but she couldn't move.

Her feet were sinking into the soggy soil, spreading terror through her body. She moaned fearfully and tried to run again, but to no avail. A sharp pain shot across her muscles once again and she tried to scream, but there was no sound coming from her vocal cords. This had to be a horrible nightmare, and any minute she would wake up. She was tired very tired and the pain, oh the pain. Why do I hurt this badly? She inwardly moaned, and before any further thoughts, she was consumed by darkness once again.

The clock was ticking away, and Arielle was still unconscious. Her father rose to his feet, his hand still stroking his wife's back. She looked up watching him, sadness spread across her beautiful face. His hand moved to cup her cheek lovingly, and she lifted her hand to cover his. She leaned against it and, closing her eyes, felt the comfort he was giving her. He bent down and pressed a soft kiss on her forehead.

"Dani, dear, I will go, let everyone know how she is doing and have a cup of tea. Would you like a cup?" he whispered, and she nodded in agreement.

Tapping of light footsteps were back again. Rolling emotions began to drop into Arielle's memory and, suddenly, she stiffened. An unwelcome memory of her captivity made the blood run cold in her veins and sent shockwaves right through her brain. Two very angry sets of eyes overcrowded her thoughts, and a chill crept down her spine. She suddenly recalled her escape attempt and the horrible beating she received from her captors, but she was still in a drab haze that obscured the clear memory of their faces. She had this strange feeling that she knew them, but nothing was coming into her memory bank right now.

She could feel the pain as she recalled the terrible plunge down the stairs, the bleeding, the difficulty trying to breathe, and the sharp pain in the back of her head. The pain! The excruciating pain! Her face fell in response to the sensation as another sharp pain shot right through her body suspending her reverie, and she groaned loudly. Terror and hopelessness of still being locked in the room brought fear that vibrated right through her. *Oh God, I must be back into that awful room. Please don't let them hurt me anymore! Where is Sebastian? Why didn't he come for me?* The tears burned the back of her eyes and started to stream down the side of her face. They signified what her life had turned out to be in a matter of seconds in the campus parking lot.

"She's coming out of it." A woman's gentle voice broke her reverie.

What? Who is she? Arielle couldn't remember a woman being part of her abduction, but before she could process the statement, the voice urged anxiously. More footsteps approached as the nurse in charge of Arielle entered the room. The same woman's voice sounded once again.

"She's in pain! Please do something!" The tension in the tone of her voice struck a chord, but the interpretation of anything at this point was way too advanced.

Who is she? Arielle's brain reeled wildly while the pain intensified, and she whimpered. She needed help, and she wasn't able to move or open her eyes. She called out in sheer desperation. *Please help me! Where am I?* She waited for a short moment, but nobody replied to her desperate plea. *Why can't they hear me? I'm screaming!* Suffocation was the closest feeling she was experiencing at this moment. Silence stretched. She was isolated, and her fear was that she was still locked in that room.

Immediately, a drugged, warm sensation surged through her limbs and body, and the pain vanished as she was enveloped in pleasant comfort. Her eyelids felt heavy, and no matter how hard she struggled to open her eyes, she failed. *Why don't I hurt anymore? Am I dead?* She asked herself, but the silence from her mind was deafening. Finally, a new voice, gentle like the soft whisper of a spring breeze, disrupted the solemn silence.

"This will take the pain away and help her sleep peacefully."

What? Whom was she talking to? No one seemed to reply to her requests or hear her screams for help, so she was sure that she couldn't connect with the people in the room cognitively or emotionally. Suddenly, the fog swept through her mind again, and everything went dark.

It was dusk, and she felt lonely...a huge meadow in the far-reaching twilight just before the dawn. She walked slowly through the meadow, feeling inexplicably isolated. Her feet started to feel heavy as if she were dragging them through the mud. She tried to find someone or something familiar, but to her dismay, all she could see was darkness. It was as if in the blink of an eye, she had been transported to a different universe.

This has to be a dream. *She stopped in the middle of the meadow and closed her eyes. If this was a dream, she could change it just by wishing away the darkness. She prayed hard and opened her eyes as she held her breath. She smiled wide as her eyes fell on a beautiful meadow that was now being bathed in the brilliance of the sun, crammed with a vast amount of the most exquisite flowers in all colors and all shapes. They swayed in the light breeze, creating a moving sea of colors. She lifted her eyes toward the sky, and pleasure filled her senses. Where in the world am I? It all appeared so very strange but so beautiful.*

Her gaze fell into the distance, and her smile faded away when she noticed a huge wall of fog at the end of the meadow. But how could that be possible? It was sunny and bright over the meadow. Almost as if someone had taken a pen and drew a line starting at the sky and ending on the ground, splitting her world in two. One was a brilliant, beautiful world, and it ended at the beginning of another, not-so-brilliant, not-so-beautiful, bleak and obscure one. She lifted her eyes again toward the sky and followed the clear blue color out to the distance, and it turned dark and hazy exactly at the line of separation.

Confusion spread quickly through her mind. Tears pooled in her eyes again, and she lowered her gaze to the edge of the meadow. Startled, she noticed a man standing right in front of the foggy wall, waving eagerly for her to come. She strained her gaze, but couldn't clearly see his face. She held her hand up, shading her eyes against the sun, and started to walk toward him. It wasn't long before his face became vivid, and she grinned in delight. "Sebastian!" she screamed and started to run toward him. He held his arms open, ready for her to fall in. She closed her eyes in sheer delight as she reached the edge of the meadow, but when she opened them again, he was gone! "Sebastian!" she screamed, and tears streamed down her face. Why didn't he wait for her? She made a quick decision to follow him and stepped right over the line and into the haze and everything became dark.

She had no further thoughts. The meds pushed her into a deep sleep.

"Thank you, Miss Walker," Danielle Lloyd murmured, glancing at the nurse thankfully. The nurse had just administered a strong dose of pain reliever to Arielle.

"She is awfully peaceful now," the nurse said and gave her a reassuring smile. "She'll sleep for a while longer. The doctor should be in shortly to give you all the details," she continued, her voice laced with compassion.

"I'm sure she will need pain relievers for a few more days," Danielle murmured as if she spoke to herself.

"Yes, she will, and the doctor will prescribe what she needs," the nurse replied and, smiling gently at Arielle's parents, she left the room discreetly.

They both sank into the two chairs next to the bed and sat quietly. James Lloyd reached over and clasped his wife's hand with one of his, and with the other, he took Arielle's hand and held it tenderly. His heart was breaking. It was quite clear that he needed a great deal of strength to bear the pain for both himself and his wife. He saw tears streaming down Danielle's face.

"Dani, darling," he murmured, trying to keep his voice steady. "She'll be fine. Let's see what the doctor says." He released her hand to wipe her tears away. She gazed at her husband lovingly and nodded in agreement. He started to say something but closed his mouth as the doctor came in, a soft smile on his elderly, kind face. James Lloyd stood up as the doctor approached.

"Good evening. I'm Dr. McKenna."

"Good evening, Doctor. I'm James Lloyd, and this is my wife, Danielle. We are Arielle's parents. How is she doing?" he asked eagerly.

"Arielle is a strong and healthy girl. However, she has received serious trauma to her body and face. She has four cracked ribs, and her body is pretty bruised up. She took some bad hits on the face, and her eyes will be closed for a couple of days. The bruising and the swelling on her face will eventually go away. She received a two-inch laceration on the right side of her face with a sharp object," he said softly and pointed to Arielle's face. "I used small sutures to close the cut, and that will reduce scarring after it heals. She took a bad hit in the back of her head, and she has a large bump that will be sore for a couple of weeks." He gave them a gentle smile. "She will be fine. She just needs tender loving care," he added. "The people that did this beat her up pretty severely."

"Good Lord, who could do that to a young girl?" her mother murmured, completely stunned by the news.

"That would be a good question for the authorities," the doctor replied.

"Thank you, Doctor," Mr. Lloyd said and shook the doctor's hand.

"I'll check back with her in the morning, but I'm sure we'll keep her here for a couple of days," Dr. McKenna said and left the room, shaking his head in clear wonder.

Arielle woke up in a heavy black cloud. Nothing to see, nothing to feel, just this unresponsiveness of her whole body. But where was she? What happened? Was she dead? Was she dreaming? Why was it so dark? She attempted to sort her thoughts, but they remained confused. There was a clear inconsistency between what she was feeling in her heart and what she was thinking in her head.

A distant noise drew her attention. It sounded like a steady beeping, like a machine monitor. She tried to move, but she couldn't. She tried to open her eyes, but she couldn't. *God, what is happening to me? I can't open my eyes!* She inhaled deeply, and a cold feeling began to creep through her. She shivered, and her muscles contracted. Something was happening, but what?

She tried to think, but absolute silence was coming from her brain. As if her thought processor had ceased to function. She panicked, as anxiety took over, and she started to hyperventilate. *What in God's name is happening to me?* She tried to move again, but nothing worked. She struggled to open her eyes. She heard distant male voices and footsteps approaching. Arielle stiffened and remained perfectly still. *They are coming back,* she thought, and fright took her breath away. *What now? I don't want to be raped, and I don't want to be hit again, and oh! God! Where is Sebastian?* She was going to die in that awful room—*alone.* She moaned softly and felt her mind hazing away once again.

Sebastian burst into the hospital room. He approached the bed with a few long strides and gazed down at Arielle's small frame. His eyes widened in sheer horror. It was his fault that she was in here. His body ached, his eyes burned, and he thought he was losing his mind.

"Sebastian, dear!" The soft voice of acknowledgment came from the other side of the bed. He caught Danielle's eyes, as her mouth quirked into a half tormented smile that stilled him. He saw the depth of sadness that painted her face and, glancing next to her, he saw James Lloyd sitting quietly, his expression completely crushed. Danielle dropped her eyes to Arielle's battered body and uncontrolled tears entwined its way down her face. She clasped her hands together in her lap and sat completely motionless like a statue.

Sebastian was lost for words. He dropped to his knees and, leaning on the bed, he rested his head on his folded arms. His love for Arielle was infinite.

"Oh, baby," he muttered. A surge of sullenness coursed through him, followed by a long unbearable pause. "It's all my fault. I'm so sorry; I shouldn't have left you alone," he murmured in clear distress. He drew in a shuddery breath and mentally cursed the horrible situation he created for Arielle once again. His gaze swept the room that swirled hazily before his eyes. He reached over and took Arielle's hand gently. Raising it to his mouth, he brushed his lips softly across it without disturbing the IV attached to it. He then placed it tenderly against his cheek and leaned into it, wanting to feel her warmth against his skin. He had no idea how long he remained in that position. He was utterly lost. He finally lowered her hand back on the bed and, closing his fingers over it affectionately, he held it, as if he was holding a lifeline.

A soft hand touched his shoulder and jerked him out of his reverie. He saw Arielle's mother who had left her seat, and she was now standing right behind him and caught his breath.

"It's not your fault, Sebastian. We'll find the people that did this to her," she said sympathetically.

Recovering his poise with extreme effort, Sebastian shook his head. "I should have been with her. I shouldn't have left her alone," he said bitterly.

"Sebastian, you can't be with her all the time," James Lloyd said quietly from the other side of the bed.

"Has the doctor been here?" Sebastian asked.

"Yes, he just left. He said she'll be all right; it will just take time," Danielle replied.

Sebastian glanced from one to the other, and letting go of Arielle's hand; he rose to his feet. Pulling a chair close, he helped Danielle to it. He then walked around the bed and took the seat next to James Lloyd. They just sat quietly without speaking, staring at Arielle's pale, distorted face.

It seemed like a century passed slowly, agonizingly. He wanted to scream from anger, from anxiety, from frustration. James and Danielle had their eyes closed, and their lips were moving to a soundless prayer. Sebastian closed his eyes in distress and wished he could go back in time and change everything.

A soft moan broke them out of their reverie. Startled, they opened their eyes, and their gazes rested on Arielle's face. Tears were streaming down the side of her face and disappearing into her ears and down the bed sheets.

"James! James!" Arielle's mother called out. "I think she's coming around," she murmured and inched the chair closer to the bed. Sebastian sprang to his feet and stared motionless at Arielle's face.

"I think she is still asleep, Dani," James replied quietly.

"No, no, she's not asleep. She's trying to open her eyes. She is moving her eyelids, but she doesn't know that her eyes are swollen shut," Sebastian said, anxiously. He wanted to fall on the bed and hold her tightly in his embrace, but he didn't move. He wanted her parents to have time with their daughter. He would have her for eternity.

James Lloyd clasped Arielle's hand in his and leaned closer. Gazing on his little girl's face, his heart was breaking. She was the love of his life. His pride and joy, everything that meant anything to him in this life. Danielle Lloyd walked around, draped her arm around her husband's shoulders, and let her tears flow freely down her face.

Chapter 14

ARIELLE TRIED TO MOVE her arm and a sharp pain shot through her. Her head hurt, her chest and arms were hurt, and her face was burning up. Her throat was dry as the desert. She was thirsty, and she needed to open her eyes. Why was she still draped in this awful darkness? She was groggy and confused.

A soft hand landed on her forehead, and a warm voice whispered in her ear. "Arielle, it's Mummy, darling, I'm right here. Daddy and I are here."

Where is right here? She thought. *How could my parents be here? How did they find me?*

"Mummy!" Arielle mumbled due to her swollen lips. Tears flowed freely down her face while trying to squeeze the hand that was clutching hers. "Where am I?"

"You're safe, dear. You're in the hospital," her mother replied joyously.

"The hospital? Ho—how—who brought me here?" she whispered, her pulse-elevating.

"Ian brought you into the hospital, darling!" Danielle replied reassuringly.

"But—but—," she started to say and stopped for a long moment. She tried to open her eyes once again, and her unsuccessful attempts made her eyelids jerk back and forth. Sweat started to form on her forehead, and she frowned. "Sebastian…" she murmured. "Where is

Sebastian?" Tears still flowing uncontrollably down the side of her face.

Danielle's eyes shifted to Sebastian as he inched closer and, bending down, he pressed his forehead against hers. Arielle heard the intake of his breath.

"I'm here, baby. I'm right here," he murmured, and his lips brushed hers softly. She wasn't sure if Sebastian was truly there or if she was hallucinating. He was her only love, her sanctuary.

"Oh! Sebastian!" she whimpered. A faded smile painted her swollen lips.

"Yes, baby, don't try to talk; you're safe. Are you in pain?" His voice was filled with raw emotion.

"Yes, everything hurts, and I can't move my hands," she muttered anxiously. "And...and...and I *can't* open my eyes," she whimpered.

"You have IV's in both hands, baby, so you need to stay still. I'll call for the nurse to give you a pain shot."

"But why can't I open my eyes? What is happening to me?" she asked again, soft sobs quivering her body.

"Please don't worry, sweetheart. It's temporary," he murmured.

"I don't understand; what happened to me?"

"You took a hit on your face, and your eyes are swollen shut," he said bitterly. "But like I said, it's temporary."

"How did Ian find me?" Tears kept streaming down her face, and a broken smile painted her lips.

"I think you need to try and relax, and we can talk about all the details when you feel a bit better," he said and pressed his lips against her once again.

"Is my dad here?" she whispered.

"I'm here, pumpkin," James Lloyd said, jumping on his feet and leaning closer to his daughter.

"Daddy!"

"Yes, darling. I'm right here with your mother and Sebastian. All your friends and Sebastian's parents are in the waiting room. We're all here for you, but you need to rest now and try to get better," he said, and his voice trembled.

"Sebastian!" she murmured.

"Yes, baby."

"Do I look really bad?"

"No, darling, you are just as beautiful as ever," he said and, leaning down, he pressed his cheek against hers. A sense of déjà vu crashed back into his memory, overwhelming him with remorse and anxiety. She had been hospitalized four times since they met. Three times attacked by people that had vowed to keep them apart and once when Matt tried to rape her. *Why did I ever decide to bring Arielle into this awful world of mine?* He thought and cringed. He remained silent as he reached in the deep corners of his memory and the facts hit him like a dreadful windstorm. He was not worried about the Russian Mafia any longer. He was going to abolish that organization shortly, but that wasn't going to be the end of Arielle's torture, not as long as Annabel and her mates were still alive.

Gazing down on Arielle's battered body, he silently vowed to her that he would deliver the final blow to each and every one who had hurt her or would try to hurt her in the future.

"I'm thirsty," she sniffed and grimaced.

Her mother reached above her bed and pulled the cord. The nurse entered the room a few minutes later, a soothing smile on her face.

"Oh, she's awake!" Miss Walker said, her voice skillfully low. She glanced with a calm smile between Danielle and James Lloyd, but a flicker of movement drew her attention, and her eyes fell on Sebastian. The smile faded away slowly, her mouth fell open, and her eyes widened in sheer astonishment. She forgot how to breathe, overcome by a fascinating sensation. Their gaze locked and Sebastian's brows rose.

Dear Lord! She thought to herself, trying to recover her faculties. For a fleeting instant, she thought he was an illusion. She shut her eyes, but when she opened them again, he was still there. He had to be the most beautiful man she had ever set eyes on—in her twenty-nine years on this earth.

Danielle's eyes followed the nurse's gaze and understood Sebastian's effect on her. The nurse was standing temporarily speechless at the stunning sight of Sebastian. She managed to repress her astonishment and, jerking her eyes away from him; she blinked rapidly.

She then turned her flushed face back to Danielle Lloyd to find her watching her inquiringly. She gathered her disarrayed thoughts and coughed to clear her throat. She approached Arielle's bed and stared down at her.

"Did she say anything?" the nurse asked Danielle.

"Yes, she's in pain," Danielle replied, resisting the urge to say something about the effect that bewildered the nurse's wits. Instead, she added, "And she's very thirsty."

"Oh, that's a very good sign," she said gracefully. "I'll be right back." She then made a beeline for the door. She came back shortly carrying a small tray. She set it on the side table, and taking a decanter; she poured some water in a small plastic cup. She pressed a button on the bed control panel and raised the upper part, bringing Arielle to a sitting position. Placing her arm around Arielle's neck, she helped her take a few sips of water through a straw. She then gave her a pain shot and ran her cool hand over Arielle's forehead. She was sure that Arielle was not running a fever. "Best lie back and rest," she murmured kindly. She then fluffed up her pillows and helped her lie back down, lowering her bed to a horizontal position.

"Thank you," Arielle sniffed.

"You're welcome, dear," the nurse replied. "Do you need anything else?"

"No...," she said, muffled.

"The pain shot will work quickly, and you'll feel a lot better," she said softly. She then pressed Arielle's hand reassuringly. She released it and, nodding at her parents, she left the room, strongly rejecting the temptation to glance in Sebastian's direction.

When the door closed behind her, Danielle stared at Sebastian. "Dear God! Does this happen everywhere you go?"

"What happened?" Arielle asked groggily.

Sebastian smiled and nodded at Danielle. "I'm afraid it does," he said.

"Wh—what?" Arielle insisted, her voice barely audible. The shot seemed to be working.

"The nurse nearly went dazed when she saw Sebastian," her mother said, amusingly.

Arielle snorted mildly.

"Go to sleep, baby; relax," Sebastian murmured against her ear.

His nearness overshadowed every other thought. He was there, and she trusted him. Groggily, she mumbled. "Everywhere we go…" and that was the last thing she said.

"Really?" Danielle exclaimed.

"That seems to be the case," Sebastian muttered.

Danielle shook her head in clear wonder. "I think Arielle is asleep," she said softly, staring down at her daughter.

"Why don't you both go home?" Sebastian suggested. "I'll stay with Arielle tonight. You need your rest," he added, looking at the Lloyds.

Danielle leaned over her daughter and kissed her on the cheek. "I love you, baby," she whispered to her sleeping daughter.

"Thank you, Sebastian," James Lloyd said, feeling mentally and emotionally exhausted. He stood up, and bending over Arielle; he pressed a soft kiss on her forehead. "I'll be back in the morning, pumpkin," he murmured in her ear, even though he knew she was asleep and couldn't hear him.

Danielle hugged Sebastian thankfully, and James shook his hand in appreciation. He then wrapped his arm around his wife and left the room. Turning back, he pinned Sebastian with a warm glance. "My boy, we'll be back here early in the morning, and you can have a break."

"I'm fine, sir; don't worry about me," he said.

When they left, Sebastian stood helplessly staring at the closed door. His self-control was being tried. He had been in this situation twice before. Once following Arielle's birthday after Savanna broke her ribs and tried to kill her by poison. The second time at Saint Jean de Luz, following Annabel's attack that nearly killed both Arielle and Eva. He didn't even count the two times she landed in the hospital because of an old flame of his, Paola Gordioni, and the rape attempt by a university student, Matt Winston.

He lowered his head and pursed his lips at the agonizing thoughts; the pain in his chest was intense. He grimaced again, fists clenched by his sides. He drew in a deep breath and started to pace back and forth, finally halting in front of Arielle's bed. He gazed down at her, and immediately, he was overcome by a blinding emotion of deep love and passion. He reached down and touched her face lightly by running his finger down her cheek, across her swollen bottom lip, and back up again. He then bent down and pressed a soft kiss on her lips. Excitement surged through him as his lips lingered over hers a bit longer, and his muscles went taught, just as they did each and every time they touched.

Slowly, he buried his face into the crook of her neck, and his lips pressed against her pulse point. He felt the quiet thudding that beat in sync with her heartbeat as the blood surged through her veins. His skin infused and resonated through his body like a shockwave. He was overwhelmed with the powerful sensation that held him captive to Arielle's enchantment. "God!" he whispered out loud. "I love her; I love her more than life itself."

Pulling back, he knew that he had to gather his wits and face two facts that were not favorable to Arielle.

He needed to uncover and abolish the leaders of the treacherous plot that the Russian Mafia was running against him and his company. He also needed to deal with Annabel and her coconspirators. His lips were trembling with emotion when he stared at her battered body and swore that he was never going to allow anyone to hurt her— *ever* –again. "I love you, Arielle," he muttered softly and pressed his lips against her forehead.

Arielle was still deeply asleep. He decided to walk into the waiting room, talk to his parents, and update his friends. They didn't need to stay there any longer. He strode to the door and pulled it open. Turning back, he allowed himself a loving glance at Arielle and left the room.

Everyone looked up when he entered the waiting room. His

expression spoke volumes. His eyes lingered for a moment between his friends and his parents. Gabby, Eva, and Isabella glanced at one another and frowned at the worried expression on his face. His parents and Loren stood up and pulled him into their embrace.

"How is she?" Olivia murmured eagerly.

"She is pretty bruised up and in pain," he said and grimaced, furious that he left Arielle on campus unprotected to meet Dylan.

Loren fell in his arms, and he held her tight. "I'm sorry, Sebastian," she whispered to her brother, devotedly. "We love you so much. Please don't worry about Arielle; she'll recover."

Sebastian followed her words and merely nodded his head. An instant later, he said. "I know…I know…and I love you all for being here." He stared out the window and saw the daylight vanishing. "Mum, Dad, you don't have to stay here any longer. She can't have visitors anyway, but I'll stay with her through the night."

"All right, son," his father said and patted him on the back reassuringly. "We'll come back tomorrow to check on Arielle." They hugged him once again.

"Loren, are you coming with us?" Olivia questioned, glancing at Loren still in Sebastian's embrace.

"Yes," she replied and, pressing a kiss to her brother's cheek, she fell into step alongside her parents. She waved back to her friends, and they walked out.

Sebastian shifted his gaze to his friends. They were sitting on the other side of the room quietly, giving him time alone with his parents.

"You guys don't have to stay either," he said softly.

Eva jumped to her feet, and the others followed. They all approached him thoughtfully.

"How are you?" Eva asked, reaching up to give him a hug. "You do look like hell, dazzle boy," she added, trying to ease the tension around them.

His eyebrows went up, keeping his face pokerfaced. "What do you mean?" he asked.

"Your clothes," Gabrielle said as she came up to give him a hug. She didn't have to elaborate; she just waved her arm up and down his body.

Sebastian stared down at himself, and even though he was not in a joking mood, he understood that his friends were trying to make him feel better. "I think I look great!" he said, composedly.

"You just seem emotionally drained," interjected Isabella, who took her turn in hugging Sebastian.

"I know..." he murmured and nodded in agreement. "But I'm staying here tonight. There is no place that I would rather be. I need to be with Arielle," he said bitterly. "It's my fault that she's here," he added and grimaced, running his hand through his hair.

"Sebastian, it's not your fault," Eva said. She hesitated for a short moment before she reached out, and clasping his hand; she pressed it warmly.

"Thank you, Eva, but I don't feel that way," he murmured. He took a shuddering breath and shut his eyes.

"What did the doctor say?" Isabella asked.

"He said that she would recover with time." He heard the deep relief coming from Eva, Gabrielle, and Isabella. He then strode toward Troy, Ian, and Christian. "I don't know how to thank you guys," he said, and reaching out, he shook their hands. "You're great friends."

"We wouldn't want to be anywhere else," Troy declared firmly.

"Ian, did you talk to the police? Did they come to see you?" Sebastian asked.

"Yes, two detectives showed up and talked to the doctors first. Then they came to me and asked me for my side of the story. I told them exactly what you told me to say," he stated.

"And what did they say?"

"They wanted to know where I found her, and I told them. I was sure that you cleaned up after your mess," he said, glancing between Troy, Christian, and Sebastian, his lips curving up to a half a smile. "I also told them that I didn't know anything more and that they would have to talk to Arielle when she came to."

"And?" Sebastian pressed on.

"Well, they said they would come back to speak with her."

Sebastian seemed to ponder his words. He then turned to his friends and smiled, thankfully. "Guys, go home. Tomorrow you'll be able to see her. She will be here for a couple of days, if not more."

"Sebastian, Arielle needs to know the story before the cops come to see her tomorrow," Ian said, anxiously.

"Don't worry, Ian. I'll talk with her as soon as she wakes up. Thanks again," he mumbled.

"Okay, we're heading out," Troy said and patted Sebastian on the back. "See you tomorrow."

The girls hugged him once more before the six of them walked out holding hands. Sebastian followed them out of the room and stood unmoved, watching their backs until he couldn't see them any longer.

Slowly, he turned and went back to Arielle's room. She was still asleep. Pushing the door closed, he scanned the room. Moonlight filtered through the window blinds, and the room was bleak. Sebastian sank onto the chair next to her bed quietly, and clasping her hand in his, laid his head on her bed and closed his eyes.

He grasped the quiet moment to think.

Centuries were spent on this earth, but nothing seemed to be as long and as painful as the few days spent in hospital rooms after each attack on Arielle, and all because of him. Repressing a grimace, he sucked a ragged breath. There was no doubt that he was going to kill every single person involved with the assignment that landed Arielle in this hospital. A burning volcano of fury was sweltering deep inside, and it would erupt as soon as they located the rest of the assassins.

 *Chapter 15*

HE SHIFTED HIS CHAIR closer to the bed and, lifting Arielle's hand, he brought it to his lips. He could sense the warmth sweltering from her soft skin and a shiver coursed along his nerves from the sudden sensation. He kept his lips pressed on her hand and closed his eyes, and he groaned inwardly. He felt tired...angry...and worried.

He was jolted awake by a soft voice. His eyes sprang wide open and, pushing back, he swung to face the person standing behind him. He was utterly disoriented.

"Sebastian dear, you are exhausted!" Danielle Lloyd's soft gaze met his.

Sebastian blinked and coughed to clear his throat. Slanting a glance toward the bed, his gaze dropped to Arielle. She was still sleeping. He coughed again. "Did you come alone?" he asked, his voice throaty.

"No, James is getting a cup of tea," she replied, her expression composed.

"Oh..." It was all he said. His body felt numb. He stood and stretched his limbs, trying to start the blood flowing through his veins again.

"Sebastian, why don't you go home for a while, dear? I know you'll feel a lot better after a warm shower and some fresh clothes," Danielle said.

He nodded in agreement. It was already morning, and the early light was slipping through the window blinds.

His eyes shifted to the bed once again and noticed Arielle moving a little.

"Sebastian," she murmured drowsily.

"Good morning, baby, I'm here…I'm right here," he murmured, leaning over her bed and pressing his lips to her forehead. "How are you feeling this morning?"

"I hurt, and I still can't open my eyes…" she whimpered.

"Soon, love, soon…" he assured her and pressed a feather kiss on her lips.

"I love you, Sebastian," she murmured, searching for his hand.

"I adore you," he said against her lips and intertwined his fingers with hers. "Your lips are better today," he said softly.

"Oh, what about my face?"

"A bit swollen, but better than yesterday," he chuckled softly.

"I wouldn't win a beauty contest then, would I?" she joked.

"Yes, you would. You're still gorgeous," he said joyfully. He was happy she was up to joking this morning. "Your parents are here, baby."

"Mummy!" she said quietly.

"Yes, dear, I'm right here. Daddy is getting some tea. He'll be right in."

"Sebastian, did you stay all night?" she asked.

"Yes, he did," her mother, interjected. "He appears exhausted. You need to make him go home to shower and put some fresh clothes on."

"Yes, Sebastian, please do that for me."

"But I want to stay with you," he replied.

"Please…go. My mum and dad are here now."

"Yes, go, Sebastian," her mother insisted. "Miss Walker is on her way in to give Arielle a little sponge bath."

Sebastian sighed. "Okay then. I'll go, and I'll come right back. Don't go anywhere until I return," he chuckled against her ear. He ran his lips across her cheek, over her jaw line, and back up to her lips, pressing a soft kiss there and lingering for a short moment. "God, I love you, Arielle," he murmured.

Arielle made a poor attempt at smiling. This was the voice that hit the core of her soul like a sublime note from a great composer.

"Hurry back..." her voice trailed.

Sebastian's brows lifted in amusement. "Ah, you sound eager, are you?" he purred.

She smiled softly but didn't make another remark. Sebastian turned to gaze at her mother; her expression would yield nothing. Sebastian held her eyes for a short moment.

"I take it you all want me out of here," he chuckled. "However, as I said before, I'll be back soon," he added, his tone meaningful. He turned and strode out of the room. Stepping outside the revolving doors, he took a deep breath of the cool morning breeze.

It wasn't until he walked into the house that he realized he never had a chance to speak with Arielle about what story to use with the authorities. Blinking aside his frustration, he cursed inwardly. A frown covered his face. He was not ready to acknowledge that he messed up. Swallowing, he decided that he would have to go back to Arielle's side before the authorities did.

He showered in a nanosecond, but he couldn't show up in the hospital this soon. Her parents were there, and he didn't want to make them suspicious. He lay on the bed and closed his eyes, mulling over in his head all that had taken place the day before. If he could only turn back time and change the outcome, he would do it in a second. His body was relaxed, and before he knew it, he was fast asleep.

His eyes snapped open; an uncanny feeling washed over him, bringing him to his senses. Slanting his unfocused eyes toward the digital clock, he blinked. He did a double take and swallowed a curse. "Christ!" he screamed. "I'm bloody late!" He had slept through the morning. He jumped out of bed and, grabbing a pair of jeans and shirt; he moved around the room like a tornado. Sebastian was in his car and on his way in no time at all.

Back at the hospital, Arielle was becoming more aware of her surroundings. Her vision was still blocked by her swollen eyes and the pain resonated from her head to her toes.

"Mum, how long have I been here?" Arielle asked apprehensively.

"Ian brought you here yesterday afternoon, dear."

"Am I going home today?"

"No, I don't think it'll be today, darling. The doctor is coming this morning to examine you. He'll then let us know when you can go home," her mother said and applied a cold compress over her eyes.

The door opened, and Miss Walker stepped inside. Approaching the bed, she spoke softly. "Good morning, Arielle. I'm Miss Walker, your nurse; I'm going to raise your bed to a sitting position," she said and, reaching out, she patted her hand.

"Good morning," Arielle murmured.

"I'm going to take your temperature, dear, and then I'll give you a pain shot. As soon as the pain subsides, I'll give you a sponge bath. How does that sound?" she asked brightly.

"I...I guess fine," she replied, unexcitedly.

James Lloyd walked in, holding two cups of tea in his hands.

"Good morning, Miss Walker," he said and approached his daughter's bed.

"How are you this morning, Pumpkin?"

"Hi, Daddy!" Arielle mumbled.

He set the teacups on the side table and, leaning over his daughter, he pressed a kiss on her forehead. "You sure look better this morning!" he said softly.

"Liar!" Arielle muttered.

Her father chuckled and gave her another kiss on the cheek.

"James, I'm afraid we'll have to drink that tea in the waiting room. Miss Walker is getting ready to give Arielle a sponge bath. Let's go, dear," she said, and taking one of the cups, she headed for the door.

"We'll come back, pumpkin," her father said and fell into step beside his wife.

"Okay..." She let her voice fade. She hated been in the dark, but what was the point of complaining about that, over and over again? All anyone could do about that was put cold compresses and wait... She repressed a sigh and, laying her head on her pillow, she tried to wipe every thought out of her mind.

Sebastian came to an abrupt halt as six pairs of eyes pinned him as soon as he entered the hospital room. Arielle's parents seemed to be in the same place he had left them earlier that morning. Two police officers were standing next to Arielle's bed. Their expressions were clearly surprised, and their eyes widened at the sight of Sebastian. But Sebastian's expression was poised. Inwardly, he cursed, and a muscle in his jaw clenched. He wondered how much Arielle had told them, and if any of that fell within the story he and his friends had laid out to make sure nothing became complicated.

He strode into the room unhurriedly and smiled gently to the Lloyds.

"This is Arielle's fiancé, Sebastian Gaulle," James Lloyd said, stepping forward and making the introductions. "Sebastian, my boy, these two officers are here for some information from Arielle," he said.

Sebastian didn't say anything; he just nodded and approached Arielle's bed. Leaning down, he placed a loving kiss on Arielle's forehead. His hand clasped hers and squeezed it gently. "Hi, baby, how are you feeling?" he whispered.

"Better now that you're here," she murmured, and her lips curved slightly up. She did seem much better, and the swelling was down. The puffiness in her eyes had diminished, but the blue and yellow bruising appeared ghastly.

He then took a seat next to her bed, still clasping Arielle's hand in his. He gazed over at the two officers and waited.

They seemed completely stunned, and Sebastian knew that his immortal appearance threw them off a bit. He watched them swallow hard and cough to clear their throat. The younger officer looked in his early thirties while his partner was an elderly gentleman. The officers knew very well who Sebastian Gaulle was. He was well known in London and around most of the world for being one of the richest bachelors and successful businessmen.

The younger office stared at Sebastian, and said firmly, "Mr. Gaulle, do you know if there is someone that may want to harm your fiancée because of you? By that I mean, do you think there maybe someone who wants something from you and your company, or maybe someone who is jealous of you?"

Sebastian shrugged, totally unruffled. "I operate a very successful company. I can't honestly rule out the possibility of ransom. Dylan Jamison, the head of Interpol Intelligence, has all the details on the case," he stated clearly. The young officer's eyes widened in surprise, but he didn't say anything further; he just made a note in his notepad.

"Where were you yesterday afternoon?" the older officer asked as if he didn't hear Sebastian's statement, pinning him with a quizzical gaze. Sebastian's eyebrows furrowed in disbelief.

"I was in a meeting with Dylan Jamison, along with Troy, my coworker. I was notified by our friend Ian that Arielle was brought into the hospital. I came here straight from the meeting," he said curtly. He didn't appreciate the tone of the officer's voice.

"I'm sorry, sir," the officer said. "I didn't mean to sound as if I were accusing you of something. What I wanted to know is," he paused and took a deep breath, "Mr. Gaulle, I was wondering if you knew her abductors?"

"No, I don't," Sebastian replied, his expression calm and open. "Didn't Arielle see their faces?" Sebastian asked masking his expression.

"I didn't see their faces," Arielle said, pressing his hand softly.

"Baby, didn't you see them when they were beating you up?" he asked, pretending surprise.

"No, the room was dark, and they were wearing masks," she said firmly. "I texted Eva when I heard them leaving the house, and I was hoping she would find me before they came back," she said in a high-pitched voice. She was still affected by the memories.

"We did go to that location yesterday after we spoke to your friend," the younger officer added, "but we didn't find anything that would give us a clue. The place was all cleaned up but for some damage to an interior wall. The place was abandoned."

Sebastian was thankful for making sure the bodies were disposed of, and everything was put back in place before they left. He did wonder about Dylan's detectives and what became of them, but he knew that Dylan was not going to discuss the details of this case with the authorities. He wouldn't want them to interfere with this important case.

"We'll do everything we can to try and find them, and we'll keep you informed," the older officer said to James Lloyd. The officers thanked them and left the room.

Arielle focused her thoughts on Sebastian. She could feel his hand pressing softly on hers, and his sweet scent consuming every sense awake.

"Sebastian, are they gone?"

"Yes, baby, they just left."

James Lloyd leaned over her bed and pressed a kiss on her cheek. "Pumpkin, now that Sebastian is here, we are going home. We'll be back later this afternoon," he said, lovingly. They both patting Sebastian on his back and walked out.

As soon as the door closed behind them, Sebastian bent down, trying to scoop her in his arms carefully without disturbing the IVs.

"Arielle, I missed you so much. I'm going out of my mind. I hate that you're here and in pain. I want you home with me," he purred.

"I feel better when you hold me," she whispered.

"I'll hold you for eternity if that makes you feel better," he murmured and gave her a soft squeeze.

"I need to see your face more than I need to breathe," she whimpered.

"You will, baby, I'm not going anywhere." His lips pressed hers softly, and she grimaced. He immediately pulled back and laid her carefully back down. "I can't stand seeing you this way," he moaned.

She reached up slowly, repressing the sting from the IV, and traced with her fingers the beautiful features of his face. A mixture of sensation and love coursed through her, alleviating every ache, every worry, every thought, away from her brain.

"Kiss me!" she said.

"I don't want to hurt you, my love," he murmured, his voice passionate.

"Please...I've missed you," she whimpered.

He pulled her back into his arms and his lips covered hers with restraint. She sank into his embrace, and she was unable to mask her desire. She forgot all about the pain, and her lips moved awkwardly but demanding against his. He groaned and pulled his lips free.

"Stop, you'll hurt yourself," he moaned and laid her back on the bed. He was trying hard to rein in his desires that were screaming to be unleashed.

"I want to go home," she pleaded.

"Arielle, you need to be here," he said. He was breathing deeply, and his voice was filled with frustration. "For what I have in mind, you'll need to be completely healed and strong" he snorted.

"And what is that?" she asked. Flinching, she forced a smile.

"Ah…that's a surprise."

"Hmmm…" she giggled softly.

"Well, if you won't kiss me, then tell me what happened?" She pressed her lips together and grimaced again as she felt the pain sipping into her brain. "I need a pain shot."

Sebastian jumps off his seat, and before she knew it, Miss Walker appeared at the door. Her eyes fell on Sebastian, and she halted for a moment. She stared, mystified, once again at the stunning man. Sebastian's brows narrowed quizzically. She shook her head, exasperated, and gathered her wits. She refocused, and her eyes turned to Arielle as she stepped inside the room and approached her bed.

"Arielle, dear, I have your pain shot," she said kindly.

"Thank you, Miss Walker."

She gave Arielle her pain shot and swung toward the door. Drawing a deep breath, she felt a powerful urge to run as she swept passed him. He was standing too close not to be a distraction. *What in bloody hell is going on with me?* She thought. The sound of the door closing behind her made her blink, and she exhaled in sheer relief. She rubbed her hand over her eyes and groaned. She picked up her pace and disappeared around the next corner.

"What was that?" Sebastian wondered out loud.

"What was what?" Arielle asked.

"Oh…your nurse acted strange toward me," he added.

"Oh, and you're wondering about that?" she snorted.

"Whatever do you mean?" he asked, clueless.

"Sebastian, every woman acts weird around you. I included," she snorted again.

"You are beautiful, but you're mine," she added.

"That's true," he murmured, and leaning over her, he pressed his lips to hers lovingly. "Is the pain gone?"

"Yes...I feel much better," she said joyfully.

"Arielle, I'm so glad you never said anything about who the guys were to the police officers. We wouldn't want them to become involved with this problem."

"Sebastian, I did know those guys. They were the same guys that Gabby and I met at a club, while you, Troy, and Nathan were in Brussels the first time."

"I know...I know all about them. Unfortunately for them, they tried to hurt you, and they are not going to hurt anyone ever again."

Arielle recoiled. "Are they...are...are they dead?"

"Yes, they are, and so are the two men that came to help them torture you. Arielle, they were going to kill you if I didn't give up the documents. I'll make sure they are all eliminated before I'm finished with them. I thought Dylan was going to do that for me last year, but he didn't finish the job. Now... Troy, Christian, Ian, and I are going to make sure it is done."

"Are you leaving me again?" she asked anxiously.

"No, not until you are well and at home. But you do know that I have to do this, don't you?" Leaning down, he pressed another feather kiss to her lips. "I have to do whatever it takes to keep you safe," he whispered against her lips.

Arielle remained silent. She was not sure she liked him going away, but she also knew that this couldn't go on.

"Baby," he murmured, "I don't want you to overthink this. It'll be an easy job for us."

"I'm always worried about you," she said.

"I'm the one that should be worried about you, not the other way around. I had been out of my mind ever since I received the call from Ian that you had not attended class." He stopped and bending down he kissed her again. "My beautiful angel!"

Arielle smiled. "So tell me everything?"

"Well, Troy, Christian, Ian, and I were told by Dylan that some more assassins were flying into Brighton to assist with the extortion," he said and swore under his breath. "They were going to force me to give up the company documents by threatening your life." He took a shuddering breath.

"What is it?" Arielle asked, and her arm stretched slowly reaching for him.

"Oh, Arielle." He pinched the tip of his nose, and his lips quivered. He clasped her hand and intertwined his fingers with hers. "Can't you see that I'm the reason you ended up in this hospital? For God's sake... Arielle, it has always been my fault. I'm a selfish man. I was going to risk everything, including your life to have you. I love you! I'm hopelessly in love with you!" He drew a quivery breath and continued speaking, "I can't bear the thought of you with someone else."

"Why would you ever entertain such a thought?" she asked, intrigued.

"You have been the joy in my life, the oxygen that I breathe, the reason that wakes up each morning. You have filled my life with passion and excitement. Loving you is pure bliss. I have never known anyone like you. I want you for my own. I want to protect you, but as you can see —so far— I don't seem to be doing a very good job of it," he said sadly.

"Sebastian." She squeezed his hand. "I feel the same way. You're everything to me, I want to be in your life, and I don't care about anything else. I don't care about the people that want to hurt me. I can't live without you, don't you see?"

"Arielle, you are in the hospital. I have brought nothing to you but chaos. I have brought immortals and humans that want to hurt you because of me," he said, his tone filled with frustration and rage. "I never believed that being with me would turn your world upside down. If I had thought of it, I wouldn't have made that mistake. I'm so sorry, baby."

Arielle immediately releases his hand. "Sebastian, if you keep talking like this, I don't want you here. If you think that being with me was a mistake, I want you to leave," she said forcefully.

He felt her words sipping through his veins and he was mortified. "I'm not going anywhere," he said firmly and swallowed against the bitter taste in his mouth.

"Then you have to stop talking nonsense and continue with the story."

He took her hand again, and she let him. "All right then, you adorable creature you!" He gathered his thoughts and continued with the story.

"Dylan found out through his surveillance that the two goons that kidnapped you from campus were to meet the men that were flying in from Belarus at the airport. Then the four of them were going back to the location they were holding you." He took a deep breath and pressed her hand softly. "I wanted to kill them at the airport, but I needed them alive so they could lead me to you. We heard their conversations, so we knew pretty well what they had done to you and what they were planning on doing." He paused again for a moment. "Their words were slicing right through every muscle in my body, and anger took over. It took Troy, Ian, and Christian to keep me calm. When we arrived at the house, Troy and Christian climbed to the second floor. Ian and I went around the back. We found you in one of the basement rooms, and you were unconscious. Ian brought you to the hospital while Troy, Christian, and I finished up all four of the assassins."

Arielle jerked aware at the words.

"You're safe now, baby," he said warmly.

"I thought you were not going to come for me," she whimpered.

"Arielle, I wouldn't stop until I found you. How could you ever think something like that?"

Tears were streaming down her face once again.

"Why are you crying, sweetheart?" he whispered against her lips and brushed his thumbs against her cheeks, wiping the tears away. "Are you in pain? Where do you hurt?"

"No, I'm fine," she sobbed. She felt the gentleness of his touch leaving her with an unexplained aching feeling of loneliness. "Why am I so tired?"

"Baby, they have given you meds to help you relax, and they make you sleepy," he whispered closed to her ear.

"Please stay with me."

"Oh, you don't have to worry about that. I'm staying right here until you're ready to go home with me," he said softly, gazing at Arielle's bruised body. Putting his elbows on his knees, he leaned closer and whispered, "I love you, baby." He hated the thought that there was nothing he could do to make her feel any better.

Arielle was starting to feel sleepy again. "Stay with me. I thought I'd never see you again," she said, lethargically. Another stream of tears rolled down her face, and Sebastian reached out and took her hand in his. "Sleep now baby; I'll be right here."

Miss Walker came in to check on Arielle, but she was already asleep. "I'll take care of her," she said. "I mean if you need to go."

Sebastian scoffed, quietly. "I'm staying right here," he said firmly.

The nurse scowled but chose to remain quiet. She checked Arielle's vitals and adjusted her covers, throwing a sidelong assessing glance at Sebastian she walked out.

It was a couple of days later when Arielle finally was able to open her eyes. She was a lot better, and everyone was thrilled to have her back to normal. The swelling was down, and the IVs were removed. The bump on her head had receded, and the bruises had turned purple and yellow, slowly disappearing. She was released from the hospital five days after she arrived with a couple of prescriptions for pain from the broken ribs and the sutures on her face. She would have to go back in two weeks to have the sutures removed.

Sebastian was thrilled to death to take her home. He had filled the house with freesia.

Chapter 16

ARIELLE HAD BEEN HOME for over a week now. She was feeling quite well and ready to take the world by storm. She opened her eyes and winced at the unexpected exposure to daylight. A ray of sunshine brushed across her face while still lost in a slumber haze. She threw her arm over her eyes to block the light. *Why is it so bright in here?* Lifting her arm, her gaze drifted toward the window. The curtains had been pulled wide open. She blinked against the brightness of the day. *What in the world?*

Her glanced drifted to the digital clock on the nightstand. It was only seven o'clock. Awareness sipped slowly through her mind and cleared away the sleep smog. She didn't have a class until ten, so there was plenty of time to enjoy the morning with Sebastian.

She closed her eyes and smiled wide. She rolled over and her arm stretched looking for his warm body, but the bed was empty. An unclear inciting of alarm stormed her thoughts. Her eyes snapped wide open, and she scowled. *Where is he? This was getting to be a bloody daily routine.*

Coming home from the hospital had not turned out to be what she expected. Every night Sebastian worked late in his office and by the time he went to bed she had fallen asleep. Every morning she woke up alone and every morning tears pooled in her eyes. Something had changed, but she didn't know what that something was. She grabbed his pillow buried her face in it and groaned out loud. She swallowed hard and rolled on her back, letting an invisible current of hot fiery anger flow through her muscles.

She placed the heels of her hands on her eyelids and pressed hard, trying to set her thoughts in order. She stood there for a long moment, lost in thought. She needed to get up. She was not going to go another day like this. She couldn't take much more of what she considered an unmitigated rejection on his part. Tears pricked the corners of her eyes.

They had not made love for twelve days. He was treating her like a porcelain doll. "I have to put a stop to this before I go completely out of my mind," she muttered mulishly.

She kicked the bed covers away and sat straight up. The pain from her still aching ribs ripped through her muscles like a cyclone and the air whooshed out of her lungs, leaving her breathless. Her face paled, and she cringed at the pain.

"Sebastian!" she whimpered, but there was no answer. She laid there for a long moment waiting for the pain to subside. Then she scrambled off the bed carefully. She didn't bother to put any clothes on and headed toward the kitchen. Sebastian's voice caught her attention as she passed his office. The door was cracked open, and he was on the phone.

His voice was firm and concise. "Yes, I think that it will be wonderful to have them all here."

Have them all here? Who is he talking to? Moving closer, she pushed the door open and peered into the room. Sebastian was sitting in front of his desk, facing the large window away from her. He was leaning back, his feet crossed ankle-to-ankle and resting on the top of the desk. He was shirtless with only his pajama bottoms on, and he was mouthwatering. She could lose herself at this magnificent Adonis that was hers, she thought, and only hers, *but was he?* He hadn't touched her for days.

A shiver of lust coursed along her spine, and the intensity made her lips tremble. She leaned against the door frame, crossed her arms in front of her, and waited silently. She drank him in, reining in her wits that seem to be scattered all over that room.

"I would like them to cover the western part of the continent," Sebastian continued. "Jon, Pier, and Jacques will take the eastern part, leaving the rest of us to take care of all the other locations," he said flatly.

What in the world is he preparing to do?

"No, no, we don't need to do that. I'm sure that we have enough people to have the job done sufficiently...yes... I do appreciate the information. I'll see you in a couple of hours."

Sebastian shut the phone, drew his feet off the desk, and sat up. He placed the mobile on the desk, gathered the papers that were spread in front of him, and put them in a folder. He then slipped the folder inside the top drawer and locked it.

What in bloody hell is this all about? It sounds like he is getting ready to leave again.

She cleared her throat. "Where to now?" she asked quietly.

Sebastian swiveled the chair around to face her, and he stilled. Their gaze was locked, green to blue, a most intoxicating mixture of colors. His jaw dropped at the sight of her naked body. She was a sight for sore eyes. His mouth went dry and gasped inwardly. All he wanted to do was pick her up, take her to bed, and make passionate love to her.

But he remained unmoved for a long moment. He gathered his wits with extraordinary effort. And even though he was hungry for her body and eager for their passionate encounters, he stayed away. It was the hardest thing he had ever done, but he knew that she was in pain. Her stressful facial expressions, her cringing, and the tears that pooled in the corner of her eyes each time she made a sudden move never escaped his incredible immortal senses.

He watched her carefully and the corners of his lips quirked up in a sweet smile. His voice was breathy and shaky. "Good morning, baby; how did you sleep?"

She ignored his question. "I woke up alone, *again*." She emphasized the word again.

Something flickered in his eyes as he pushed his chair away and rose to his feet. His pajama pants slipped lower and hugged his hips in a sexy way. Her heartbeat accelerated, and her strength faltered. He was strikingly handsome.

"But did you sleep well?" he asked again, trying to keep his voice even.

"Fine," she said her voice clipped. "Where are you getting ready to go now?"

Sebastian's eyes shot up in surprise at the tone of her voice. He raked a hand through his sandy hair. *What in the world has come over her?* "Well, first, I'm taking you to class and then I'm going to the office."

"I don't need you to take me to class. I seem to be getting along quite well without you lately."

He stood rigid, words unspoken, but they were lingering in his heated gaze. "What's wrong?"

She humphed and, pushing away from the door frame, she moved into the study. "Should there be something wrong?"

"I don't think so, but you sure seem and sound angry."

"You seem to be the great observer," she said, unable to keep the sarcasm from the tone in her voice.

Sebastian frowned. "What's wrong, baby?"

She raised a rigid chin. "Don't call me baby. I have not been your baby for over twelve days. And you haven't answered my question."

"What question was that?"

"Sebastian, don't be obtuse. Where are you going?"

Sebastian understood that Arielle was angry with him for not being sexually involved with her. He resisted a strong, inexplicable urge to reach for her and pull her hard in his embrace. *God, I want her.* He closed his eyes and let calm wash over him before he opened them again. Obviously flustered, he let out a deep groan.

"I told you that I'm taking you t..."

She raised a hand up to halt his words. "I don't mean this morning. I mean the phone call. Where are you planning on going?"

"That was Nathan," he said pointing to the mobile on the desk. "We were discussing business."

She opened her mouth to speak but thought the better course of action would be to remain quiet. She didn't want to fight.

"I don't want to hurt you." The words had left his mouth before he was able to stop them. The swelling of her face was gone, but for the sutures on the right side of her cheek. The bruises and the contusions were gone. Her skin was again smooth like silk, and she was just as beautiful as ever.

She advanced toward him, lips pursed, and Sebastian's lungs locked. It was hard enough for him to stay away, but Arielle was relentless. She was putting Sebastian through torture.

She stopped in front of him, and he inhaled sharply. Seconds elapsed, and she trembled with anticipation. "Sebastian, I need you," she whimpered. She reached up and cupped his face with both hands. "I'm going out of my mind. I don't think I can make it another day." She stood on her tippy toes and brushed her lips against his. "Just kiss me, Sebastian," she whispered her words against his lips.

He sucked in his breath. "Arielle, I'd do anything for you, but I'm not going to touch you until the doctor says you are back to normal."

She threw her hands up in the air and groaned out loud. Sebastian's brows rose, and the corners of his lips kicked up.

Arielle watched him as he stepped even closer. Hands on his sides, a sexy smile lingering on his face. He towered over her, and she drew a deep breath. He lowered his gaze and their eyes locked. He managed to keep his voice level. "We need to come to an agreement."

"What do you have in mind?"

"All I can suggest is that you stop sulking. We have to deal with this issue, keeping in mind what is best for you right now."

She humphed. "And you think that you know what is best for me?"

"Yes, I do. And the answer to your question is no."

"No? No? I haven't asked for anything."

"Arielle, I know what you want and the answer is...No."

Arielle's face fell, and tears pooled in her eyes. She turned up and met his eyes. "Don't you love me anymore?"

His jaw twitched and his eyes closed for a short second. She heard the intake of his breath. Slowly his lips curved and, swooping down; he captured her lips in a soft tender kiss. She immediately moved closer, breast to chest, to take advantage of the situation, and he chuckled into the kiss. His hands came up, and he slowly eased her away from his body.

Arielle drew a deep breath, stepped back, and blinked. She met his eyes once again and held his gaze a puzzled expression on her face.

"What was that for?" she asked, entirely frustrated.

"That was because I love you, but the answer is still no."

"But, Sebastian, I'm fine!" she yelled, totally frustrated.

"No, and I mean no," he said. "I think you need to either go back to bed or dress for class." He walked past her and out the door. "I'm going to take a shower," he said.

"You're enjoying this, aren't you?" she called out. She heard his quiet laughter and then a door close. She knew that he was already in the shower, and she scowled.

"Bloody man..." her voice trailed and, turning, she stomped toward the kitchen. She decided to stop torturing herself and Sebastian, and just see when he decided that she was healthy enough for his touch. She cringed and stomped her feet on the floor a bit harder.

In the shower, Sebastian leaned against the tiled wall and, taking a sharp breath, he let out a deep guttural moan. He almost lost his composure at the sensation of Arielle's body against his and the softness of her lips beneath his. It had been twelve days of pure torture. Every night the extreme proximity of her luscious body drove him insane. He would lie silent for hours after she had fallen asleep, debating if he should leave the bed and sleep in another bedroom, but he knew that was out of the question. Something like that would hurt her deeply. So he would choose to take cold showers in the middle of the night to ease his needs and settle back into bed to see the nights through to the unpleasant end. In the mornings, he would roll over and watch her sleep, wanting nothing more than to wake her up and make passionate love to her. But in the end, he would slip away quietly.

The guilt was immeasurable. Was he doing the right thing? He had spoken with her doctor before they left the hospital, and he advised him that he needed to be very careful with her for a couple of weeks until her ribs were starting to heal. He was not going to be the reason Arielle suffered longer than she had to.

He let the scalding stream of water pulsate off of his body as he tried to shake the worrisome thoughts away. After all, he was supposed to be this incredible immortal, stripped of human emotions. His thoughts reverberated against the walls of his brain. Who was he kidding? When it came to Arielle, he was weak, desperately in love, and filled with emotions that he never knew he had until he met her.

He turned the water off and grabbed a towel as he stepped out of the shower. He quickly patted his body dry and wrapped a small towel around his waist, he stood in front of the mirror to shave. He lifted his arm, shaver in hand and froze in mid-air. The door opened, and she walked in. His eyes followed her in the mirror. He marveled at her beauty, and her scent was intoxicating. She turned and met his smoldering eyes, and he heard her swift intake of breath. She didn't say a word she just stared for a short moment. Passion flared in her eyes, but it was gone just as fast as it came. The silence was heavy she didn't miss the lust expression on his face. He raised an eyebrow, and his lips kicked up at the corners. She didn't smile back; something flickered in her eyes and she shut them as if she was in pain. He tried hard to keep his hands to himself. She brushed past him, and he inhaled deeply. She took a couple of steps and moved into the shower, pulling the glass door shut behind her.

Sebastian groaned inwardly. He needed to finish and leave the bathroom. Her scent was drifting through his veins and settling into his bone marrow. He didn't think he was going to be able to wait another second. It was a good thing that she didn't reach for him, because if she had, he would have lost control. He was burning up with scalding heat of pure desire.

He quickly escaped into the bedroom. He sat at the edge of the bed and took a few deep breaths trying to clear his head. He rested his hands on his thighs and growled quietly. He craved her touch, and he needed her more than ever. He tried to ignore his arousal that was driving his senses to a maddening universe. He lifted his arms and rubbed the muscles on the back of his neck with his hands. *God help me! Two more days—long—long—days.* He dressed quickly and in an effort to divest himself from the blistering thoughts about sizzling encounters; he escaped into his office.

He unlocked his desk drawer and took out the brown folder. His eyes flicked at his watch. It was seven-thirty. He slumped into his favorite recliner and proceeded to read the detailed report he received from his private investigators. He was surprised to find that there was so much more information out there, that he never saw or heard before, about the people that were trying to destroy his company. He made a few notes and put the envelope back in the drawer and locked it. He feared that the information would fall into Arielle's hands. He loved her so much, and he didn't want her to know the lengths that the Mafia was ready to go, to destroy him, his company, his friends, and their families.

The information provided by his private investigators told him that Rainer was furious. There had been two unexplained incidents, and he had lost a few of his better men. Something was happening, but he couldn't put his finger on it. He was now carefully reorganizing to make sure this was the last and final stroke that would put Sebastian completely out of business and give him the documents he needed so badly.

Sebastian was gathering his immortal friends, preparing for a strike against the Mafia rings across the globe to end the madness. He already told her that he was planning on taking care of all the people behind her abduction, but he couldn't let her in on every little detail. She had already been through a horrible experience and all because of him. This report was creating concerns about her safety. He needed to move fast.

Today would be the first day Arielle was returning to class since her abduction at the parking lot, so he was sure that she was going to be in an unpleasant state of mind once, and they reached the campus. He was going to make sure she was in a class safe and then he would leave after talking with Christian and Isabella. They were going to remain close to Arielle until he would come back to take her home.

The next time he glanced at his watch it was eight-fifteen. He stood up and decided to go and get Arielle. He heard noise in the kitchen, so he headed that direction. He had sawed her before he entered, and a shiver of passion rushed through him. Arielle turned and gave him a slanted gaze as she lifted the toast to her mouth. A palpable silence fell and stretched until it reached a painful point. He cleared his throat and smiled sweetly. "Are you still mad at me?" She stopped herself from scoffing outwardly. "Whatever for?" she muttered, unable to hide her sullenness. "Because I want you and you turn me down at every turn?" she snapped.

Sebastian winced at her words and his smile faltered. He met and searched her gaze, and all he could see was sizzling passion. Her words didn't match the emotions that were touching her eyes. He had centuries of experience with women, and he was sure he was reading her senses correctly. He sensed turmoil and heard her gasps of breath. He was affecting her, and he was going to use that to calm her down.

He took a few steps into the room and halted in front of her. Their gaze was still locked. Pleasure took her breath away, and she gasped, feeling a bit lightheaded. He moved even closer and she drew a shuddering breath. His lips kicked up again and spread into a dazzling smile across his face. Arielle blinked, and her heartbeat increased, and the blood rushed through her veins like thunder. *She is not as mad as she wants me to think,* he thought, and a wave of arousal washed over him.

Awareness crackled between them and intensity peaked. He put his finger under her chin and tipped her head up. His mouth came down on hers, and she parted her lips, drawing him in with hunger. Passion swelled as their tongues swirled in a wild dance, tasting, savoring, rejoicing, and relishing each other. He raised his hands, and gently framing her face, he tilted it slightly and deepened the kiss.

"I love you," he murmured into the kiss. "I…"

"I know," she interrupted lightly.

Sebastian tilted his head to the side and his eyebrows furrowed. "Then why are you so upset?" His arms came about her and pulled her softly into his embrace, breathing in the sweet freesia fragrance in her hair.

"Because I missed your touch," she whimpered.

"You missed me?" He tried hard to keep the amusement hidden.

She gave a little snort. "You know better than to ask me a question like that."

Sebastian shook his head and closed his eyes tightly. "Oh God,

Arielle, you have absolutely no idea what these past two weeks have been for me."

"For you?" she exclaimed. "What about me?" Lifting herself on her tippy toes, she reached up and touched his lips with the tip of her tongue. Sebastian groaned with pleasure, and bending down; he took her mouth in a searing, passionate kiss.

"There is nothing in this world that I want more than you."

Arielle closed her eyes, desire flooding every part of her body. After a long moment, he pulled back and let her go. "Please, baby, finish with your breakfast and put some clothes on so I can take you to class."

"You're not coming with me?"

"No, not today. I have a very important meeting at ten."

"Okay," she said gently. She seemed to mull over his reply, and the next statement came out of nowhere. "But after we see the doctor, I expect you to make it up to me," she said, significance flashing through her eyes.

"I promise," he said wittily.

"See that you do." She gave him a sexy look and smiled.

Sebastian couldn't help it. He laughed out loud. He sank back into the softness of her mouth stealing her breath away and leaving her witless, mindless. Eventually, he drew back again. "I promise," he repeated. She laid her head against his chest and closed her eyes nothing more needed to be said.

After a few moments, she pulled away from his embrace and went back to finish buttering her toast. Sebastian took a seat at the counter picked up the newspaper and turned to the sports page to wait for her to finish her breakfast. She then grabbed a glass of milk, walked around the counter, pressed a soft kiss on his cheek, and headed toward the bedroom. "I'll be ready in a few," she said with her mouth full.

Sebastian watched her retreading naked back until she disappeared into the bedroom and chuckled out loud.

"Not funny!" she yelled back

Sebastian ran a hand through his sandy hair and snorted. She took his breath away. No power on earth could ever keep him away from her. She stirred feelings in him beyond simple desire. She was a drug more powerful than Salve that he needed daily to survive. He closed his eyes and stroked his chin thoughtfully. He finally opened his eyes and proceeded to finish the article in the newspaper.

Barely fifteen minutes passed before she walked right back into the kitchen, dressed and ready to go. He flipped the paper shut and rose to his feet. He turned his emerald eyes to her, and she inhaled deeply. She held his gaze and lifted a quizzical brow.

"Are you ready?" she asked.

He grinned and made a low bow. "At your services, my lady."

Her only response was a wide smile that warmed his heart.

They rode to school in a comfortable silence. Sebastian placed her hand on his thigh and covered it with his. His thumb stroked her knuckles gently back and forth. As they approached the parking lot, he gave her a sidelong glance. Arielle swallowed and pressed her lips together. Sebastian noticed the tension on her face and sensed her discomfort. This was going to be her first day back to school since the horrible incident.

He squeezed her hand softly. "Are you going to be all right?" he asked.

A light, reluctant smile touched her eyes. "Yes, I'll be fine," she said quietly.

Sebastian stepped out of the car and surveyed the area around them carefully. Arielle couldn't stop herself, and she glanced about as well. The odds of something happening while Sebastian was with her were remote. They walked across the parking lot with his arm wrapped around her protectively. Arielle was not completely surprised that she made it to class with very little fear. She always felt safe in Sebastian's presence.

"I'll be here to pick you up. Please stay close to Eva and Loren." Bending down, he pressed a chaste kiss on her lips. He escorted her into the auditorium and left after he saw her safely seated between her friends.

Sebastian saw Christian on his way to the car and asked him to make sure he kept an eye on Arielle.

"Sebastian, I'm going with you to that meeting," Christian insisted. "Isabella will take care of Arielle. She will go to every class she has today, and I know that Loren and Eva are keeping a close eye on her. So I'm going with you. I want to be part of this job."

"All right, Christian, let's go."

"What about Troy and Ian?"

"I'm to meet them in my office. Do you want to ride with me?"

"Yes, I left the car for Isabella, in case I'm not back by the time she's ready to go home."

"All right then. Let's go." In the car, Sebastian smiled blissfully. He was on the way to start a war against the people who wanted to see him destroyed. He already knew the outcome of that fight, but he was excited about the feeling of satisfaction of delivering and witnessing their demise.

Chapter 17

AT THE SOUND of the elevator door, Madeline turned and fell into a pair of startling green eyes. Those eyes had haunted her dreams ever since she accepted the job as Sebastian's private secretary.

He stepped out of the elevator in his usual graceful way, followed by Christian. Madeline swallowed hard as millions of butterflies invaded her stomach.

"Good morning, Madeline."

His musical voice traveled through her body and settled deep into her soul. Her eyes were locked on his, unable to keep the heat from rising and changing her cheeks from pale to crimson. She had spent entire nights tossing and turning, thinking about Sebastian and what it would be like to spend one night with him. Silently, she thanked God that she was sitting down because her knees began to tremble.

Sebastian's eyebrows furrowed. "Are you okay?"

Overcome by both embarrassment and desire, she struggled to find the voice that was buried under her inappropriate thoughts.

What in the world is wrong with me?

"Yes...yes, I'm fine," she replied, her voice breathy. "Good morning, sir," she mumbled.

His lips quirked in response, knowing exactly why Madeline was a bit lost. To Sebastian, her thoughts were an open book. He could read every human thought. This was the same expression she held each and every time he came to the office.

Madeline blushed again, and her gaze drifted to Christian. "Good morning," she said, her voice more stable.

Christian gave her a full smile, and she gasped. "Good morning to you, too," he said in that soft, musical immortal voice.

Good God, he is just as beautiful as Sebastian.

"Any messages?" Sebastian's voice broke her errant thoughts.

"Yes, sir." She grabbed a handful of notes from the top tray and handed them to Sebastian with a soft smile. "Mr. Vasser, Mr. Bristow, and Mr. Shilton are waiting in your office."

Sebastian's fingers brushed hers lightly as he took the messages, and she shivered. He thumbed through them, and her thoughts ran wild again. She could have placed them on his desk for him to find. She could have sent his daily schedule to his computer, but she did neither. She wanted—*needed*—that small interaction with him. She was living and breathing for that small connection, no matter how senseless it was.

Sebastian was the perfect man. She drank him in and waited until he was through going over each one of the notes. He finally placed the pile back on her desk.

"Please make the appropriate phone calls and set up meetings with everyone except for Focal Industries. I am not interested in meeting with them, so make up some excuse." Tapping lightly on her desk, he added. "Also, please hold all my calls this morning."

"Yes, sir."

Sebastian and Christian left her desk and walked with that seamless immortal walk toward his office. Before he entered, he turned around and said, "Madeline, hold all my calls but for Arielle. If she calls, pass them through to me right away."

Madeline nodded. "I will."

She gaped at the closed door for a long time. *How strange!* Clearly unable to stop her overwhelming thoughts from swirling wildly, she forced her mind to concentrate on a few bothersome questions. What about the uncanny similarity between the five men in Sebastian's office? They had perfect physical appearances, seamless walks, and magical voices. And what about the fact that Sebastian never had anything to drink? Her brain was recollecting the fact that he never asked for coffee or tea or any other refreshment for that matter.

The few times that he had asked for refreshments for visitors, they were not part of his group of friends. She shook her head. She couldn't keep her mind from drifting toward Sebastian's gorgeous muscled physique, his snug fit jeans, and his stunning smile. She was daydreaming over a man that she would never have in this lifetime. Inwardly, she groaned and turned back to the computer screen. She didn't want to work, but she had to if she was going to keep her job. Her fingers started running over the keyboard as she let out a deep sigh.

Christian followed Sebastian into his office and shut the door behind them. The instant the door closed, three pairs of eyes turned and focused on them. "Ah, there you are," Troy said, rising to his feet. Ian and Nathan moved to stand on either side of Troy.

"Good morning," Sebastian said and flashed a grateful smile to his friends. They were there to selflessly offer their support.

Christian had only visited Sebastian's office once before. The first time was under very stressful conditions, so this time, he took a minute to take in his surroundings.

Sebastian's vast office was elegantly decorated, providing a comfy but masculine environment. His desk was decorated with classic molding with fluted columns and acanthus carved trim. It was made out of different kinds of exotic woods —ebony and Carpathian elm-- and took up a large portion of the east side of the room. Three enormous leather sofas and four massive recliners anchored the lounge area, along with five armchairs with numerous side tables to support a drink. A mahogany table stood at the west side of the room, twelve similar chairs surrounding it. The paneling made this masculine space inviting. A huge flat screen TV was set high on the wall above the table and directly across from the sofas. The north wall was a solid sheet of thick glass from floor to ceiling, overlooking Parliament St and the river Thames.

Sebastian paused for a short moment then waved everyone to sit. He crossed the room, and rounding the vast desk; he sat behind it. The only emotions lingering in his eyes were those of pure determination mixed with frustration. He bent down and unlocked the bottom drawer. He pulled out a brown folder and set it on the top of his desk.

"More photos?" Nathan exclaimed.

Sebastian pushed away from the desk and rose to his feet. He swung on his heels grabbed the folder and crossed the room. He sunk into one of the cushioned chairs and let his gaze linger on Nathan's face. "No, not photos. It's a video."

Nathan's eyes widened. "A video!"

"Yes, a video."

Glancing around, he could see the quizzical expression on his friend's faces, but he didn't expound. He set the folder on the small table next to him and stood up. He shoved his hands in his pockets and walked over to the window. He stared down at the river, and his eyes squinted against the sun's brilliance. He longed to be rid of this problem today, but he knew he had to establish a plan. Hundreds of scenarios raced through his mind, as he turned and glanced between his friends. "We all know what needs to be done," he said calmly. "Now we have to have to establish a bulletproof plan."

Troy stood up and walked to stand next to him. "So what's on your mind?" he asked.

Sebastian's lips pinched, and he frowned. "I've been climbing the walls for over two weeks now, ever since Arielle's abduction, trying to come up with the best method to handle this situation. I'm not happy right now with the results, but I know that I will be once we are done."

Christian's turn to interject. "What does that mean?"

"Christian, I'm not happy that the goons that want to destroy my company and those I love are still alive and planning their next move against me. I want everyone involved in this dirty quest abolished from the face of the earth." The tension that flashed through his eyes momentarily gripped Nathan.

"All in good time, Sebastian," he said coolly.

Sebastian studied his face for a moment, and then he nodded. He pushed away from the window and halted in front of the small table where the brown envelope rested. He picked it up and waved it in front of his friends. "We need to review the contents and make a strategic decision."

"Have you receive anything from Jorrit's team lately?" Nathan asked.

"No, not since the last extortion note before to Arielle's abduction. I think he's trying to find out what happened to his men and what happened to Arielle."

Troy's lips lifted and arched a brow. "Oh, I'm sure there is chaos in their headquarters. There have been two incidents that keep them utterly perplexed. They think that the three men they lost in Brussels were a revenge killing. But they can't explain the disappearance of the four men in Brighton. They are never going to find their remains, and that will create a troublesome unsolvable puzzle for them. This makes me giddy."

They all nodded in agreement, and wide smiles spread across their immortal faces.

"Are the investigators immortals?" Christian asked quizzically.

"Yes, they work for my parents."

"Are we going to view the video this morning?" he further probed.

"I think we should wait until the rest of the guys are here and that should be first of next week."

"Oh! Who else is coming besides Jon, Pier, and Jacques?"

"There are three more guys coming from Italy. They are Troy's friends who have become my friends as well. They came to help with Annabel at St. Jean de Luz. A total of eleven men will partake in this endeavor, but I think we will have to include Loren and Isabella because there are thirteen central locations that we will have to invade."

"What about Eva?" Ian asked.

"No, not Eva. I want her with Arielle while we are gone. I never know Annabel's whereabouts, and I can't trust her. I can't imagine leaving Arielle completely unprotected."

"Yes, I agree," Ian replied. "I didn't think about that."

Nathan let out a slow whistle. "With that number, we can take on a whole army. When are you planning1 this invasion?"

"It will be sometime next week. I hope that you'll be here, Nathan. I have included you in the count."

Nathan grinned. "I wouldn't miss this for the world. When do we ever experience this kind of excitement?"

"I want us all to view the video and then work out a plan because the Mafia cells are spread around the globe, and we will have to split up and make sure we carry our attack on the same day and at the same time. They will have no idea what hit them, and we will give them no time to communicate with each other."

"Sebastian, it will make absolutely no difference if they speak to each other and if they warn each other. There will be no escape for any of them when we are done." Troy's words were firm.

"I understand," he said, "but I think a plan is what we need to do this right. I will be the one to take on Jorrit and Rainer."

"What about their boss?"

"That goes without saying. I will move up until the last guy is down."

"Do we know where they are all located?"

"Yes, I have a detailed list, not only of the locations but the number of people in each location, their names and addresses, their offices and ranks, and a video of their activities."

Christian let out a long whistle of appreciation. "When did you gather all this?" he asked, eyes wide open.

"The investigators brought the information to me yesterday afternoon. I was thinking about viewing the video, but then I decided that it would be best if we all viewed it together. Each one will have useful suggestions that we will take and form our perfect plan. I know that we all have military experience, and that is an additional advantage in forming that faultless strategy of attack. I also understand that our experience is from centuries ago, but the changes through time in the high-tech weaponry and the fighting capabilities might of have created issues for a human being, but it will have no effect on us."

"What day are you friends arriving?" Christian asked Troy.

"They are all coming the first of the week. Antonius is in Australia, so he is coming in on Tuesday. But Girard and Giani will be here Monday."

"What about your guys, Sebastian?"

"They will all be here Monday. I don't want to prolong this. I want it over before Ian and Eva's wedding. I don't want something like this to spoil their special day. I am sure that they would love to create chaos during a huge wedding gathering, thinking that they could succeed in achieving their goal."

Ian smiled appreciatively. "Thanks, Sebastian, I have to agree. A wedding with all of us there would be exactly when they would think it's the best time to execute their dirty scheme."

Sebastian raked his fingers through his hair and pinched the tip of his nose.

"We are going to bring this to a prompt and successful end."

The change of plan in viewing the video turned the discussion to various other issues about the Russian Mafia. Sebastian distributed a copy of the list to each one of his friends to become familiar with Nikola's people and the locations they occupied.

He spent the next hour answering questions and discussing small details included on the lists he provided.

"Are we to take everyone's life in the organization or just specific members?" Christian's question brought everyone's gaze to him.

Sebastian paused for a moment. The question swirled in his thoughts, and he finally focused on Christian. "I am afraid that if we don't, they will regroup and come back. They are relentless, and I will not allow this to go on much longer. To make things worse, I have Annabel that will not give up her ghastly plots of trying to make Arielle's and my life miserable. I have made a mess of Arielle's life, and I have to fix this. She has done absolutely nothing, and she has the Russian Mafia and Annabel, both trying to hurt her because of me." He shut his eyes against the revulsion that Annabel's vivid image brought him. A concerned look crept across his face. "There is no other possible course but the one we are going to take right now," He furthered though gritted teeth, and his eyes darted from one side of the room to the other. Everyone nodded in agreement. They knew that come next week things were about to become a whole lot more interesting. Silence fell and stretched for a very long moment.

Suddenly Nathan's voice broke the quite. "Where did the time go?" he said glancing at his watch. "I have a meeting this afternoon with the engineers that brought the new security system."

"All right," Sebastian said rising to his feet. "Troy, Ian, Christian and I have to go back to the university. We have to pick up the girls."

It had been four hours since they assembled in that room, and they decided it was time to disperse and come back together again when the rest of their friends arrived in town.

Arielle was sitting in the fifth row of the huge auditorium between Gabrielle and Loren, fumbling with her mobile phone while listening to Professor Allworth going through next week's assignments. Her eyes wondered around the room aimlessly and suddenly locked with a pair of soft brown eyes. They belonged to a handsome guy with brown hair and wide shoulders. He was watching intently, a pleasant smile touching his lips. Arielle frowned and stared back at him in stunned silence. After a long moment of intent stare, she shifted uncomfortably. *Could he be another immortal?* She thought as she broke eye contact. *What in bloody hell? He seems safe, but is he? Why is he watching me?*

She glanced between her two friends, but they were oblivious to the guy's stare; they were watching Professor Allworth. *This is utterly ridiculous. I can't be having these crazy thoughts every time someone is staring at me.*

She had no intentions of satisfying her curiosity, but as absurd as it sounded, she couldn't help herself from glancing at his direction once again. He was now holding a wide smile across his face and appeared quite amused. She raised a single eyebrow when he motioned for her to join him at the empty seat next to him. He watched her, expecting a reply. Arielle repressed a shiver and quickly turned to face Professor Allworth. *Maybe he was a nice guy, but is he?* Lately, it seemed that everyone around her had some motive to hurt her. Could he be working for the same people that abducted her? She couldn't remember seeing him before, but then she didn't see anyone around her but for Sebastian. She was finally realizing that the fact that she couldn't recognize all the people in her classes was outrageous but true. Being in love with Sebastian had not been an easy task, but then nothing worth having is. She knew the difficulty, the fear, and the agony she would have to face if she chose to love him, but she did.

Lost in her thoughts, she was startled to find that the lecture was over, and her friends were standing watching her quizzically while she was still sitting utterly unmoved.

"Are you coming or are you staying?" Gabby chuckled.

Arielle shook her head and slowly straightened up. "Sorry, I lost track of time," she stammered, nearly forgetting where she was.

"You always lose track of time when Sebastian is not with you," Gabby said giggling.

The corners of her mouth turned up, clearly pleased with Gabby's statement. She gathered her books and followed her friends down the steps of the auditorium and toward the exit. They had just crossed the exit when she turned to check on her. She was shocked to find the strange guy walking extremely close behind her. For a moment, her heart stopped, and her face tensed. The intensity of fear was so strong she felt bile rising to her mouth. Her hand came up to grab Gabby or Loren when she fell into a hard wall of muscles. A pair of strong arms wrapped around him and Sebastian's warmth pulled her right into his safe sanctuary.

"Are you searching for me, baby?"

She drew in a shallow breath and gazed into Sebastian's emerald eyes. His heat seeped into her skin and spread across her body. Her uneasiness did not escape him.

"What's wrong?"

Arielle took a look behind her, around her, but the young man had disappeared into the thin air. "Strange!" she murmured.

Sebastian pushed her hair away from her face and met her gaze. "What's strange?"

Arielle noticed that their friends had left, and they were walking toward the parking lot. She took Sebastian's hand and guided them toward that direction.

"Can I have a kiss?" Sebastian asked. He snaked his arm around her waist and pulled her closer, surrendering his mouth to hers. A soft sigh escaped her, and his arm tightened around her. Pulling himself away, he peered into her eyes. He then bent his head and whispered into her ear. "I love you, Arielle. You are mine."

She reached up and stroked the side of his face, and let her fingers slide along the length of his jaw. "I love you, too."

"So what was so strange?"

"There was a guy in the auditorium that kept staring at me. I have never seen him before, and it scared me."

"And what is so strange about that? I see a lot of guys staring at you."

"Well, his stare was intense. I was sure that he was closing in on me while on our way out of the auditorium. I felt that he was reaching for me when I fell into your arms."

"I didn't see anyone reaching for you," he said.

"Well..." her voice trailed. "That's what so strange. One minute he is right behind me and then the next he is gone."

"Well, don't worry about him any longer. I'm here now, and he's probably upset that you are with me," he whispered with a chuckle.

"I suppose you're right. I don't understand why I'm always so jumpy."

"Arielle, you have every right to be. There are people out there that want to hurt you, because they know that you are the only person in the world than means everything to me, and I mean everything." He flinched as if a bad image passed across his eyes. "I have made a mess of your life, and I'm going to fix it. I will take care of those issues, and you'll never have to worry about anything but how you can spend every moment of your life with me."

She squeezed his hand and smiled. They were now at the parking lot, and their friends waved as they climbed into their cars.

"Let's go home, baby," Sebastian said and held the door open for her.

"How did your meeting go?" Arielle asked breaking the silence.

"It went well. We will meet together again on Wednesday next week when all the guys are in town."

"So they are coming, just as they did in St. Jean de Luz?"

"Yes, all."

"Is Christian going to join you?"

"Yes, it will be a total of eleven of us."

"Oh my! Eleven immortals? Are you taking on an army?"

"Well, we are not sure how many we have to face. But I have a strong feeling that they are many."

The rest of the drive was quiet. Arielle let her fears wash away, happy to be sitting next to a man that meant more to her than anything else on this earth or in any other universe for that matter. She chuckled inwardly and turned her eyes to scan the busy streets. The windows were down and the cool air whipped through her thin blouse sending a shiver across her body.

"Are you cold?" Sebastian asked, reaching over and taking her hand in his. "Did you bring a jacket?"

She turned to look at him and smiled. His jaw and mouth were set in a soft line, waiting for her answer.

"No, I didn't bring one. It was quite warm when we left the house. But I'm all right."

Sebastian remained unconvinced. He reached up and with his fingers he felt the material. "This material is way too thin," he said. He reached into the back of the car, grabbed his coat jacket, and handed it to her. "Please put this on."

Arielle was happy to slip her arms into Sebastian's jacket. It smelled just like his immortal sweet scent, and she felt as if she was engulfed in his embrace. She closed her eyes and sighed deeply.

"What are you thinking?" he asked.

"It feels like when I'm in your arms," she said giggling.

"That's a good thing, right?"

"That's a great thing," she murmured with a throaty voice, as unexpected desire spreads across her muscles.

The amulet on her neck prevented Sebastian from reading her thoughts, but he was very sure what she's thinking. "You heard Dr. McKenna. You have to wait."

"But, Sebastian! I'm fine. I need you."

He sighed deeply and shook his head in denial. "No."

"It's my body, and I say yes," she spats out mulishly.

Sebastian responded with raised eyebrows. "Oh! I thought it was my body, too," he said his voice amused.

"Sebastian, I'm not joking. I've waited for two weeks now. I am not going to wait any longer."

Sebastian chuckled inwardly and remained silent. She leaned back in her seat and closed her eyes once again. She would have to make her move on him as soon as they reached the door. She wasn't going to let him stop her this time. She smiled pleased with her decision. She had no regrets for choosing to spend her life with Sebastian no matter how many angry immortals or humans she had to face because of him.

At the house, he helped her out of the car and held her against his warm body. "Now, what were you saying about being in my arms?" he chuckled. His arms snaked around her waist, and he pulled her even closer. His mouth came down on hers, and their lips melded together, and their tongues fell into a sensuous dance. He leaned over and deepened the kiss leaving her breathless. The kiss was filled with pure passion and desire. His long, strong fingers moved firmly across her body and stroke her senses alive. Her skin burned with desire, and her knees gave in.

He finally broke the kiss and took a step back. "Oh, no...no...no... Not on your life, Gaulle. You are not going to stop now," Arielle growled. She moved into him with incredible passion. Her hands weaved into his hair and pulled him down firmly until her lips found his and the kiss turned scorching hot. Sebastian groaned into her mouth in defeat, and his tongue pressed her lips apart, and he delved into the softness of her mouth. Arielle arched her body, pressing her full length against his. Heat coursed through him, and he knew he was not going to stay strong. When they finally broke apart, he took her hand and drew her across the threshold. There he swung her around once again, and his mouth came down on hers with barely controlled ravenousness. Swiftly, he leaned down and scooped her into his arms, moving with impatient strides toward the bedroom. "Let's finish what you started."

Arielle blinked at his intense gaze. "I started?" she began to say.

Sebastian chuckled and, bending down, he muted her words.

 *Chapter 18*

SEBASTIAN'S HUGE OFFICE seldom appeared so full, and even more seldom so animated, as it did Wednesday morning. Eleven incredible immortal men and two striking immortal women occupied the vast space, standing around, waiting, with rigid expressions on their beautiful faces. They all knew why they were there and what they needed to do, but they were missing the rules of engagement.

The tension was high. Hard faces were staring intently at Sebastian waiting for his instructions. They all exchanged glances of understanding. They were there to help Sebastian rid of a major difficulty in his life, and they seemed like warriors ready to go to battle. The resolve and the immense energy inside the room seemed to infect Ian. This was going to be the first time he was taking part in such an enormous and complicated conflict since he became immortal. Sebastian scanned the room and noticed the resolve on each face. But he also knew that he needed to lay out a comprehensive plan.

He walked up to his desk and retrieved the brown envelope that contained the CD with the details on the Russian Mafia organization. He then swung around and sauntered to the center of the room to face his friends. His lips lifted briefly and his jaw set. He had spent nearly a month displaying patience he didn't have. He wanted this over with. He looked down at the envelope and then up again. "Before I present this documentation," he said, and topped at the top of his desk, "I want to thank you for coming once again to support me as you all did in St.

Jean de Luz. This, however, will be very different than going after immortals. It will be an easy task for us, but it requires precise timing of execution at all the locations. This particular organization is spread across the world with central locations in all the continents."

A long low whistle slipped from Antonius' lips. "How many continents are we talking about?" he asked.

"Almost all of them," Sebastian replied. "I need to abolish this nightmare from the face of the earth. I want to eliminate the entire organization that has devoted so much time to destroying me and those that I love. The best way to succeed is to hit all central locations at the same time, and I couldn't possibly do that without you, no matter how fast I can move. Once we destroy their central locations, we can concentrate on the final clean up with the low-rank criminals. Attacking their significant command posts will create chaos, and they will lose communication with their leaders. "

Sebastian scanned the room and noticed that all his friends were nodding in agreement. He motioned for everyone to take a seat while he walked back to his desk and pressed a button on a small device, and at the far wall of the room, a large screen dropped from the ceiling. He then pressed another button, and dark shades lowered, covering all the windows, turning the room completely dark. Darkness was not an issue for the immortals. Their vision was perfect in the night as it was in the daylight. He then took a seat and slipped the disc in the computer. He pointed a remote at the screen and clicked. A large figure of a stocky man with thick brown hair, dark brown eyes, and a shrewd expression on his face covered the screen.

"This is Nikola Vasilovitch, the top man of the organization and my daily nightmare. He only answers to the Prime Minister. However, that does not mean that Nikola keeps him abreast to all of his dirty undertakings. I'm also sure that the Prime Minister has no idea that Nikola is after my company or the reasons behind it. In my research, I found out that Nikola is a selfish man, and there is a motive behind everything he does. And that motive is always to achieve his goals, which will only profit him. He has to be taken out."

The next image was that of a tall, handsome man with sandy hair and green eyes. "This is Rainer Heinrich. He reports directly to Nikola. I'm not sure how I can describe this man. From all the movies I have watched, all the conversations I have heard, and all the researched I have done, he provides a confusing profile. He portrays the hardened criminal that he should be; however, his actions and directives to his people contradict that portrait. He is always pressing the point of not killing the people they are after. He demands that his people do not harm anyone in their captivity. Things do not always turn the way he wants them, but his demeanor has me puzzled. If it was not for Rainer, I'm sure that Arielle would have been raped and badly abused by those goons while in their captivity. I'll be the one dealing with Rainer as well."

Sebastian raked his fingers through his hair, clearly frustrated, and shook his head, dismissing his bothersome thoughts. He then pressed the forward arrow, and two other men appeared on the screen. "These two are Rainer's right-hand men, Larue Legrand, and Hahn Dussel. They are the experts in decoding top-secret documents, invading computer privacy, extortion, and manipulation. They have numerous kills under their belts. They are unethical, heinous, and heartless killers. Since I'll be taking on the St. Petersburg command center, I'll be dealing with those two as well."

Sebastian took a long breath. "Now I'm going to show you photos of all the men that hold leading command locations in each country and share information on each one of them." He continued flipping through images on the screen, giving his friends clear views of the people they would have to eliminate.

"The reason I want you to see their faces is that I don't want innocent people to die. They have employees at those locations that are completely unaware of their filthy undertakings. They are just employees used to mask a corrupt business. I don't want those people killed." Sebastian emphasized the last words. "Before we leave this room, each one of you will receive a folder that contains all the pertinent information that you'll need. The folder will contain details on each one of the men that will be targeted along with their photos."

Next, a huge world map covered the screen. Red dots appeared over the cities that were to be part of this invasion. The immortals scanned the map, making mental notes of the locations. The cities seem to be spread across six continents and included Berlin, Paris, New York, Cairo, Ankara, Athens, Brussels, Toronto, Tokyo, Sydney, Milan, Rio and St. Petersburg.

"Wow! They are spread across the globe," Pier noted.

"Yes, they are," Sebastian agreed. "That's why I need your help." He rose to his feet and pressed a button on his desk. The shades came up, and bright daylight flooded the room. He leaned over the desk, picked up an arm full of folders, and brought them back dropping them onto the large table in the middle of the sitting area. "My private investigators prepared and provided these folders," he said pointing at the small pile on the table. "I need for you to discuss and chose what city you wish to handle. Then take the folder for that country. Please make sure you go over them tonight. You will find accurate details of the daily schedule for every command leader, their right-hand men, and the people that carry out their dirty work. There are also details of the offices they occupy in those buildings. My investigators did an incredible job in providing all this information."

"Yes, it sounds like they did a remarkable job," Troy said, as they all inched closer to the table.

An animated discussion began, and soon enough, they had all agreed as to what country and what city they were going to handle. They picked up the folders and walked back to their seats. The folder for St. Petersburg was left on the table for Sebastian. A smile tugged at the corners of his mouth as his gaze swept over his friend's faces. He let out a long breath and crossed the room once again to reach his desk. His calm exterior didn't fool his friends; they sensed the anxiety, and the eagerness to see this endeavor come to an end.

"Jorrit is a piece of work," Troy said.

"It's the whole bunch under Nikola's radar that's dirty and corrupted to their core," Sebastian stated.

His finger pressed down on a small unit attached to the desk, causing the screen to disappear into the ceiling. Resolve spread across every muscle in his body. With his eyes slanting downward, he approached the table, picked up the last envelope, and sank into the sofa. He opened the flap and thumbed through the detail sheets for a long time.

It was his voice that made everyone's gaze dart toward him and stares in astonishment.

"I'm not sure that killing everyone under Nikola is the right thing to do," he said as if he was talking to himself. "But it's the only way I know to rid the world from goons that participate in kidnapping, beating, and murdering innocent victims for their own gain. Every moment that we sit back and wait, they will use it to reorganize and come back every bit as vicious as they were the first time around. I'm not worried about any one of us in this room. I'm worried about the humans we all love: Arielle, Gabrielle, Paul, and Nathan's wife, Jasmine. I can't sit here and wait for them to take another shot at the company or one of them."

"Who is going to stay back to protect them?" asked Girard.

"Oh, I've asked Eva. She's more than capable of keeping them safe from Annabel or anyone else that might come along." He paused for a short moment; he glanced at his watch and shook his head. He then fixed each one of his friends with a firm stare full of determination. "This should not take long," he added.

"When are we leaving?" Gerard asked tapping a pen against the armrest.

Sebastian rose from his seat and moved to the window. He took in the amazing view of London. He then turned to face his friends. "Due to the variance in the time zones, I suggest that we should plan to attack at four PM London time. Some of us will have to leave early tomorrow morning for the countries that are way ahead of our local time. If you chose countries with later time zones, then you can leave a bit later in the day. We will use our immortal ability to arrive at our locations. This is too important to rely on human transportation. I also suggest that we arrive there around three PM London time to familiarize ourselves with the buildings and the surroundings. I want you to make sure you locate your targets and leave the innocent people untouched. We'll synchronize our watches, and when we are in place, we will text each other, and I will give the signal to move in and strike simultaneously precisely at four o'clock. Do you agree with the plan?" Sebastian checked around the room and saw everyone nodding in agreement, a smug grin on their faces. His lips kicked up at the corners, and he leaned against the window. "We'll take no prisoners!" he said.

"We'll treat this as a cleanup job that will rid the world from the lowest filth on this earth," Troy added.

"Sebastian, if you think that we might need a few more to take part in this, I have friends that will be willing to come on a moment's notice," Antonius said.

Sebastian pinched the tip of his nose. He took a few steps away from the window. With his hands in his pockets, he glanced around the room. "Does any one of you need any help?" Everybody remained quiet. They were given all the facts about the assignment, the attack was seamlessly planned, and they were good to go with no additional help.

"I think we are okay, Antonius, but thanks for the offer," Sebastian said appreciatively.

They discussed the strategies with excitement and eagerness for adventure. It was now early afternoon, and they all seemed to have all their questions answered.

"Well, I guess we're all set. Let's meet in this room tomorrow morning for any last questions or details. Is there anything you want to ask before we conclude this meeting?" Sebastian asked.

Silence met his question once again. "All right then. Jon, Pier, and Jacques, you are staying with Arielle and me unless you have other plans." The guys shook their heads.

"No, no plans. We all want to see Arielle." Jon's statement was met by soft laughter. The immortals loved the girls.

Troy turned to face Antonius, Girard, and Giani. "I know a girl who is waiting anxiously to see you again," he said and chuckled. All three nodded, a delighted expression spreading across their faces. They loved Gabrielle; they were happy with their best friend's choice.

Sebastian turned to face Nathan. "Nathan, tell Jasmine hello, and that I'm sorry I have to take you away from her once again."

"I'm sure she'll understand," Nathan said with a kind smile. It was obvious that he was delighted with his wife's wonderful personality. They were newlyweds and madly in love.

Sebastian thanked Ian, Christian, and Isabella once again. He then hugged Loren and pressed a soft kiss on her cheek. "Give Mum my love, and tell her that Arielle and I will come to visit after this is over," Loren smiled returning her brother's kiss.

Sebastian strode to the door. "I'll see you all tomorrow at six in the morning for any last minute questions before we leave for our locations," he said. "And if any questions come up tonight, I'll be home."

Now it was a simple matter of waiting untill morning

Sebastian arrived in St. Petersburg a little before three PM. A smile that did not touch his eyes lingered on his lips. By now, all of his friends were on their way or had already arrived at their respective locations. A fresh breeze brushed across his face, and he glanced at his watch one more time. His expression changed to that of sullenness at the thought of eliminating someone's life, but this had to be done. By three-fifteen, he had received text messages that they all had arrived at their specific locations. They were going to probe inside to locate their targets. Then they would be waiting for his text message to move in. Sebastian smiled with clear satisfaction. *So far so good.*

Rainer and Nikola's office buildings were about two kilometers apart. He chose to stop at Rainer's office first. He slipped his phone into his jean pocket and approached the building.

The lobby was busy with employees and visitors moving in and out. Guards were stationed on either side of the receptionist area as well as by the entrance to the elevators. Sebastian used his immortal speed and in nanoseconds, he had crossed the lobby and reached the inside staircase undetected. He scaled the stairs in large strides and went through each floor, making mental notes of every person and their exact locations. He arrived at the top floor and paused behind the closed door for a short moment. All he could hear was absolute silence. He grabbed the door handle and, leaning against the door with his right shoulder, he turned and pushed quietly. The door was locked.

His lips kicked up with amusement. *Like this is going to prevent me from going in.*

He chuckled inwardly, and the lock gave to his immortal strength. He stepped inside and found himself standing in the middle of a vast, extravagantly decorated waiting room. An enormous ornate desk occupied the middle of the sitting area. He took a quick look around, but there was no one in sight. Sebastian knew that this floor was exclusively allocated to Rainer and his two scummy right-hand men. He decided to peer inside each room along the long corridor, but every office was empty. After glancing quickly into an empty conference room, he reached the last door that had Rainer's name plastered on it. The door stood halfway open, and he stopped to listen. A woman's soft voice reached him, and he inched up close to pick inside. He saw Rainer's secretary on the phone. Her picture was included in the video provided by his private investigators. She was stunningly beautiful. Sebastian knew from the detailed documentation in his hands that she was an innocent girl. She was bent over Rainer's desk searching for something, the phone glued to her ear. He drew back and leaned against the wall.

"I don't see the folder on your desk."

Sebastian heard the deep male voice at the other end. "Check inside the top left drawer."

He caught the swishing of a drawer being drawn out. "What am I searching for?" she asked, thumbing through the folders.

"It should be titled 'Sebastian Gaulle,'" the man replied.

Sebastian frowned at the sound of his name. He peeked through the door and saw Georgiana still bent over the desk scanning through folders. He pulled back once again and waited. There was a bit more ruffling of paper, and finally the drawer shut.

"I have it," she said, satisfaction and something more coating her voice.

"Perfect. Please bring it to Nikola's office as soon as you can."

"All right, I'll leave right now."

"Thank you, Georgiana."

From the sound of their voices, Sebastian could sense a special relationship between the two. His acute awareness also told him that the man on the other end was Rainer. Georgiana sounded breathless, emotion coating every word she spoke. There was something special that this woman felt for Rainer.

He glanced at his watch. It was now 3:35 PM. He made a decision to follow Georgiana and take care of the top men first and then come back to clear this location. Georgiana's high heels clicked on the floor as she made her way to the door. Sebastian slipped into one of the empty rooms. Georgiana walked down the corridor clenching a wide folder under her arm. He let her footsteps fade down the hallway and waited. First, there was the sound of the computer keyboard being shut down and then the ping of the elevator arriving. The swish of the door opening and closing and the absolute silence that followed told Sebastian that the coast was clear. He moved down the hallway in his immortal speed, and he was outside the building before the elevator with Georgiana in it reached the lobby.

He waited away from the main door and watched her walk in a fast pace to the parking lot and climb into a small sports car.

She drove beneath a clear sky toward the main road along the river Neva. Sebastian moved in his immortal speed and arrived at Nikola's building where he watched Georgiana pulling into the parking lot. She stepped out of her car and made her way through the glass revolving door. She stopped for a short moment and talked with the guard at the entrance. He checked the card she handed him, and soon he stepped aside and let her in.

Sebastian used that time to move in and reach the emergency staircase at the other side of the lobby. He grabbed the handle and with no difficulty, he opened the locked door. He scaled the steps in a fast pace, and he was on the top floor in no time at all. He waited behind the door and listened. The sound of the elevator arriving made him anxious. He glanced at his watch, and it was now exactly 3:58 PM. He fished his mobile out of his jean pocket and texted two words to his friends, "Move in." He then shut the phone and slipped it back into his pocket.

He pushed the door slowly and peeked carefully. A young woman in her early twenties was sitting behind a vast desk that occupied the center of the room. She was on the phone and writing something on a piece of paper. She glanced up as the elevator binged and smiled wide at Georgiana as she entered the room. The young woman held her finger up for a short second as she concluded her phone call.

"Hi, Georgiana," she called out joyfully and put the phone down.

"Hi, Belinda," Georgiana replied, a wide smile spread across her beautiful face.

"How are you? It has been a while," Belinda said.

"I know! I'm sorry for not keeping in touch. My life has been a bit crazy lately," she said apologetically.

"Oh, anything you want to talk about?"

Georgiana pressed her lips together and sighed. "Yes, but not now. I have some papers from Rainer. He wants them right away. I assume they are quite important," she added, pointing to the folder in her hand.

"He said you were coming." She pulled her center drawer open, and taking a small card; she handed it to Georgiana. "This is for access to Nikola's office."

"Thank you," Georgian said, reaching for the card.

"Don't forget to use your handprint on the first door," Belinda added.

Georgiana nodded with a smile and disappeared around the corner as the phone rang once again and Belinda picked it up. "He's busy right now, but I can take a message," Sebastian heard her say. He pushed the door open and stepped inside. He moved quietly in his immortal speed and disappeared behind the corner undetected by Belinda. It was a winding hallway that was brightly illuminated, but there were a couple of dark corners perfect for his use. Georgiana was already at the end of the hallway and had stopped in front of a large door. She pressed her hand against a screen panel on the wall that seemed to analyze her fingerprint, and the door opened with a swish. She crossed the threshold, and the door swooshed shut behind her, but not before Sebastian made it through as well. She kept down another short corridor, turned a corner, and stopped in front of another door. A large sign displayed the name Nikola Vasilovitch. She slipped an electronic key into the slot to the right of the door panel, and the light turned green. She entered the room, but the door remained open.

Sebastian inched up and heard Nikola's deep voice.

"What the devil is wrong with you?"

"What are you talking about?" someone replied.

"Rainer, you're either dumb, or you are playing dumb. Can't you see that there is something very wrong with this whole Gaulle thing? How can people vanish into the thin air? How can they disappear from the face of the earth with no trace at all? Did you find what happened to the men in Brussels? And what about the men in Brighton? Don't you find that a bit peculiar?"

"Yes, I do find that quite peculiar, but I have no explanation. Maybe the men decided to leave."

"Leave?" His voice roared and bounced angrily from the walls. "What the hell are you talking about? Those worthless pieces of shit were getting paid well, and I was providing a better life for them. Why would they want to leave?" There was a short silence, and his voice rumbled once again. "Rainer, you know there is no way out. Once you sign up for this organization there…is…no…way…out." His last words came out staccato. "Find them and do away with them, or I'll do away with you." Something in his voice drove a shiver down Georgiana's spine.

Rainer's next statement rolled out of his lips before he could stop it. "Nikola, I'm tired. I don't want to do this anymore. If the morgue is the only way out, then let it be." He stood there facing Nikola, brushing off any concern, acid mood settling over him.

A loud intake of breath made Rainer turn and face Georgiana. She was staring at Rainer, her anxiety palpable. Rainer's eyes softened, and a smile painted his lips.

"I brought the file," she stammered.

Rainer moved closer and took the folder, brushing her hand with his fingers. "Thank you, Georgiana," he said quietly.

Time was up. Sebastian moved quickly and stood at the door

opening right behind Georgiana. He took a quick survey of the people in the room. There were four men, and they were all on his list. Nikola was standing behind his desk, glancing down at a piece of paper, a cigar in his right hand. Rainer stood with his back to Nikola, his eyes locked with Georgiana's. Sebastian could feel the passion between them. Larue and Hahn were seated on the sofa across from Nikola's desk thumbing through several documents on their lap. They didn't seem to acknowledge Georgiana or take part in the heated conversation between Rainer and Nikola.

"That'll be all. Go back to work," Nikola barked without looking up, dismissing Georgiana. His voice was harsh.

Georgiana gaped at Nikola's words, shocked by the tone of his voice, but he completely ignored her presence. She couldn't mask her embarrassment, and she bit back her anger. After a long moment, her gaze moved away from Nikola and settled on Rainer's face. His eyes were a burning green, penetrating. Georgiana shivered and took another step closer.

Sebastian moved his hand and the door sung shut behind him with a loud bang.

Chapter 19

RAINER'S INTENT GAZE moved away from her face and focused somewhere past her shoulder. Georgiana watched his strong jaw drop, his face paling, and his expression darkening. She followed his eyes, turning around slowly, and immediately regretted it. She let out a muffled scream, and her eyes went wide. *What in the world?* She shut them tightly, willing herself to believe that the stunningly beautiful man standing in front of her was nothing more than an illusion. For a long moment, she merely stood unmoved. She then forced her eyelids open and fell into the icy gaze of Sebastian's mossy eyes. His expression was hard and angry emotions were flashing through those eyes. Her mouth felt dry like the desert, and she found it hard to breathe.

Rainer took a sharp breath, but he said nothing. His focus was intent on Sebastian's face. He knew who he was from his photos, and he had a gut feeling this was not going to be good. He had not shared those photos with Nikola because Nikola had only asked to see a photo of Arielle.

"Well! What are you waiting for?" Nikola shouted. He glanced up and blinked. His eyes widened beneath his furrowed brows. His gaze fell on Sebastian, and he gasped, completely shocked. He regarded him in silence for a long moment and recovered quickly. "Who the devil are you?" he shrieked. "How in the hell did you get in here?"

At the sound of his words, Larue and Hahn's heads shot up simultaneously. At the sight of Sebastian, they both leaped to their feet. They knew exactly who Sebastian was. They exchanged quick glances, and their gaze glided toward Rainer's direction. Utter confusion was spread across their faces, but Rainer chose to ignore them.

Sebastian shot them an icy look just before he moved farther into the room. His attention was focused on Nikola's arrogant face. He could read the surprise and the confusion in Nikola's mind, but strangely, there was no fear. He had no clue as to who Sebastian was or why he was there. But clearly, he was not there for a friendly visit. Sebastian sensed movement to his right, and his eyes quickly flew over Larue and Hahn. They had taken a step toward Sebastian, but Rainer's hand was extended in front of them, stopping them in their tracks. Sebastian could practically feel the anxiety pumping off them in huge waves. He resisted the temptation to deal with them right off. He was going to kill them soon enough. They heaved a dry gasp and broke their stare as if they could read Sebastian's thoughts.

Sebastian's gaze lingered over them for a moment and then fell on Rainer's face. He was pale, but there was a strange tranquility that emanated from him. It was more like relief. Sebastian eyebrows shot up as he read Rainer's thoughts, now pouring out of him like lava from a volcano. Rainer was waiting for the day that he could finally put an end to his horrible life of crime and corruption. And he had a strong gut feeling that this was going to be the day of reckoning. He was only worried about Georgiana as he raked a hand through his hair.

Georgiana gazed numbly at Sebastian, paralyzed from fear. Stony silence hung heavily in the room, the air full of the smell of cigar smoke. Everyone seemed to be lost for words.

Suddenly Nikola's voice bounced off the walls like a boomerang, snapping everyone from their deep thoughts, "Who the devil are you?"

Sebastian's face creased, and his gazed settled on Nikola. Fury flashed in his eyes; he seethed with rage. He stalked across the room to stand only a few feet in front of him. His lips curved slightly. "I'm Sebastian Gaulle." His voice was calm but icy cold.

Nikola's mouth dropped opened, and he paled. His eyes grew wide, and disbelief spread across his face. He recovered quickly and coughed aloud, trying to clear his throat. He crossed his arms over his chest arrogantly and leveled his gaze on Sebastian. "Well? What do you want? Did you come to surrender the documents in person?" he asked with a deep chuckle.

Sebastian quickly glanced at his watch. It was now four-ten, and he had to move and finish the job. The realization that he was finally here, ready to end this miserable game, had amusement trickling through his veins, drowning the heave of fury. He suppressed his irritation, stoked his chin nonchalantly, and smiled. "No, that's not the reason I'm here."

Nikola uncrossed his arms and cocked his head to the side. "I'm close to losing my patience," he hissed. "What in the hell do you want? Speak quickly as your time here is limited."

Sebastian's smile widened. He had not missed Nikola's move earlier. He had pressed a button on the side of his desk. He knew that security was on the way up. "I'm here to kill you," he replied calmly.

Nikola's eyes shot up in disbelief. "You and who else?" he said, glancing around the room for more assailants. A roar of laughter left him, and he slapped the desk with his fist several times. "That is the funniest thing I've heard today." He stopped laughing just as fast as he started. The tone of his voice turned arrogant. "You are delusional if you think you can walk into my office, one man alone, and threaten me."

Fury coiled in Sebastian's stomach. Before he could reply, the door burst open behind him, and three guards poured into the room.

"It's about time you got here!" Nikola shouted, his eyes darting to the door. He strode around his desk. "Take this fool out of my office," he roared, pointing with his finger at Sebastian dismissively. His lips curled in a smirk. "Take care of him," he added. The undertone in his voice made everyone in the room, but Sebastian recoiled. They knew how Nikola took care of business.

"Let's go," a voice called from behind Sebastian and a hand clamped around his upper arm.

Sebastian turned slowly to face the guards. His eyes moved slowly over the guard's hand on his arm and flitted upward to scan the hostile faces that were staring him down. Sebastian pinned them with an arctic look that shot a shudder through their bodies. The breath caught in their throats, and confusion spread across their faces. What in the world was happening to them? They struggled to rein in their wits.

"What the hell are you waiting for?" Nikola bellowed, snapping them out of their haze.

Their befuddled gaze flew to Nikola's face. The guard holding Sebastian coughed, trying to clear his throat. He shifted from one leg to the other and tugged hard at Sebastian's arm. "Move...you don't want me to remove you; trust me on that," he spat out, and with his head, he made a motion toward the open door.

A slow smiled crept across Sebastian's face. "Can you?" he asked with mockery.

The guard's eyes widened. "Can I what?"

"Remove me," Sebastian replied, his face impassive.

They never saw him move. Sebastian's hands clamped around the guard's neck, and he squeezed effortlessly. The guard's eyes rolled up in his head, and when Sebastian released him, he dropped onto the floor like a rock. The two guards stared at the lifeless body of their friend, utterly stunned. They bit back the bile that rose to their throats and took deep breaths to calm their heaving stomachs.

Sebastian watched as they moved their hands from their gun belts and drew, taking a bold stand, ready to shoot. The next few moments were a blur. They watched in dismay as Sebastian took their guns in his hands and squeezed until the hard metal turned to scrap metal and slipped between his fingers, scattering all over the floor.

Their eyes widened like huge saucers. "What the hell..." one of them shrieked. His eyes flickered up and down Sebastian's body inquiringly. "What the hell are you?"

"I'm your destiny," Sebastian replied through clenched teeth, and taking one step, he grabbed each guard by the throat and squeezed. They fought hard to free themselves, but Sebastian's hands were like merciless steel vices. They wobbled on their feet, and it wasn't long before they took their last breath.

A sob brought Sebastian around to face the others, dropping the lifeless bodies from his hands. His eyes swept the room and noticed that nobody had moved an inch. They all seemed lost for words, stunned by the sight of the three dead bodies. They all knew by now that there was something very special about this man.

Nikola drew a sharp breath and stared Sebastian squarely in the eye. He knew that something was not right, but he had to push that aside and stand up to him. He had no idea how he found the last remnants of strength to mimic coolness, which he did not possess. "Make no mistake that I will personally kill you," he spat out.

Sebastian could read his mind and knew that he was scared to death. He was desperately trying to stop his heartbeat from pounding painfully in his chest and to block the fear spreading slowly but steadily across every part of his body. Sebastian moved in his immortal speed and stood only inches from Nikola. The sharp intake of breath told Sebastian that Nikola's fear increased by leaps and bounds. "You basta..." Nikola started to say, but he never finished. Sebastian moved again like lightning and grabbed a stunned Nikola by the neck. His balled fist came back and flew forward, landing hard in the middle of Nikola's chest. The eerie sound of shattering bones bounced off the walls and settled like a death blanket over Larue, Hahn, Rainer, and Georgiana.

Nikola's body fell limp, ready to crumble, but Sebastian's hand held him upright. The pain was unbearable, and his breath came out in excruciating gasps. Sebastian gave him a hard push and let him go. Nikola stumbled backward, tripped over his chair, and landed onto the floor. He sat there unmoving for a long moment, sputtering and coughing blood. His face splattered with blood, and he finally moved. He snarled something inaudible. He brushed the damp off of his mouth with the back of his sleeve, and grabbing the side of the chair; he struggled to rise to his feet. Filled with rage and vision blurred by fury, he screamed. "I'm going to fucking kill you. You...you son of a bitch."

Sebastian's next punch came quickly and caught Nikola in the middle of his face, breaking bones and sending him flying across the room, screaming from pain. His body collided with the wall, and he dropped to the floor. Sweat was dripping from his forehead, mixed with blood that was pouring out of his nose and mouth.

Sebastian sauntered across the room, ignoring the others for the moment, and stood over Nikola. He was a bloody mess, trying to breathe, but he could only manage short gasps. There was no air flowing through his crushed lungs. He gasped and wheezed for another moment, and then he let out a long eerie, gurgling sound before he choked in his own blood and keeled over. Sebastian stared down at him for a short second, and he then turned around to face the others. Larue and Hahn were frozen in place while Rainer stood tense and confused.

His arctic looks immobilized Larue and Hahn. Icy fingers crawled down their spines and their breath stilled as they struggled to slow the heaving in their chests. They shivered, sensing his intent deep into the marrow of their bones. They barely had a chance to blink and Sebastian was standing closer. They swallowed nervously the bitter bile climbing and threatening to leave their bodies. Hahn gathered his wits first and leaped, lifted his leg in a roundhouse kick targeting Sebastian's middle. Sebastian grabbed his foot in mid-air, pulled him forward, and knocked him off balance. With his foot still in his hand, Sebastian turned his wrist sharply to the right and broke Hahn's femur in two. A curdling scream escaped Hahn's lips, and he tumbled to the ground, moaning in sheer pain.

Larue stormed to his friend's aid and ran into Sebastian with all the power he possessed. His body bounced back, sending him flying across the room and landing against the far wall to crumble to the floor with a painful groan. The pain was unbearable. *What the hell?* He couldn't think a rational thought. He couldn't explain any of it. When his body collided with Sebastian's, he felt as if a speeding train hit him square in the chest.

Sebastian's gaze changed from irritated to furious. He glanced at Hahn on the floor and, leaning down, he picked him up by his throat and squeezed. His face contorted in a grimace of fury; it hardened, and slowly his muscles twitched. Blood dripped from the sides of his mouth as he tried to take a breath, but no air was getting through. His eyes widened and finally rolled back on his head, and he was gone. Sebastian let go of him, and he dropped to the floor lifeless.

Larue flinched at the sound of Hahn's body hitting the floor. He stared from across the room, eyes wild with fear of the unknown. He needed to do something; he couldn't let this man kill him without putting up a fight. Sweat slid down his back, adding to his fear. What kind of a man was he? He was not a normal human being. There was something very peculiar about him. Larue pulled himself off the floor and pushed away from the wall. His eyes were spitting fire, and his anger was overriding any reasonable thought he might have had left. "I'm going to kill you," he spat out through gritted teeth. He ran across the floor full speed. He lifted his right hand, balled his fist, and landed a hard hit catching Sebastian square in the jaw. A loud scream left Larue's lips, and horror filled his eyes as his hand connected with what felt like a concrete wall. Larue pulled back, clutching his arm and screaming in agony. His hand was completely shattered. Sebastian grimaced at the goon's stupidity, and he stared at him, face hard, green eyes icy and level.

"What the hell are you?" Larue cried out, staggering back, trying to reach the wall to steady himself. His legs gave in, and he crumpled to the floor.

Sebastian moved quickly, bent down, and picked Larue up by his shirt like a rag doll. Larue lifted his left hand to hit Sebastian in the face. Sebastian moved his head out of the way, and Larue's hand went flying by, plunging into the thin air. He never saw Sebastian's hand move, but he felt the hard blow in the middle of his chest. The blow was so strong that his feet left the floor. He flew back, crashing on his back against the same wall with a loud thud, and he groaned in pain. The sound of crushing bones drove sheer terror into his body. Before he had a chance to recover, Sebastian pulled him up once again this time by the throat and squeezed until his eyes rolled back and he stopped breathing. Sebastian let go, and his lifeless body hit the floor with a loud thump, landing only a few inches away from Hahn's corpse.

A loud gasp behind Sebastian made him swivel, and he came face to face with a trembling Georgiana. Her hand was pressed over her mouth, holding back a scream. Her eyes were wide, filled with horror, and extreme fear registered clearly on her features. When she met Sebastian's gaze, her knees nearly gave out. She took a few shaky steps backward until her back came in contact with Rainer's hard body. His arm came about her and held her firmly, preventing her from dropping to the floor. Georgiana let out a breathless whimper as a wave of nausea rolled over her. Unable to watch any longer, she turned and buried her face into Rainer's chest. He wrapped his arms around her protectively and held her close.

They were both trying to breathe, but nothing was coming through. Their lungs were locked. Sebastian could read their thoughts. Georgiana was shivering, afraid for herself and Rainer. She loved him deeply. She was ready to give her life to save his. Rainer was full of guilt for bringing her into this situation and putting her life on the line. For Rainer, Georgiana was love at first sight. He had spent sleepless nights thinking about *what if?* What if he had not chosen to take this dark path in his life? What if he had been free to make his own decisions, to love whomever he wanted to love and go wherever he wanted to go without any attachments to the Mafia? He couldn't change a thing about his life, so Georgiana would have to remain just a wonderful dream, a dream that would never become a reality. The pain of it all was excruciating, so Sebastian's appearance was a welcome event.

Something had clicked in his head the moment Sebastian stepped inside that room. Fear consumed him at first, but suddenly, everything became crystal clear. He knew what was about to happen and relief spread across his brain. He had no illusions about Sebastian. He knew that the intruder was there for revenge, and he was ready to be on the receiving side. The casual effort, the speed, and strength with which he killed seven people were almost unnerving. Strangely enough, the fear he originally felt was gone, and a peaceful wave spread across his body. He was glad that he was next, and Sebastian would put an end to his miserable life. He didn't want to do this any longer. The only way out was the morgue. Nikola had said that phrase over and over again. *How ironic? Here he was facing the end of his miserable life.* He only had one regret. He wished he could have had a chance with Georgian.

"I'm sorry, Georgiana," he whispered. "If I knew, I would have never asked you to come here."

"It's okay. I want to be with you," she sobbed and moved even closer.

Rainer closed his eyes and opened them again, hoping that all this was just a hallucination. He knew that one day he would meet

Sebastian and yet, somehow, he had never imagined anything tenuous like this. Sebastian eyes widened as he watched Rainer push Georgiana softly behind him, shielding her body protectively. Something tugged deep in Sebastian's chest that made his anger slip away slowly.

He held Georgiana's gaze for a short moment and then his eyes turn to Rainer, who had not moved an inch. He was still standing with his arm around his back, holding Georgiana close to his body. Sebastian wanted to understand the man that was providing such a confusing profile. He stood there watching him carefully. He could read his mind, and he saw no fear, just relief.

"Please do not hurt her. She is innocent," Rainer said quietly.

"You know who I am?" Sebastian asked.

"Yes," Rainer answered simply.

"Why are you not afraid?"

"This was inevitable, and it's the best way," he said, gazing into his eyes.

"No, no, it can't be. I love you," Georgiana cried out, moving quickly, and standing in front of Rainer protectively. She held Sebastian's eyes for a long moment. Tears were cascading down her face and soaking the front of her blouse. Her voice came out broken, pleading, painful. "Please, sir, don't hurt him. If you need to kill someone, please take me."

Sebastian dismissed Georgiana's plea and moved his gaze to Rainer. "What do you mean this was inevitable?"

Rainer looked tired, broken, his shoulders sagging and his expression blank. "I never wanted to be part of this horrible life. I was deeper than I thought I could ever be and then it was way too late. There was no way out. I became a thug and an assassin by name." He blew out a breath and ran his hands through his hair. "A few years back, I tried to run away, but when Nikola's men caught up with me, they taught me a lesson that I would never forget. He gave me another chance, but he said that if I ever tried that again, he would be sending me to the morgue. Death was the only way out for me, so go on and get it over with," he said, closing his eyes and pressing his lips together. "I don't want to hurt people anymore. I don't want to see the pain on people's faces when they lose their loved ones. I hate this life, and I hate myself." He stopped talking for a short moment and opened his eyes to face Sebastian.

"I was envious of you, Gaulle. Yes, I was envious of you and your life. Free to love and free to be the man you want to be. I wanted the same for Georgiana and me, but I never dared to let her know how I felt. I was afraid to bring her into my world. The world that is muddy revolting, filled with crime and sadness." He pulled Georgiana around to face him and wrapped her in his arms.

It was as if the world faded away and he was alone in that room with Georgiana. He held her gaze and, bending down, he locked their lips in a scorching kiss. When he pulled back, there were tears in his eyes. "Georgiana, I love you. I have loved you from the very first moment I laid eyes on you, but I was afraid to tell you. You are so innocent, so beautiful, and I'm not the man for you. Remember that I will always love you." He bent down once again and locked their lips together. He then pulled back smiled tenderly and pushed her aside. "All right, Sebastian, I'm ready." He closed his eyes and remained still.

"NO!" Georgiana screamed, stepping forward and dropping to her knees in front of Sebastian. "No, please don't hurt him." She sobbed hard.

Strong arms gripped her gently and pulled her to her feet. Sebastian's eyes were soft, even tender. "Don't worry, Georgiana. I'm not going to harm Rainer."

Rainer's eyes snapped open as he stared at Sebastian rooted in place, lost for words. "But…" his voice trailed. "I was responsible for Arielle's abduction."

Sebastian nodded. "I know. I also know that you gave strict instructions for her not to be touched."

Rainer's eyes widened. "How do you know?"

"I know."

Rainer glanced around and gulped at the sight of all the broken, lifeless bodies. He was not prepared for this. "You mean you're letting me go?"

Sebastian strode into the room and stood in front of Rainer. "Take Georgiana and go away from here. Somewhere when you can build a new life together."

Rainer was astonished. He had never envisioned this type of outcome. "But they will find me. And when they do, they'll kill us both," Rainer said anxiously.

"No, they will not."

"But how?"

"Rainer, you're wasting precious time."

The confusion and desperation in Rainer's eyes made Sebastian stop for a moment. "All right, if you really must know, in the next few minutes, there will be no one left that will know you or your association with this organization."

The hard intake of breath told Sebastian that Rainer understood the meaning of his words and the reality made him shiver. He swallowed hard. "I don't know how to thank you," Rainer said. "I owe you my life."

Sebastian smiled and placed a hand on his shoulder. He was amused by Rainer's stunned expression.

"Are you leaving St. Petersburg?" Rainer asked.

"Not just yet, but I should be on my way shortly."

"Thank you," Rainer murmured and, grasping Georgiana's hand, he pulled her toward the door. He never felt so alive. Georgiana sent Sebastian a warm smile of appreciation. He watched them go, feeling pleased with the results.

He heard their footstep rushing down the hallway and chuckled. He glanced at his watch and was shocked to find that only thirty minutes had passed. He fished his phone out of his pocket and texted his friends. "Are you all finished?"

The reply was unanimous. "We are heading home." He smiled into the screen, and closing it shut; he slipped it back into his jean pocket. He was pleased. He made a quick sweep at Nikola and Rainer's buildings. He was finally rid of one bad nightmare, and he felt vindicated. His plan had been executed successfully. His fear of the Russian Mafia harming Arielle had washed away as he stepped out onto the pavement. He was on his way back to Brighton by five-fifteen.

Sebastian arrived home, reeling from his encounter with the St. Petersburg lot. His mind was consumed by thoughts of Arielle. All he wanted was to hold her and let her know that she was safe. His heart soared as he came through the door and she fell right into his arms.

"Oh, Sebastian... where have you been? Everyone else is already here. Are you all right?"

"I'm fine," he said gently. He raised his hand to her face and pushed a lock of hair behind her ear. He then tenderly brushed her cheek with his fingers. Her eyes burned stormy and passionate. Her face was soft, warm to his touch. He moved his other hand at her back to enfold her waist and pulled her hard against his body possessively. Her body did unfathomable things to his mind. Without another word, he bent down, and with his tongue, he traced the softness of her lips before he angled his head and plunged inside to taste the sweetness of her mouth. A low growl sounded deep in his throat.

Arielle pulled back letting out a soft gasp. "Our friends are here," she whispered.

Sebastian suppressed a groan and pressed a soft kiss on her lips before he let her go. Clasping her hand, he pulled her toward the study.

Their friends had assembled in there joined now by Gabrielle, Eva, and Paul. They came together to celebrate the successful outcome of the venture and to enjoy each other's company before they left for home. Sebastian looked around the room and his gaze swept over each face. "I want to thank you for your help and to let you know that if you ever need me, I will be by your side, no questions asked."

The immortals enjoyed tall glasses of salve. Arielle, Gabrielle, and Paul each took a glass of wine and joined the group.

As the end of the evening drew near, their friends took their leave. The immortals informed Sebastian and Troy that they were not going to spend the night at their homes. They had plans of their own, and when finished, they would be heading home. Hugs and handshakes were in abundance as the group started filing through the doorway.

Sebastian slid his hand around Arielle's waist and pulled her to his side. They waved goodbye. Finally, the last car drove away, and Sebastian pushed the door shut. He yanked Arielle closer until there was no space left between their bodies. He angled his head and closed his mouth over hers, sinking deeper with passion into the kiss. Arielle quivered beneath him, and parting her lips; she let him invade the softness of her mouth. She tasted like honey and sweet wine. Sebastian broke the kiss, and swooping down; he swung her into his arms. "We're going to bed," he murmured anxiously.

Arielle wrapped her arms around his nape and drew his mouth back down to hers. Sebastian felt himself being swept away by her passion. His wits were reeling with anticipation. "You're mine for eternity," he whispered against her lips.

Arielle giggled as jolts of pleasure shot through every fiber of her body. She pulled back slightly and gazed intensely into the emerald pools of his eyes. This amazing man was hers and hers alone. Sebastian set her on the bed and, seconds after, his warm limbs enfolded her. Their encounter was powerful, and the eruption sent them to an alternate universe where they were alone body and soul, lost in the utter pleasure. Slowly, they drifted back to earth and fell into a peaceful and serene sleep.

Many hours later, she opened her eyes and found herself tightly held in his possessive embrace. He was still fast asleep. His long powerful legs tangled with hers, keeping her close to his warm body. He looked so peaceful and so breathtakingly gorgeous. She stared at his strikingly sculptured face that she so utterly adored. She let out an inward sigh, and her gaze moved slowly from his tousled sandy hair to his perfect nose and down to the lips that promised passion, desire, and pure sin. The warmth of his body sent an enticing shiver down her spine that made her blood throb through her veins. She was his, and he was hers, and there was nothing more beyond that point. Pleasure coiled as she thought of their earlier encounter. She lifted her hand and ran her finger across his bottom lip and closed her eyes in complete contentment.

"Good morning, love."

Arielle jerked her eyes open and fell right into a pair of dark green eyes filled with amusement. His voice was low and seductive, his lips touching hers and his tongue licking her lower lip.

"Can I help you?" he said chuckling.

"Um…no," Arielle replied, a wide smile painted across her lips.

He moved fast, rolling and taking her with him to land fully on top of her, his morning erection pressing against her abdomen.

"Aaaa!" she shrieked. "Sebastian! Stop doing that."

"Doing what, love?"

"Moving in that immortal way of yours. It always scares me half to death."

"I was eager," he chuckled out loud and moved suggestively against her so she could feel his want. Arielle smiled, letting his seductiveness seize her and bond her to his endless hunger.

His body surged over hers, and he dipped his head to brush his lips against hers. The smell of freesia in her hair, made him quiver. Arielle's eyes smoldered with uncontrolled desire, as his lips came down on hers with startling vigor. With his tongue, he coaxed her lips apart and plunged into the softness of her mouth like a thirsty man in a desert searching for relief. He reeled in her taste and passion ripped through his body like wild fire as the kiss intensified. He palmed her breasts with his hands and kneaded softly. Sensation built higher and higher, and she let out a low moan. She flexed her spine, with a loud moan, and pushed her upper body against his hands. Every nerve, every inch of her wanted him like never before.

He was now fully on top of her, pressing her softly onto the bed. He gazed down at her and smiled in a warm, passionate way, ready to take what was his. He wedged his knee between her thighs and he took her mouth in another hot throbbing kiss. Their tongues twisted and entwined, but it was obvious that they needed more. They were hungry for each other.

His hands moved over her soft skin like a pianist's hands over the piano keys. She moaned into his mouth, and he growled with anticipation. His lips skimmed across her jaw line down to her collarbone, pressing against the base of her throat. This was Sebastian's favorite spot. He reveled at the pulse of her heartbeat. It gave his immortal soul pleasure beyond any measure. He soon ducked his head and set his mouth onto one hard nipple teasing, suckling and lapping, sending hot waves of desire through every pore in her body. He then moved the other breast, and she nearly came off the bed. The intoxication he was spreading across her veins was utterly wild. He suddenly moved fast and hard and drove deep into her, leaving her gasping for breath.

Arielle marveled at this strength and, pressing inexorably upward; she matched his strong thrusts. A low growl sounded deep in Sebastian's throat as he reached the absolute end of his control. Sharp waves of sensation slid across his muscles, and the heat that was radiating from her drove him to absolute madness. Sebastian hissed in a breath and pressed their bodies tighter together.

"Open your eyes, Arielle. I want to see your eyes," Sebastian murmured.

Arielle opened her eyes just enough to gaze into his mossy, burning gaze. Her body arched slightly, and she locked her legs around his hips as they clung to each other with urgency and passion. Her nails dug into his back, and their breathing grew ragged, strained until they shattered as euphoric waves fractured reality into shards. They were seized and thrust beyond reality into a magnificent, timeless universe. He collapsed on top of her, unable to move. Her heart was pounding her chest like a sledgehammer, and she let out a primal gasp. Arielle welcomed his weight, held entranced by the aftermath. Slowly, their minds came back to reality, and they lay quietly wrapped around each other. Before he rolled onto his back, taking her with him, he bent down and pressed a soft, gentle kiss on her lips.

"I love you, Arielle."

Arielle snuggled up beside him, leaning her head onto his shoulder. "I love you, too, Sebastian."

Sebastian reached down and pulled the covers over them. He

slipped his arm around her protectively and gathered her closer. "We are nearing our wedding day," he whispered.

"I know," Arielle said and moved even closer to his masculine body.

"I'll be honored beyond reason to take you as my wife, Miss Lloyd—my Lizzy—in front of God, family, and friends."

"Are you sure, Darcy?" she asked, meeting his gaze.

"What do you mean, 'am I sure'?"

She could clearly read the alarm in his eyes. Arielle giggled, and her lips were on his. The kiss was gentle, full of love and appreciation for the man lying next to her. "I was only joking, Sebastian."

He gave her a playful squeeze, and she sighed with unfathomable happiness. A long life of nirvana next to this incredible man was but a dream.

"Um…I don't want to become too excited," she said. "We still have this grueling semester to go through. And then another few weeks for the holidays to be over."

"Oh, it will be but a breeze. Time will go by in a blink of an eye."

"What in the world does that mean?"

Sebastian propped himself on his elbow and stared down at her. "What?"

"Why do people say 'in a blink of an eye'?' Nothing happens in a blink of an eye. I think it's a rubbish metaphor."

"Do you want to argue about it? Or do you want to get up and take a shower with me?" he questioned playfully. He ducked his head and pressed a soft kiss on her lips.

"I'd rather spend the day in bed—*with you.*"

"Would you now?" his question but a whisper.

"Yes."

"Well, you won't have an argument from me." He lay back down and folded his hands beneath his head. "What do you want to do?" he asked, amusement coding his voice.

"I just want to spend the day alone with you." She rolled to her side and touched her lips to his throat. Sebastian moaned, a deep sound of utter pleasure.

"I can spend eternity in bed with you, baby," he breathed against her lips.

Arielle fought the shockwave of pleasure that threatened to consume her. She had found her Darcy and her dream was becoming true.

They spent practically the whole day in bed. Between hot encounters that left them spent, lost in raw gratification, they chatted about school, the upcoming holidays, and the wonderful details of their wedding that was coming up next year.

Arielle and her friends endured the grueling classes for several weeks until the autumn semester ended in mid-December. Christmas was approaching, and winter crept over the grounds. The city fell into the traditional spirit of peace and humanity. Every store and every home were decked with decorations, festoons of holly, and mistletoe. The sparkling, vibrant lights made the city look spectacular.

Arielle and Sebastian enjoyed putting the finishing touches on their own Christmas tree. They spend time with their friends during the week before Christmas, horseback riding and experiencing the joys of winter and the crisp air. Riding a horse against the wind was nothing short of breathtaking. They enjoyed clubbing, Christmas shopping, and exchanging gifts. The girls had fun sitting around the fireplace and roasting marshmallows while chatting happily and laughing carelessly about every little thing important and unimportant, something the immortals found quite entertaining.

Arielle's parents held their annual Christmas dinner party with all the trimmings. Every year seemed to be getting bigger and better. This Christmas was symbolic for the three girls and their best friend, Paul. Next year, each one of them would be marrying their beloved immortal.

On Christmas day, Sebastian surprised Arielle by enjoying the traditional cup of chocolate with her before they gave each other their gifts. Sebastian's gifts to Arielle were once again over the top. Arielle had given up trying to keep him from showering her with extravagant presents a long time ago. All she wanted was to be this stunning immortal man's wife. She felt drunk with overwhelming pleasure at the thought of their wedding day.

Annabel invaded her thoughts in spurts, creating a stinging in the back of her eyes and an intense dry feeling in her throat. She couldn't understand why the bitter immortal woman had just disappeared. What was she plotting? One thing she was sure of, Annabel would not give up, not until she had made sure that she destroyed Arielle and Sebastian's happiness. She had to be preparing something truly treacherous, but what? *Oh God! Please do not let her show up on my wedding day.* Eternity would be soon enough to have to see her again.

Time flew by just as Sebastian said it would, like rushing waters of a river. Another year was gone! January arrived, the beginning of a splendid year that was to be filled with wedding plans, joyful adventures, aches of two more grueling semesters, and exam results still to come. But it was the year of graduation and the year of their weddings, so those were huge pluses in the whole equation.

 *Chapter 20*

THE YEAR of three glorious weddings left Arielle thrilled about each one of them, but she was most ecstatic about her wedding day with the man of her dreams, *her Darcy*. It was hard for her to believe that this amazing man, this incredible immortal, was going to be her husband.

Eva wanted a late June wedding; Gabrielle had decided on a July date, and Arielle — of course — had to have the wedding in the month that she first set eyes on the man that fit the blueprint of her life's quest, August. She was excited that the plans were going to work out well, making it possible for the three of them to be part of each other's wedding without being stressed over the length of their honeymoons. This was extraordinary as they had been best friends and more like sisters all of their lives.

They made an agreement that they weren't going to assign titles such as maid of honor or bridesmaids because they couldn't pick one over the other. The agreement was that the four of them, including Loren, were going to be involved and stand by each other on that special day, and that made them exceptionally happy.

School started mid-January again. Gabrielle and Ian had another six years to fulfill their dream of becoming successful surgeons. Eva had to wait for five or six years to fully qualify as an attorney-at-law. Paul and Arielle were in for two additional years to receive their MDs.

Troy and Sebastian had decided to devote their time to the business and let them move on with their education.

Loren had decided to keep Paul happy, so she was going to put herself through more boring classes. The girl held several degrees, and she certainly didn't need any more education, but love conquered all. Arielle was happy to see Paul content, even though his father's infidelities and their family secrets were now splashed all over the newspapers. Arielle was sure that if it weren't for Loren, this span of time would have been dark for Paul.

Gabby, Eva, and Arielle were quite busy with homework and attending classes every day, but they took every spare moment they had and every weekend to work on their wedding plans, including the wedding dresses.

They made a list of items and decided to prioritize according to their importance and urgency. They placed a small box next to each item, planning to check it off as it was accomplished. Three items on the top of the list had already been checked off.

The first was the church, which was an easy choice. Their families had been linked to the parish for as long as they could remember. The second item was the reception location, and their parents had arranged those to be held at their country club on the designated dates. The third item was the photographer, who was a family friend and had produced all the family portraits over the years, making that an easy selection as well.

Loren was always welcomed in their group segments as her input was faultless. Her taste in clothes was astounding, and her family's connections to the fashion world were like something out of a storybook. The four of them spent hours at a time visiting bookstores, selecting wedding books and bridal magazines, and trying to learn how to plan their weddings successfully.

All three decided on the same wedding planner that would provide them with professional advice on the menu, the flowers, and the cake that would complement their parents' budgets. They would also coordinate the rehearsal and organize things the day of the wedding. All the other little things were going to be handled by them. Doing this together made it a whole lot easier and they didn't feel overwhelmed with the planning process.

The school was taking a lot of their time, but they were so excited that they didn't stop meeting and planning every moment available. By March, they already had ordered elegant invitations.

Eva chose her invitations in ivory silk paper with a matching translucent wrap and script print. Gabrielle chose a romantic cupid graphic design on cream textured paper trimmed with a strip of luxurious satin ribbon, and Arielle chose an elegant sweeping filigree design in black on soft bone color silk paper inscribed in sixteenth-century style calligraphy.

The guest wedding books were another item that they were very excited about. They were to be handmade from fine leather with their names engraved on the top left corner, and the pages were off-white soft bond paper. They picked the same flower vendor, and they each made a list of the flowers they loved and the colors of their wedding themes.

The wedding gifts to each other would have to remain a secret to be a surprise for each one of them on their special day. They chose the music, and they were not surprised that their taste was so similar. The menu and cake were chosen with their husbands-to-be, and that was a separate endeavor and quite a laughable matter since Sebastian, Troy, Ian, and Eva couldn't care less about food.

Arielle was extremely happy to hear that they all decided on writing their own vows. She knew she couldn't wait to tell Sebastian how he changed her life, and she was sure her friends felt the same way about their future grooms.

The only thing that remained open was their wedding dress, and, God, that was going to be the hardest thing to decide on.

Loren told them that she already had manifested her wedding dress way before she met Paul. She had attended the wedding of Princess Sofia Magdalena of Denmark to King Gustaf III in 1771, and she fell in love with her dress. She manifested something similar to that, and one of these days, she was going to take them to the Dillon estate and let them see it. They could hardly wait, as it would have to be something magnificent. They were going to have their mothers involved with their wedding gowns but not just yet.

On a weekend, the girls decided to go shopping for wedding magazines; the guys spent the morning playing golf. When they returned, they found the men sprawled in the library watching sports on the telly. Sebastian, Troy, Ian, and Paul had become very close, and their friendship was a welcome gift to the four girls. They didn't want to disturb them, so they gathered in the kitchen to go through the magazines and make plans. Completely absorbed on those beautiful designs, they were startled to hear Loren's voice break the silence.

"Do you know how the custom of placing the wedding ring on the third finger of the left hand started?" They stared at her without having a clue.

"Do you?" Arielle asked inquisitively.

Loren chuckled softly and said, "In the ancient days, people believed that the third finger of the left hand had a special vein called vena amoris, the 'vein of love,' that ran from the finger directly to the heart. King Edward VI declared that the third finger of the left hand must be designated as the 'official' ring finger. In 1549, the Book of Common Prayer sealed the deal with the designation of the left hand as the marriage hand."

"Oh, Loren, that's a beautiful story..." said Eva, and they all gazed down at their stunning engagement rings. Christmas day, Paul had given a gorgeous ring to Loren, promising to love her for the rest of his life. She was now standing mesmerized along with her friends, watching her beautiful ring with a wide smile spread across her magnificent face.

"Eva, are you going to manifest your dress or are you going shopping with us?" Gabrielle asked.

"I have a specific vision of my dress, and it will not be cheap, so I know that I'll have to manifest it if I'm going to have exactly what I want within my mother's budget." She laughed out loud, and they joined in. "I know that my mum has been waiting for the mother-daughter gown shopping day so eagerly, and I can't disappoint her. I have decided to go through the motions with her. Later, after I cancel the order, I'll tell her that I made a few changes to the design, and I know she'll be happy."

"Well…listen to you…you have it all planned out. I never thought of you as this sneaky," Arielle said, laughing. Immediately, her face changed to a more thoughtful expression.

"I'll have to be careful with the dress I pick," she said, voice extremely serious. "I don't want this dress to become a huge expense for my parents. I already know that the expenses for the wedding, like renting the country club for the night, the flowers, and the photographer, are overwhelming. I'll have to keep all that in mind while I make my selection."

"Me, too…" Gabrielle agreed with a soft voice.

"Girls…" Loren said. "Eva and I can manifest your dresses at no expense," she exclaimed, voice completely amused.

"No, Loren," Arielle said firmly. "I appreciate your offer. However, I'd rather purchase my dress. I feel this will make the wedding seem more real, as marrying an incredible immortal seems to be so unbelievable." Arielle chuckled under her breath, and she saw Gabrielle nodding in agreement.

"You seem a little worried," Loren went on.

"I'm not worried. I'm only trying to make good decisions," Arielle said.

"Arielle, you're my sister now, and you know that I can help," Loren said again.

"Thank you, Loren, but no. I'm going to do this the human way." She gave Loren a hug to show her that she loved her and appreciated her suggestion to help her with the dress.

Their attention now turned to Eva. They knew that Eva's wedding would end up being just like a royal wedding since she and Ian could manifest everything they wanted and make it extraordinary.

It was late at night when they finally left the house, and Arielle was exhausted. She jumped into the shower, and she wasn't surprised that he was there ahead of her, waiting to hold her in his warm embrace. They let the hot water caress their bodies as his lips brushed her ear and slowly moved across her cheek down her throat, and she closed her eyes surrendering in his arms. She let out a soft sigh and closed her eyes.

"What is it, baby?"

"Nothing. I'm just a little tired."

His arms squeezed her tighter as his lips found hers and locked them into a fervent kiss. "I'm so happy to see you planning the wedding. I don't think I have ever felt excitement like this before. I find myself unable to wait any longer."

Arielle chuckled. She lifted her head up and gazed into his beautiful emerald eyes. He did appear completely jubilant.

"Are you sure you want to marry me?" she asked in a playful manner.

"Right now would be my preference," he said with sparkling eyes.

They finished their shower and, slipping under the covers, became quite comfortable.

"How are you doing with your classes?" he asked.

"I'm doing a whole lot better than I thought I would." She smiled softly.

"I'm not surprised; you're very smart,"

Arielle smiled as she turned and pressed her lips at the hollow of his throat, and she heard him moan eagerly.

"Have you and your parents made a decision about the church?" he asked.

"Yes, that wasn't something that took a lot of thought. My family, as well as Gabrielle and Eva's, have been members of the same parish for as far back as I can remember. The vicar is a family friend at the Church of Saint Nicholas of Myra. It's the oldest surviving building in Brighton and the original parish."

"It sounds very intriguing."

"It's a gorgeous church with a lot of history behind it."

"What type of history?" he asked inquisitively.

"Well, this church has ten bells, and what's pretty interesting about that is that they were established a very long time ago to ring when important visitors such as monarchs or other members of the

Royal Family came to the town; a series of tablets preserved at the base of the ringing chamber give details of each 'special occasion' on which the bells were rung."

"It sounds like it will be a beautiful church for the wedding," he murmured. He pulled her closer and brushed his lips across her shoulder.

"There's also a very heartwarming love story that has been documented, and it's linked to this church,"

"Oh…a love story? I would love to hear it," he whispered. He snuggled up closer to her body, turned the light off, and encircled her in his warm embrace.

Arielle turned to face him and waited a couple of moments while her eyes were adjusted to the darkness. She could clearly see the outline of his face but not the detail of his beautiful features. She leaned in and kissed him softly with a long deep sigh. "This story is a factual love story," she said, keeping her lips on his.

"I can hardly wait," he said.

"Phoebe Hessel, a famous eighteenth- and nineteenth-century resident of Brighton is buried in the church cemetery. The story goes that she fell madly in love with a soldier, William Golding, at the age of fifteen. Against her family's objections, she disguised herself as a man and enlisted alongside William in the British Army after he was sent overseas. They had vowed to be together until the day they died. She concealed her sex so effectively that she served for seventeen years until she voluntarily revealed the truth to her commanding officer's wife, and she was discharged. She was not discovered even after she suffered a wounded arm at the Battle of Fontenoy in 1745 and was treated at an army hospital.

"They loved each other so very much that they would do absolutely anything just to be by each other's side. She became a well-known figure after moving to Brighton following the death of Golding in 1762 and lived to be one hundred and eight years old. Prince Regent granted her a special pension and she was invited by him to be part of the parade during his coronation as King George IV."

"That's an amazing story, but I don't think William loved her half as much as I love you," he whispered. His lips brushed against her ear making her shiver.

"Sebastian, I've never asked you about your religion. Do you want to talk about it?"

"I was raised Catholic, but I'm not a good Catholic." He chuckled.

"Oh...but how interesting is that? I'm Catholic, too," she said, and he laughed, quite amused.

"I'd love you no matter what you are," he said, pulling her closer, and his mouth landed on hers in pure hunger. His next statement left her totally stunned.

"How would you like to fly to Paris to select your wedding gown?"

"What?" She was taken aback.

"I'd love to have you visit some of the designer studios in Paris and see all their gowns and decide on what you'd like to wear on *our* wedding day." He emphasized the word *our*.

"Are you serious?"

"Absolutely, I've been a guest along with my mother and Loren at many big designer's fashion shows, and they have become very good friends of the family. They provide an exquisite and unexpected mix of designs that would give you a large amount to choose from."

"But...um...that sounds amazing, but I don't think I should do that," she said feeling uneasy.

"Why not?"

"Sebastian, my parents, have a set budget for the wedding, and I'm sure those gowns are extremely expensive. Therefore, I don't want to create an uncomfortable situation for them."

"Arielle, please listen to me."

She rolled over and stared at him in clear wonder. "What?"

He held her affectionately and went on. "I know that I've made a point of never talking about money with you. I find it necessary that we discuss this issue now. I want to take care of you because I'm a very wealthy man. I want you to have the wedding of your dreams, and I'm not going to accept any push back from you. I already stopped by your parent's house, and we had a long talk about this wedding. I explained to them how I feel about this whole thing and that I want to be part of it. I don't care about what the traditions are and who is to pay for what. I want you to have everything you want without worrying about money."

Arielle was in utter shock. She sat up, and reaching over; she turned the light on. She wanted to be able to gaze into his eyes. She couldn't believe what she was hearing.

"What did they say?" she asked, after a short pause.

"Well, my suggestion was strongly rejected by your father several times, but I think I tired him down with my persistence, and so he gave in. You mother was too shocked to talk." He chuckled softly. Arielle pushed her hair away from her face and remained silent. "I love you, Arielle. You're everything to me," he said, watching her carefully.

"You discussed the wedding expenses with my parents, and they are okay with you paying for my dress?" she asked, a little loudly this time. She was now shaking her head in pure disbelief.

"I didn't say they were okay with it. What I said was that I convinced them that my desire to give you what you want would mean the world to me. They weren't easy to persuade, but they finally gave up because I wasn't going to leave their house without their approval. Your father knows how much I love you and how much this means to me, so they both agreed, and now I want you to say yes."

Arielle was speechless. She felt moisture in her eyes, completely moved by his offer. "But why?" She was still shocked with his amazing generosity.

"Because it makes me happy to make you happy," he said.

Arielle raised her hands and wiped her eyes, fighting the urge to cry openly. She reached over and stroked his face and ran her finger around his beautiful lip line. His lips curved up into that immortal magical smile that he always kept just for her, and she fell apart. *God! He is so gorgeous.* She still couldn't believe he was going to be her husband. She turned the light off and lay back down, remaining silent.

"I love you, baby," he murmured. "Will you accept my present?" He pulled her close to him and held her tightly.

"You make it very difficult to refuse." She barely finished her sentence before he crushed her lips beneath his in a fevered kiss.

"Say yes," he whispered without leaving the kiss.

"Yes," she said and closed her eyes in pure contentment.

"Tomorrow you're taking a short trip with me," he said as he pulled back from the kiss gasping for air.

"Where?"

"Paris," he said and kissed her again. He held her softly as he closed his eyes and smiled in sheer bliss.

"Paris! Tomorrow!" she exclaimed.

"You're mine," he whispered. She stayed in his warm embrace and drifted to sleep. Sebastian stayed awake for a little while longer. His gaze swept over her beautiful face. Possessiveness had never felt so solid. He had never wanted anything or anyone as much as he wanted Arielle. She was going to be a never ending desire, a sheer joy in his limitless life.

He drew breath and pulling his gaze away from her face he stared at the ceiling. He chuckled at the thought of the elaborations he, Ian, and Troy had made to their wedding details. Paul, on the other hand, would enjoy the normal tradition as Loren was handling everything for their important day.

Sebastian had read Arielle's mind and discovered the names of the wedding coordinator, the flower company, and the photographer that the girls chose to handle their weddings. He, Ian, and Troy visited each one of them — including the country club — and made extraordinary agreements that left even the vendors shocked.

They were to keep their visit and their agreement private from the Lloyds, the Taylors, and Mrs. Winters. They were to charge the families a very small, reasonable amount for their services. The immortals, in turn, left very generous deposits to cover the excess cost. The weddings would have to be extraordinary, and they were to provide an extravagant type of services.

The excitement between the three immortals had been quite infectious. They were going to keep the details a secret never to be shared with Arielle, Eva, and Gabby.

Sebastian lay in bed, his arms were wrapped around what he considered his most essential treasure. Arielle was fast asleep, her warm breath brushing against his chest, sending shivers of pleasure along his spine. He pulled her closer, gazed down at her, passion flaring in his eyes. She was utterly beautiful. He reined back his self-control that could shatter at any moment. She was the most desirable woman he ever set eyes on. He wanted to kiss her until she would forget everything else in the world but him. She had taken center stage in every facet of his life. He nuzzled her hair and sighed contentedly as he drifted to sleep.

# *Chapter 21*

A **BRIGHT SUN RAY** peeked into the room through the curtains and brushed across their sleepy faces. Sebastian opened his eyelids and fell into the sapphire ocean of Arielle's eyes.

"Good morning, Lizzy! Did you sleep well?" Sebastian whispered. He leaned in and pressed a soft kiss on her lips.

"Mmmm. Good morning, Darcy!" she murmured back, and rolling away from his embrace, she stretched leisurely.

"We have to leave soon," Sebastian said quietly.

Her eyes shot open wide, and she sat up in bed anxiously. She clenched her fingers around the sheet and giggled with pleasure. "We're going to Paris!" she squealed and fell back on the bed, kicking her feet like a little kid overwhelmed with delight.

"Yes, we are," Sebastian, replied softly. Pulled her toward him and kissed the tip of her nose.

She took a sharp breath and shot out of his arms and out of bed like lightning. "I'm going to take a shower. I'll be ready shortly."

She ran to the bathroom and jumped into the shower. "Aaaaaa!!!" She let out a scream as strong hands wrapped around her body and held her tightly.

"Not without me," Sebastian whispered against her ear.

"Sebastian, honestly, one of these days, I will have a heart attack, and you will feel sad. You have to stop moving at supersonic speed. It scares me," she admonished him playfully.

"Sorry, baby, I can't help myself," he snickered.

It was not a fast shower, as Arielle thought it would be. It turned out to be a slow encounter filled with steamy passion that suspended every thought she ever had and left her gasping for air while trying to grip onto reality. Sebastian was a tireless immortal with over five hundred years of experience that had one promise to keep, and that made Arielle happy for eternity. Gazing at the expression on her face he smiled wide knowing she was deliriously ecstatic. They dressed in blissful silence.

Soon they were in the car heading to the airport. It was the same private airport gate they used the night of her birthday.

"The private jet again?" she gasped; he just chuckled but remained silent. "We're going to Paris?" she asked.

"Yes," he said, face serious, eyes glittering.

"Good morning, Sis..." She heard Loren's happy voice just as she entered the plane.

"Loren...What? Hmm..." Eyes wide open lost for words. Gabrielle, Troy, and Loren were sitting in the cabin, smiling at her. It took a while to understand what was happening, but once they explained, she could hardly contain her enthusiasm.

"Gabrielle, did you know about this?"

"No, Troy told me late last night. I wasn't to ask any questions until we arrived here. I was quite surprised."

"Who owns the jet?" Gabby asked, gazing between Arielle and Loren.

"Sebastian, of course," Loren replied, and Gabby's mouth dropped.

"You have a plane?" she asked, turning toward Sebastian.

"He has four," Loren chimed in again.

Gabby's jaw dropped, and Arielle flinched at Loren's statement. She stared at Sebastian with wide eyes.

"You have four planes?" Arielle's expression was that of disbelief.

"That's just a drop in the ocean," said Loren giggling.

"What do you mean?" Arielle demanded, glancing at Loren uneasily.

"Loren, stop," Sebastian said, glaring at his sister.

"She's going to be your wife, Sebastian. She should know who you are." Arielle was now gazing at him in utter shock.

"There is more?"

"A hell of a lot more," Loren said, still laughing as she stood up, moved over, hugged her brother in a loving manner, and gave him a huge kiss on the cheek. "Don't be mad at me, dear brother. I love Arielle, and she needs to know all about you."

"She knows all about me," he whispered, watching Arielle carefully. "She knows exactly who I am and how I feel about her. Money isn't something that would make any difference in our relationship."

Loren went back, taking her seat, and this time, she stayed quiet. Arielle rested her eyes on his beautiful face and smiled softly. He was right; she didn't care about what he had. All she cared about was that this beautiful man loved her and wanted to be her husband.

"I'm a little puzzled about something," she said. Sebastian waited for her question with a soft smile. "If you have all these planes, why do you fly with regular airlines when you have to go somewhere?"

He smiled again and replied slowly, "The planes are to be used by my executives to conduct business around the world. If they are available, I use them. If not, I fly just like everyone else. Today, this plane is in London and available, so here we are." He chuckled.

"That's if he wants to use a plane at all," Loren added and broke into a soft laughter. Gabrielle and Arielle were trying to absorb the reality of her statement. Immortals could move around the world at an amazing speed, without using human transportation. That wasn't something they could wrap their minds around. This was something beyond credence.

Arielle was lost in her thoughts. She felt his hand on her, and he pressed softly, making her face him.

"What are you thinking?"

"Oh, I was thinking about how incredible you all are. You can come and go anywhere, anyway, anyhow you choose without any constrains created by humans. That must be an exhilarating feeling," she murmured and pressed her lips together. He didn't say anything; he just pinched the tip of his nose, as if he was troubled by something, but he remained silent.

The plane landed in Paris, and soon they were on the way to somewhere unknown to her and Gabby. The luxury limousine drove leisurely through the city and arrived at Rue du Faubourg Saint-Honore.

"Here is the pulse of Paris design and fashion," Loren exclaimed. "This is the Faubourg Saint-Honore district. All you see is a narrow but ultra-coveted artery of the French couture. Most of the great designer boutiques are located here."

"Is this where we are going?" Arielle asked quietly. Loren looked at Gabrielle and Arielle with a wide smile spread across her face.

"No, Sebastian, Troy, and I just wanted to show you the place that you both might want to visit when you come back to Paris with your mothers and search for your wedding gowns. That is if you don't find something at the place we are going right now." Arielle and Gabrielle stared out the window and grabbed each other's hand in sheer excitement.

"Right now, we are going to Nemours, a small town about fifty-seven kilometers away from the city to a seventeenth-century mill-turned design studio called 'Cymbeline Paris.' Sisters Evelyne, Chantal, and Monique Joubert created it almost forty years ago, and it's on the top of the list for brides all over the world," Sebastian said in his velvety voice. "I want you to meet some of our friends and see some of the most beautiful wedding gowns in the world." His tone was a matter of fact while Gabrielle and Arielle were still gasping in clear shock. They seemed to walk in a fog as Sebastian and Troy kept their arms around them and held them close, giving them all the details about each individual they met. They spent an amazing day meeting people and going through some of the most stunning gowns they had ever seen. They couldn't wait to come back home and tell Eva about this trip. On the way to the limo, Arielle thanked Sebastian one more time.

"All I want to do is make you happy," he murmured. His lips found hers and held her to a soft kiss as she heard Loren chuckle.

Soon they were on their way home. At the airport, they thanked
Loren again for coming along. She climbed into her car and waved at
them, calling out, "See you Monday at school!"

Gabrielle and Arielle hugged each other for a long time, unable to
wipe smiles from their faces, making Sebastian and Troy very happy.
The guys shook hands, and they parted.

On the way to the car, Arielle leaned in and whispered softly,
"Sebastian, everything you are doing for me is like a dream come true,
but it feels extremely uncharacteristic of me to use your money."

"Arielle, I want you to promise right now that you won't bring
this up ever again. You're going to be my wife, and what I have will
be yours, and what you have will be mine."

"But I've nothing to give you but my little Volvo still sitting in
the garage," she laughed softly.

"Oh...But...You...Do..." He uttered the words slowly with an
amused voice. She looked at him inquisitively, and she saw a wide
smile curve his lips.

"What are you referring to?" she asked, pretending not to
understand what he meant. He just laughed out loud, and taking her
hand; he pressed on the gas. She was completely exhausted by the time
they went to bed, and after getting comfortable in his arms, she fell
asleep before her head hit the pillow. Sebastian chuckled as he gazed at
her sleepy face and pulled her body close to his and closed his eyes.

He was sure that he would never be able to sleep peacefully ever
again if he couldn't feel the warmth of her body against his. She was
perfect. She was what made the blood pulse in his veins. Her heart's
rhythm gave his life the tranquility that he never knew. He was
overwhelmed with love for this human girl.

The next day, Arielle called her friends to invite them to spend some
time together and see a film. Arielle didn't call Loren because she knew
that she was taking Paul to her parents' house. When everyone was
there, Arielle and Gabrielle couldn't wait to tell Eva all about Paris.
They were stunned to find out that Eva and Ian knew all the details

about their trip way before they knew about it. They both wondered why their guys couldn't give them a little clue before they boarded the plane.

Gabrielle walked over to Troy and sat on his lap. She wrapped her arms around his neck, and leaning in; she pressed her lips to his. Troy pulled her to him, extremely pleased with her gesture. She sank into his embrace, and their lips met again, infusing Troy with her warmth, and he shifted uncomfortably.

Arielle knew that Gabby had him hot and bothered, especially when they heard his soft moan. Immortals were sexually oriented creatures with a very short fuse. In this room, there were only two humans and four immortals, so it was no surprise that Gabrielle would have to move away from Troy quickly.

"Why couldn't you tell me about Paris and the fact that you prearranged this with Sebastian?" Gabrielle asked with glittering eyes.

"I wanted it to be a surprise, and from what I saw, it was," he laughed softly and coughed a couple of times, trying to clear his throat. He pushed Gabrielle gently, trying to nudge her off of his lap, but she seemed to enjoy his difficulty. She wouldn't budge.

Arielle now couldn't hold back laughter and Eva joined her. Troy put his arms around Gabrielle and lifted her into his embrace. He rose to his feet, put her down, and pressed his lips to hers.

"You need to stop," he whispered. Gabby laughed with delight.

She left his embrace and walked over to where Arielle and Eva were sitting. Troy's face was flushed, trying to suppress his wolfish grin. The guys exchanged amused glances.

Gabrielle's eyes glimmered; her gaze fixed on Troy's face. "Chicken…" she whispered, and they all laughed again.

Troy's eyebrows furrowed. "Payback is hell," Troy said, his voice shaky.

"Promises…Promises…" she murmured and turned to take a seat. She was startled as Troy moved in his immortal speed, lifted her into his arms, and walked to the door.

"I guess we have to discuss this now," he said with amusement. Arielle saw Gabrielle's shocked face.

"No…no…no…I was only joking," they heard her say.

"Who is a chicken now?" he chuckled.

"Sorry, I was only joking," she said again, a bit embarrassed.

"You promise no more smart remarks?" He was now completely amused with her.

"Yes…yes, I promise." He put her down and held her into his arms, locking them into a hot kiss. Gabby blushed, a little shaken up. Troy put his arm around her waist and drew her back towards their friends. Arielle could still hear Ian and Sebastian trying to hold back laughter.

"Lessons learned," Ian said, lovingly at Eva.

"Well, are we all done here?" Arielle asked, trying to bring the conversation back to normal. She stood up and asked Eva and Gabrielle to follow her out of the room while the guys turned the telly onto a sports station.

"How did you like Faubourg Saint-Honore district?" they heard Eva asking.

"Have you been there?" Arielle asked, surprised.

"Yes, I went with Ian a few times, and I must say the gowns are amazing, but I'm still going to manifest my wedding gown and your dresses for my wedding if you don't mind."

"Oh…no, not at all. We loved what you did for us on my birthday, so I am sure whatever you manifest for us will be amazing, right, Gabby?" Arielle asked, glancing toward Gabby's direction.

"No disagreement here," Gabrielle replied with a smile.

"Eva, you have to come with us next time, even though you've been there before. It won't feel right if the three of us aren't together."

"I wouldn't miss it for the world." The corners of her mouth lifted into a furtive smile.

"Great," Arielle said and proceeded to tell her about all the designers they met and how amazing their bridal gowns were. Eva seemed pleased to see both them so excited.

"When do you want to go?" Arielle asked.

"How about the weekend after next?" Gabby chimed in. "I have a couple of tests this week coming up and one the week after."

"That'll work for me as well," Eva said.

"Okay, I'll talk to Loren and Sebastian so they can make the arrangements for us."

 *Chapter 22*

ARIELLE, GABRIELLE, AND EVA had made an agreement that they would stay away from their guys for a whole week before their wedding day. This was something they thought would be fun, and it would make their honeymoon more exciting. The week before Eva was to be married; she moved in with her mother. Arielle and Gabby were sure that it would be a very difficult adjustment for Eva.

Eating wasn't something Eva or Ian enjoyed doing since becoming immortal. Ian's family flew in from Germany for the ceremony, and they were staying with Ian at their house. Ian was unable to keep salve in the house, afraid that his parents would wonder about the strange substance, so they moved Ian's supply to Gabby's house and Eva's supply to Arielle's house to keep them from running into each other before the wedding day. Gabrielle and Arielle were sure that this separation was hard on both of them, but an agreement was an agreement, and they were going to honor it. They were very familiar with the way immortals loved, and that powerful encounters were part of their existence.

Eva's wedding dress was amazing. The beautiful strapless, bone color silk gown was to die for. It was magnificently decorated with roses and jewels. Her veil was trimmed with diamonds. The train was several yards long. She looked just like a princess — stunningly beautiful.

Gabrielle, Loren, and Arielle wore the dresses she manifested for them, and they did love them. They were also strapless, made out of rich, shiny blue taffeta trimmed with floral designed lace and tastefully decorated with jewels.

The day of the wedding was thought to be the most important day in Eva and Ian's lives and a joyous one for their friends and family.

They all arrived at the church in plenty of time for dress and makeup. There were rooms designated for the bride and the groom. The wedding dress and the tuxedos had been delivered the day before and were placed in the rooms, creating a lax atmosphere.

The hour after their arrival was busy in the bridal room. The girls wore their fabulous dresses and then helped Eva with her wedding dress, veil, makeup, and hair. She was so perfect that Gabrielle and Arielle were speechless. She was just like a porcelain doll, stunningly gorgeous.

"Good God! Eva, you are spectacular!" Arielle cried out in excitement. Eva gazed in the full-length mirror and blissfully laughed out loud.

"How about you!" Eva said, gazing at the three of them and pointing at the exquisite dresses she manifested for them. They were lovely, especially Loren who had that special immortal appearance. Gabby glanced at Eva and then averted her gaze to Arielle, holding a playful smile.

"What?" Eva asked.

"A far cry from the girl on the beach searching for the bottom of her bathing suit," Gabby said. Her voice was breaking with laughter, which sent Eva and Arielle into heartfelt laughter.

Loren watched them clueless, unable to grasp the joke. They took a moment to explain and soon she was laughing with them. When they finally stopped laughing, Eva made sure the girls' appearances were perfect before making some final adjustments to her dress.

Ian was already waiting at the altar with Troy, Sebastian, and Paul lined to his left side, waiting for the bride. Loren was the first to walk down the aisle. This was the first time she was asked to be in a wedding, and she seemed to be glowing with pleasure.

Gabrielle was next, and Arielle was right behind her. Her eyes fell on the four men standing at the altar next to each other and her breath held in her throat. She gasped quietly. They were all striking. She knew that every female eye inside the church was locked on them. Sebastian's eyes immediately fastened on Arielle, and she saw his lips quirk in that smile that made her heart beat faster. He was the type of a man whose presence would suspend discussions. She felt so completely happy as she kept her eyes on him. She couldn't believe that this man was hers to love for eternity. He seemed like a fabrication of her imagination. He was rich, distinguished, and outright imaginary.

She took her place next to Gabby, and shortly after that; she heard the bridal music. Everyone's eyes turned to the entrance. Eva walked in on her uncle's arm, and both Gabrielle and Arielle gasped out loud. Tears welled up, and they reached for each other's hand. Their gasps were loud enough for the guys and a few of the guests in the front row to turn and stare at them.

Arielle felt a lump climbing slowly up her throat. Eva's uncle was the twin of Mr. Winters, and it was as if her father had come back to life to walk her down the aisle. Both Gabby and Arielle gulped and tried to control their emotions. They noticed Sebastian and Troy's concerned looks. Eva was an angel as her immortal face was flawless and her body was that of a goddess. Ian's eyes were sparkling, and his stunning immortal face was jubilant.

The church was charmingly decorated, the flowers were amazing, and the ceremony was lovely. Their vows were so warm and affectionate that Gabrielle and Arielle became quite emotional. When Ian and Eva were pronounced husband and wife, they locked each other into a loving kiss, and with big smiles, they took each other's hand and walked out beaming from exuberant pleasure. Troy was next. He took Gabrielle's hand tenderly and walked toward the exit followed by Paul with Loren and Sebastian with Arielle.

"You are stunningly beautiful," Sebastian murmured.

"I was just about ready to say the same thing to you," Arielle said. Their eyes locked, and the curve of his lips deepened, and she felt surrounded by his strength.

"What happened in there with you and Gabrielle?" he asked.

"Sebastian, we almost lost it when we saw Eva walk in with her father's brother by her side. It almost seemed that Mr. Winters was walking Eva down the aisle."

He leaned over and gave her a peck on the cheek, squeezing her softly. "I love you, Arielle, and I can't wait to make you my wife. Your compassion for people is astounding to me, and that is one of the so many qualities I love about you."

"You do know that every girl here would love to be with you, don't you?" she whispered in his ear with a soft chuckle.

"I don't see any other girl here but you." His arm was now around her waist as they walked into the reception hall.

The reception was magnificent, and the decorations were lovely. Each table had a fabulous floral center piece that carried Eva's wedding theme and each seat was designated with a beautifully designed name tag. The food was delicious and extraordinarily prepared, followed by scrumptious desserts. Eva's uncle took Eva to the dance floor for the father-daughter dance. It was quite an emotional moment. Eva's mother was openly crying, and that emotion seemed to spread like fire among their guests.

Arielle took a quick look around and didn't see a single person who didn't have moisture in their eyes or an expression of sadness on their faces. She averted her gaze to Eva, and she felt tenderness for her best friend. Eva couldn't cry anymore, but distress was clearly spreading across her face. She was trying to carry the memory of her beloved father the best way she knew how.

Gabrielle came up holding Troy's hand and stood next to Arielle and Sebastian. When the dance was over, Eva left the dance floor and made a point of going to where Gabby and Arielle stood to give them a hug and let them know how much she loved them. Everyone had an amazing time. Gabby and Arielle saw some of their secondary school friends that were attended other universities and hadn't seen them for a couple of years. They chatted and danced for hours.

Paul and Loren never left each other's arms while Eva and Ian shared their time between the guests, their friends, and their families. Gabrielle and Arielle were on the dance floor with their friends and felt extremely amused watching Sebastian and Troy being surrounded by single girls in a desperate attempt to pick them up. Their guys appeared to be totally overwhelmed.

It was quite amusing to watch the sexy mannerisms used by the girls to entice the immortals to some exchange back without success. Frustration painted their faces as they stepped away. Arielle and Gabby had been on the dance floor for a while when Sebastian and Troy walked up and cut in.

"Where you ever going to stop dancing and talk to me?" he asked Arielle quietly.

"Well, I was getting ready to do that when you came up." Arielle chuckled.

"Not true...it appeared that you forgot all about me."

"How can that be possible? You aren't exactly the type of a man that can be forgotten. I saw all those girls that came up and wanted to dance with you. Why did you not dance?" she asked.

He snaked his hands around her waist and pulled her flush against him. "I don't want to dance with anyone but you," he said firmly.

"Really?" Her giggling was like a remedy for his soul.

"Yes, really." His arms tightened, and she stopped breathing.

"Troy and I waited to see how long it would take you both to come back and dance with us, but we finally realized that we may have to wait all night, so here we are."

The lighting was soft and the music amazing. She stretched up on her tippy toes, searching for his lips, and he was more than happy to accommodate her. Their lips melded, their tongues twisted, and they both moaned softly.

"I love you, baby," he breathed without leaving the kiss. "You make me a happy man." His scent was intoxicating, and his lips tasted like sweet honey. The kiss deepened and they moved to a slow song with their eyes closed. When the song was over, the four of them walked back to their table.

Loren and Paul were there, whispering sweet nothing to each other, making them smile. Eva and Ian walked up, letting them know that they were getting ready to leave. They hugged each other and wished them a safe and wonderful honeymoon.

"We'll see you in a couple of weeks," Ian said with a wide smile on his face, holding Eva lovingly.

"Don't do anything we wouldn't do," said Gabrielle laughingly, and they were surprised to find Sebastian and Troy completely amused by her statement.

"What do you mean by that?" Troy asked.

"You never heard that before?" Gabby asked, totally surprised.

"No, I must say I never have. Have you, Sebastian?" Troy turned to Sebastian.

"No, I'm not familiar with that expression, but I find it very amusing."

"Well, you both are pretty easy to amuse I must say," Arielle said. Troy leaned in and whispered something in Gabby's ear, and she flushed. They all now turned their attention toward Eva and Ian as they walked away waving and smiling at them.

"Have fun!" Arielle called out.

"We will," they heard Eva's jubilant voice.

They were flying to Fiji tonight. They seemed so happy, and her friends were extremely joyful for them.

"We will see you in a couple of weeks," the newly married called to their parents as the entered the limousine bound for the airport.

"How human of them…" Arielle said.

Gabby shot her a sincerely stunned glance. "What do you mean?"

Arielle laughed. "Let's face it, Gabby; they don't need to catch a plane to Fiji. They can be there before the plane takes off."

Gabrielle started to laugh, and soon enough Troy, Sebastian, Paul, and Loren joined in. Mrs. Winters approached with her brother-in-law and his wife by his side. She was beaming from head to toe knowing that her daughter was now married to a wonderful young man.

"Her father would be so proud of her," she said in a soft voice.

"He is…" Arielle entered in a very matter of fact voice that made all of them except for Gabrielle stare at her in wonder. Gabrielle remembered just as well as Arielle did Eva's summons and her father coming back, stating that he would be by her side every step of the way, so they were sure he was there.

Mrs. Winters smiled and gave Arielle a hug, stating that she was sure her father was watching from above. She introduced them to Mr. Winters' twin brother and his wife. They seemed to be very kind individuals that loved Eva and her mother immensely. Ian's sister and parents approached their table, and after short introductions, they talked for a little while about their trip to England and the excitement of the wedding. Ian's father had lived in England in his younger years, so this wasn't his first time in the county. It wasn't long before Arielle and Gabrielle's parents walked up and, after the introductions to Ian's parents, they all spent a little more time discussing the beauty of the wedding and the happiness of both Eva and Ian.

Mr. Taylor's strong, happy voice came from across the room. "I guess we'll be seeing each other quite a lot in the next few weeks as we have to repeat this a couple more times, right?"

"That's right…" Arielle's father replied with a jubilant laughter. He then turned to Sebastian. "Sebastian, my boy, are you ready to take the plunge?" His voice dripped with mirth.

"Yes, sir, I sure am," he replied with a wide smile on his face, and reaching over, he put his arm around Arielle and pulled her close.

"What about you, Troy?" Mr. Taylor asked, turning to face Troy.

"I've been ready," he muttered, sending a warm smile to Gabrielle.

"Good…good…that's Good to know," he mumbled and gave Mrs. Taylor a kiss on the cheek. Paul and Loren took off before anyone else did.

Around ten, the remaining guests stood in the country club's brilliantly lit parking lot talking away when Arielle had a strong feeling that someone was watching her. She shivered as she rapidly scanned the parking lot, trying to pierce through the dark shaded areas, afraid of what she might see, but she couldn't see anything at all. She bit her lip and tried to suppress the feeling. But it came back much stronger, making her tremble as she pulled herself closer to Sebastian. He immediately wrapped his arms around her and cradled her, thinking that she might be cold.

"What's wrong, baby?" he whispered, holding her gaze. Bending down, he pressed his lips on her forehead. He didn't push her for a reply; he just waited. Arielle hesitated because she couldn't explain the weird feeling, but it was still there. His eyes narrowed, and she heard his soft voice one more time. "What is it?"

"I'm not sure, but I have this strange feeling that we're being watched," she said. Her voice dropped to a soft whisper. He pulled her closer and held her tighter against his warm body. He rested his soft gaze on her face one more time, lips curved, face relaxed, spreading relief through her.

"There is nobody watching us," he chuckled, giving her a soft squeeze, and she forced a smile. The conversation continued, and it grew pretty animated now as Gabrielle pressed Troy to tell her the secret location of their honeymoon. Troy kept shaking his head, totally unyielding to her hugs, kisses, and requests. Arielle laughed as she started to relax, and soon enough, she threw herself enthusiastically into the conversation.

"How about taking this argument home?" Troy asked with a chuckle and pulled Gabrielle towards the car.

"I was just about to suggest the same thing," Sebastian said with a smile.

"Goodbye, Arielle!" She heard her father's voice, and she turned towards the club entrance. She saw her parents descending the main staircase along with Gabrielle's parents, waving at them. She blinked as the bright lights in the background and the shadows of the night prevented her from having a clear view of their faces. She waved in their direction, smiling. Suddenly a fast movement caught her eyes at the club entrance, and she felt her body go rigid. Sheer horror crept up her spine as she zeroed in on the beautiful woman who was standing behind the huge glass doors.

She was Arielle's most horrifying nightmare. Her face was partly obscured by the shadow of a pillar, but even in the weak lighting, Arielle could make out her smug expression, and she recoiled. A man stood right next to her with his arm around her waist, but she couldn't see his face. Despite the peculiar familiarity about him, her eyes were glued to the woman. She managed to draw breath as bile climbed her throat.

Annabel... she gasped as her breath held in her throat, and she felt her heartbeat hammering in her chest, creating enormous pain. She started to shake uncontrollably, feeling faint, and the ground seemed to sway under her feet. Sebastian's strong arms instantly tightened around her body and held her upright. Otherwise, she would have sprawled on the ground, utterly petrified.

"Arielle...what's wrong, baby?" he asked with clear concern. She tried to speak, but all she could do was wheeze over and over again.

"What...?" Sebastian asked again, watching her carefully as she lifted her hand and pointed towards the club entrance. They all turned back, gazing at the direction she pointed, and that's when she heard both Sebastian and Troy gasp at the same time.

"Annabel..." She heard Sebastian's voice as he turned to Troy and she saw their lips moving but couldn't hear a single word. The next few seconds were a blur. Sebastian pulled her in his arms, pressed his lips softly on hers, and passed her to Troy like a rag doll. "I'll be right back; miss me..." She heard his voice, and he was gone before she had a chance to see even him move. Arielle was frozen, astonishment to her face, gazing in the direction that she last saw Sebastian being swallowed by the night.

"What in bloody hell is going on?" Gabrielle asked in a shocked voice. "Where did Sebastian disappear to?" She was now gazing between Arielle and Troy.

"Annabel is here," Troy said, voice low

"Annabel...?" Gabrielle's eyes went wide with disbelief.

"Annabel is here," Troy repeated carefully with his eyes fixed toward the entrance.

"That bloody bitch!" Gabrielle hissed. Troy and Arielle turned toward her, stunned by her icy, frantic voice.

"It's okay, baby," Troy whispered. "Arielle is safe. Sebastian went after Annabel, and it's not going to be good for her."

"How is he going to find her?" Arielle asked Troy. Her heart was hammering her chest, creating enormous pain.

"There is a certain scent that we follow with other immortals, and it'll not be easy for Annabel to shake Sebastian off her path."

"I wonder what she was doing here?" Gabrielle mumbled, frowning.

"I'm sure she wanted to frighten Arielle, and she succeeded," Troy said. He put his arm around Arielle and gave her a reassuring squeeze.

"I'm a little surprised that my friends in Italy didn't give me an advance warning that she was coming this way," Troy said. He appeared disappointed at the thought and remained silent, shaking his head. He finally gazed down at Gabrielle, who was still watching him in shock. Putting his other arm around her, he pulled her close and pressed his lips to her forehead. "It will be okay, Gabrielle," he murmured in a soft, unruffled voice. He then averted his gaze at Arielle and realized that something was terribly wrong. She seemed to relax briefly in his arm, but suddenly, she tensed, struggling to take a breath, and shut her eyes in sheer anxiety. He pulled her harder against his side keeping her upright.

"What is it Arielle?" he asked, alarmed.

"The man—the man— with Annabel…I think I know the man," she whispered, trembling.

"The man? What man? Are you sure there was a man with her?" Troy was searching Arielle's eyes. "I didn't see anyone. I only saw Annabel for a short second, and she was gone," Troy said.

Arielle pressed her lips together in frustration. "You can let go, Troy. I am doing a little better," she said. She was trying hard to evoke her memory. "There was a man with his arm around her. I'm very sure about that. There were both watching us." Troy let go of her, and she took a deep breath, trying to collect her thoughts.

"Are you okay?" Gabrielle asked with a worrisome expression on her face.

"I'm doing much better, but I don't mind telling you that Annabel is my worst nightmare." Her name caused bile to rise up her throat, and it was hard to ignore the bitter taste in her mouth. Troy moved closer to face her.

"So who was the man? Was he immortal? And if so, how do you know him?" Troy kept on trying to learn a few more details.

"The sight of Annabel terrified me, and I didn't have a good look at him. But I'm almost sure that I know him." Her eyes darted toward the entrance one more time.

"Well? Think…Arielle, it's very important," Troy pressed on. Arielle paused. Her heart hammered her chest so hard that she thought she was going to have a heart attack.

"Think, Arielle." Troy's voice was steady and strong. She stared up at him, and her face twisted in agony, trying to take a deep breath.

"I know that you'll think that I'm crazy, but I am almost sure that it was Gaston Bertaud. Sebastian grew up with him; he was his best friend."

"Gaston Bertaud!" Gabrielle gasped, and her jaw dropped. Troy's body stiffened, watching Gabrielle's expression. He pressed his lips together in astonishment.

"Gabrielle, how do you know him?" Troy was stunned. Gabrielle didn't seem to hear Troy's question because she was focused on Arielle's face.

"Are you saying that the guy we met in Calais on your birthday was here tonight with Annabel?"

"Yes, that's exactly what I'm saying. I told Eva, and I thought I told you that he was immortal. I recognized his scent, his appearance, his voice, and everything about him told me he was immortal."

"Did Sebastian know then? And does he know now?" Gabrielle asked while Troy was speechlessly trying to understand their conversation.

"I told Sebastian about Gaston when we came back. He was utterly surprised, as he had no idea that he was immortal. They were together almost every day for sixteen years, but Gaston never acted any different. He had no reason to suspect something so incredible, especially back in the fifteen hundred."

"I wonder if Sebastian saw Gaston with Annabel," Gabrielle said as if she was talking to herself.

"When we turned toward that direction, Annabel was alone," Troy interrupted. "But, Gabrielle, you never told me about this guy when you came back."

"Well, it was of no importance at the time. We met a lot of people at that ball, and he was not someone that I would remember," Gabrielle said in a low voice.

"He had dark hair and striking blue eyes," Arielle started to say, and she stopped mid-sentence in disbelief.

"You said you didn't have a good look at him, but you saw the color of his eyes?" she heard Troy's surprised voice. She was completely perplexed about that statement.

"Of course not," she replied. "I've no idea why I said that, but for the fact that there was an extraordinary familiarity about his presence." Arielle was now staring down at her toes, a bit confused. She was unable to comprehend how and why she was sure that the guy was Gaston. There was no way from that distance to be able to see a person's face clearly, especially the color of their eyes.

"I think I'm going out of my mind," she mumbled.

"It'll be all right, Arielle. Sebastian should be back shortly." Troy's voice was soothing, but she couldn't shake the icy feeling away.

"Thanks," she said, and Troy embraced both Gabrielle and her.

"Annabel should know that Sebastian is very fast, much faster and much stronger," Troy murmured, clearly talking to himself as he picked up his mobile and pressed a number. "Hey, Antonius, it's Troy."

The next few minutes were a fast conversation in Italian. Arielle didn't understand a single word that was said, but she did hear Annabel's name, so she was sure that he was discussing tonight's events. Gabrielle was fluent in Italian, so Arielle moved closer to ask details about the conversation, but Troy was then off the phone and looking totally perplexed.

"What is it?" Arielle asked anxiously.

"Antonius was surprised that Annabel showed up here, knowing that Sebastian is determined to kill her. He and his friends have been visiting every possible place that Annabel and her friends frequent, but she has been a no-show for a couple of months. Antonius was angry that they didn't know that she left Italy, and he was wondering what she was up to." Troy was stumped.

"Oh, I can answer that," Arielle said in distress. "I'm pretty sure that she is plotting to destroy our wedding plans. She is plotting to kill me in some unexpected and extraordinary way. She wants

Sebastian to suffer in the worst way, and she isn't going to stop until she succeeds." Arielle was so overwhelmed that she didn't realize that tears were dripping down her face. She finally broke down and cried uncontrollably. Troy moved close and held her in his arms.

"Don't worry, Arielle, you have a lot of immortal friends and family that are here to protect you. I'm here, and if I remember well, I've a pretty good record in saving your life." He chuckled, and putting his finger under her chin, he lifted her face to his and gave her a soft squeeze, trying to make her smile. Arielle blinked blankly up at him.

"I am committed to keeping a perfect record, so there's no way I'm going to let anyone hurt you," he said and winked. "Sebastian will be back shortly, and we'll be on our way home and can forget about this incident."

Gabrielle started to say something when Troy's mobile went off. He flipped it open, and before he had a chance to say hello, it seemed that the person on the line was already talking. Troy listened intently for a short minute, and his face lost its softness. He pinched the tip of his nose in frustration and shut the phone.

"Go home and stay there," he said, glancing between Arielle and Gabrielle. His voice was firm, sharp, but Arielle could hear a hint of panic in his tone. He pulled Gabrielle into his arms and kissed her passionately before he let go and darted toward the same direction where Sebastian had disappeared into the dark. The ladies stood frozen in place, completely dumbfounded. Gabrielle was the first to move. She took Arielle's hand and pulled her toward the car.

"Let's go, Arielle. We need to leave this place. We are all alone in this parking lot." Arielle shivered at the thought, and they both ran to the car. Gabrielle slumped down behind the steering wheel, and Arielle jumped in next to her on the passenger side, pressing down on the locks. Gabby sped out of the parking lot, heading toward the highway. The ride home was a quiet one as they both stared out the window, drowning in their own thoughts. Arielle had tons of questions, but no answers. Fear crept up, making her tremble at the thought of something happening to Sebastian. Where was he? What if Annabel had a lot of friends with her and she was waiting to ambush him? The moments were slipping away and there was nothing Gabrielle or Arielle could do. Gabrielle pulled into the garage. She ran out of the car and into the house. Arielle followed right on her heels. Gabby picked up her phone that was sitting on the counter and, thumbing through the pages of a small brown book, she found what she was searching for and pressed the number on the keyboard.

"Who are you calling?" Arielle asked. Gabrielle turned, and putting her finger on her lips; she made a motion to keep quiet.

"Hello!" Arielle heard her voice shaken with anxiety. "Antonius, this is Gabrielle; I need your help desperately. Please, help...." She emphasized her last words. "Sebastian and Troy have gone after Annabel, and we think they are in trouble." She was now sobbing, and Arielle moved closer because Gabrielle was unable to continue.

Arielle picked up the phone and put it to her ear. She hears Antonius saying, "We'll be right there." The phone went dead.

Arielle pulled Gabrielle to the study, and they both sank down on the sofa, holding each other, not knowing what else to do. She wasn't sure how long they remained there, but suddenly a sturdy banging on the door startled them. They ran to the door, shocked to see Troy's best friends Antonius, Girard, and Giani with an fourth unknown man. Antonius embraced them and introduced the fourth guy as Arturo, Giani's younger brother.

"Don't worry. We'll find them. I'm sure nothing will happen, but I'm glad you called. You need for you to take us to the location where you saw them leaving so we can follow their scent." Arielle and Gabrielle drove them to the club parking lot. The four immortals stepped out of the car and ran toward the corner of the building, disappearing in the dark.

"Go home and stay there," Antonius's voice came loud, clear, and commanding from somewhere in the dark. Immediately, the girls headed home.

"I am so worried," Arielle said, without realizing that her voice dropped to a soft murmur.

"I hope nothing happens," Gabrielle said as if she didn't hear a word Arielle had spoken. The anxiety was contagious. Both remained silent for the rest of the drive. At the house, they made sure that the doors were locked and moved into the study. They sank onto the sofa, holding each other, too frightened by the night's events to be alone. There was nothing to do but wait for someone to come or call. Both wished that Eva and Ian were home.

A Sneak Peek at the eighth book
in the Immortal Rapture Series,

ARIELLE IMMORTAL RESOLVE

 *Chapter 1*

SEBASTIAN PULLED ARIELLE in his arms gave her a soft peck on the lips, and whispered softly in her ear, "I'll be right back baby, miss me..." Following Annabel's scent, he darted toward the corner of the country club.

Sebastian tracked Annabel carefully, trying to remain calm while anger and loathing filled his lungs. Tonight he was determined to kill Annabel; he was committed to ending this part of his life and ridding Arielle of Annabel's relentless terror. He was willing to die if that's what it took to make sure Arielle was safe. He was responsible for pulling Arielle into this frightening world of immortality. He was responsible for making her live in constant fear of a crazy immortal woman's unwavering desire to kill her for vengeance. Sebastian was now ready to end it all one way or another.

The skies were clear and the moon illuminated the night. Sebastian made his way through several miles of the club grounds at an inconceivable speed, and when he reached the end of the property line, his sharp immortal eyes caught a glimpse of two people way in the distance. One of them was Annabel. The other was a man, but he couldn't see his face. His sense of smell became stronger as he grew closer to them and his nostrils were filled with their thick immortal scent. They were running next to each other and seemed to pause for a short second, taking a look-back and scanning the darkness carefully. Sebastian crouched behind the wall that surrounded the property line and watched them intently. They seemed to be satisfied that they weren't being followed as they turned their heads and started to run at a slower pace.

They ran for quite a long time through the dark streets of Brighton and Sebastian followed at a safe distance, guzzling down fresh air to help his thoughts remain on the right path. He wanted desperately to end this tonight; he didn't want her to slip away like she did back at the cemetery in St Jean De Luz. Suddenly they stopped running and remained totally still. They had reached the edge of a park that stretched for a couple of miles ahead and ended in a large square surrounded but beautiful homes. They scanned around them carefully one more time and, finally, they began to cross the manicured lawns of the park toward the square in slow strides. When they arrived at the other side of the park, they stopped again, and they seemed to carry a short dialogue. Then the man turned and darted in the opposite direction. Sebastian never had a chance to take a good look at him, but he wasn't interested in the guy right now. Annabel was ready to step into the square when suddenly she paused at the curb and looked back, piercing through the dark.

Sebastian held his breath, consumed by an uneasy feeling that Annabel realized she was being followed. He hid behind a large tree trunk on the other side of the park with teeth gritted, filled with resentment and loathing for this woman who had created chaos in his life.

He waited patiently in high hopes that tonight this part of Arielle's nightmare would be over. He wasn't going to let his anger guide his actions this time around. He needed to find out who she was working with and what they were plotting.

Annabel stood completely still for a short time as if she was contemplating whether to move forward or to abort reaching her destination. Sebastian took a long breath of relief when he finally saw her crossing the square and taking a little side street for a couple of blocks and stopping in front of a small house.

She again scanned the area around her carefully before she reached up and pressed the button at the gate twice. The lights came on, and Sebastian's immortal hearing picked up a young female voice on the intercom asking the person's name. Annabel gave her name and immediately, a tall, young girl came running out the door and across the garden, taking the padlock off the gate. Sebastian could unmistakably hear their conversation while they were still outside.

"Are they here yet?" Annabel asked.

"No, not just yet, but I'm sure they'll be here shortly. They wouldn't break an agreement with you; they know better than that," the young girl chuckled.

"Jane, I do have to run out for a short moment. If I'm not back in time, I want you to tell them to wait for me." Together they walked up the few steps and crossed the threshold, shutting the door behind them. Sebastian moved swiftly and soundlessly across the cobblestone square and reached the corner of the dark street in a few strides. The street sign displayed the name York Street.

The house that Annabel entered looked a bit run down, and he noticed tall hedges surrounding the walls, preventing access view from the outside. Sebastian looked at the large metal chain and padlock that held the iron gate secure and chuckled under his breath. His immortal strength could crush the deadbolt to soft powder, but he chose to hurdle over the tall fence and move quietly. He pushed carefully through the hedges and stood behind them, avoiding any unnecessary racket.

The night sky was dark and thick shadows surrounded the house. He stood in that darkness, right by a huge window that would give him a perfect view of the front room. The room was dark, so he waited patiently. Suddenly the light came on, and his breath rushed through his lungs so fast that it made him a bit lightheaded.

He took a few deep breaths and inched closer. Peeking carefully through the sheer curtains that were pulled shut, he saw Annabel and the girl that she called Jane engaged in an animated conversation. Annabel was giving her directions about the people who were arriving to meet with her. Then she turned, walked toward the stairs that led to the upper floor, and started to scale the steps two at a time. She was almost at the top landing when Sebastian heard Jane's voice one more time.

"We did install the secret pass you requested. Do you want to see it?" Jane inquired. Annabel paused and, looking down at Jane, she followed her finger that was pointing at the opposite wall. Sebastian saw Annabel's eyebrows narrow as a short smile crept up her ghastly face. She leaped down the stairs and dashed swiftly toward that wall. Sebastian saw Jane blink with a shocked look on her face, unable to follow Annabel's immortal speed. Jane crossed the floor in fast strides trying to keep up. Annabel had already reached the wall at the far end of the room and waited impatiently for Jane to catch up. Jane lifted her hand, and with her palm, she pushed against an invisible spot on the wall. Sebastian watched in utter astonishment as the wall parted, revealing a secret entrance.

It wasn't so much the secret entrance that surprised Sebastian, but its location. This was a rundown, dilapidated house, not quite where anyone would expect to find secret passages. Annabel seemed to hesitate for a short moment and then moved quickly through the gap in the wall with Jane by her side. They both disappeared behind it, leaving no signs that would disclose what Sebastian had just witnessed. The opening had closed instantaneously, leaving what now seemed to be a normal wall.

Sebastian's mind was whirling with wild thoughts, trying to make sound decisions in a matter of milliseconds. His loath for Annabel was increasing by the minute, but he decided to do the right thing. He pulled his mobile phone out of his pant pocket and pressed Troy's number. He picked up on the first ring.

"Troy," Sebastian said, his voice dropping to a mere whisper. "Where are you?"

"I'm on my way," Troy said. "Give me the exact location."

Sebastian gave Troy the address and added, "Listen, Troy, I'm going in. I want to go ahead and deal with Annabel in a swift and conclusive way. Come and find me in case I need help. There's something very peculiar about this run-down house. I saw Annabel and a human friend of hers go through a secret passage. The house is very small, so I think that this opening leads to some secret cellar. The location of the switch is on the wall. It's located approximately one-point-five meters from the northeast corner and two-point-one meters high."

"Sebastian, I'll be right there."

"Thanks, Troy," he said and didn't wait for his friend's reply. He ended the conversation and slipped his mobile back into his pocket.

The door was locked, but that wasn't an issue for Sebastian. He soon found himself standing in the middle of the front room, which was poorly furnished and completely quiet. Quickly he moved and scaled the staircase to the upper floor. He was going to clear any obstacles rapidly and leave Annabel as his last and most revolting elimination. This was the best and most shrewd way to approach this attempt on Annabel's miserable life.

Four fully furnished bedrooms graced the upper floor, and they all looked lived in. He was now sure that more people were in this house besides Annabel and Jane. Sebastian was standing in the last bedroom, one filled with Annabel's scent. He was getting ready to walk out when he heard footsteps and froze in place. It was but a few minutes before Jane walked in with a laundry basket in her hands. Sebastian was standing behind the open door; he didn't want to hurt her, but he would have to do what it took to carry out his mission.

Jane set the basket on the bed, started to take clothes out, and put them carefully in the dresser drawers. She was nearly done when Sebastian's phone went off, and she spun around to face a very angry immortal. Her jaw dropped, and her eyes reflected an intensely frightened look.

Sebastian was stunned for a short second as the silence stretched and he forgot about the phone when she suddenly darted toward the door. Finding her voice, she was preparing to scream. Sebastian moved with unfathomable speed, and his next move was unavoidable. He grabbed Jane by the throat, muting her scream forever. His strength broke her neck, and when he let her go, she dropped lifelessly to the floor. Sebastian pulled her body in the small closet and shut the door. He felt dreadful killing a human, but this was the choice he made. She was getting ready to alert the house occupants that something was wrong, and he couldn't allow that.

Leaving the room, he moved like a ghost along the upstairs corridor and descended the staircase carefully. He crossed the room on the main floor, walked down a small hallway, and noticed two doors, one on either side. He went into the first door on his left and found himself in a small study full of books and boxes and a foul odor that had to be a combination of several things. He backed off and shut the door behind him, shaking his head to rid his nostrils of that awful odor. He moved down the hall and opened the second door. Again, he was struck with the most god-awful smell. It was a sitting room that was connected to the kitchen area. Both rooms were poorly lit, giving Sebastian's perfect immortal eyes a sharp view of a disgustingly dirty area.

The smell came from the kitchen floor that was clogged with garbage bags, animal food, and feces, making the odor intolerable. Sebastian held his breath, moved quickly out into the hall, and shut the door behind him, shaking his head again in pure disgust. He was now moving soundlessly back to the front room, and he stood in front of the wall where he watched Annabel and Jane had disappeared. He looked for a noticeable spot, but there was none. He ran his palm across the wall, feeling every little bump and scrape until he encountered a small rise.

He pressed, holding his breath, and he was delighted to see the wall parting, exposing the opening. As he listened for any sounds, he quickly decided his next move. Sebastian knew that Annabel was there, but was she alone? And if not, how many immortals would he be facing? Pulling his mobile from his pocket, he glanced at the screen. A smile spread across his face when he saw Arielle's text. *"I'm worried to death. I love you more than life; please be careful."* His arms ached for her, but he had a serious issue to deal with, so he set the phone to vibrate and slipped it back in his pocket. Troy had to be getting close, so he decided to go for it.

Quickly he crossed the opening and forgot to breathe, consumed by total shock. He found himself on the landing of a still staircase that seemed to spiral down to a dark corridor. Taking a deep breath, he filled his lungs with the stale air and descended carefully, one step at a time until he reached the down to a damp floor. His immortal vision gave him a well-defined view of the place, and he gasped in astonishment. How could a small house like this conceal such a large cellar? Sebastian scanned the area and noticed several doors on either side of the long corridor, but they all appeared dark and soundless except for the last two doors on the right. A thin streak of light was escaping from a tiny crack in the first door.

Sebastian moved slowly, listening for any noise, but all he could hear were his own footsteps. He exhaled slowly as he reached the door, pausing to listen. Men's muted voices and low laughter whispered to him. Sebastian set his eyes on the crack and saw three men sitting around a small table, playing cards. They seemed completely engulfed in their game and totally unaware of Sebastian's presence.

Sebastian moved away quietly and approached the last door. His breath held in his throat as the air thickened with Annabel's scent. He waited, totally still while his mind assessed his position and his desperate wish to rid the world of Annabel for good. His nerves jumped, and his breathing quickened as he turned the knob and pushed the door wide open.

Sebastian focused his startled eyes on Annabel, who was sitting in a large chair, watching him intently with a smug look on her face. She crossed her legs and clasped her hands in undisguised amusement.

"Welcome to your prison, my love," she said. Her laughter rang with clear pleasure.

Note to the Readers

Thank you to my fans. It is the most rewarding and surreal experience to receive your wonderful feedback after reading my books. To the future readers, thank you for loving books and making my book your choice. This is the seventh novel in my *Immortal Rapture Series.* I hope you will enjoy it.

Contact Information
My website: lilianroberts.com
My Twitter: @lilian3roberts
My Blog: lilianroberts.blogspot.com

ALSO BY LILIAN ROBERTS

Arielle Immortal Awakening
Arielle Immortal Seduction
Arielle Immortal Passion
Arielle Immortal Quickening
Arielle Immortal Journey
Arielle Immortal Fury